ONE
WINTER
NIGHT

ONE
WINTER
NIGHT

From the Editors
Of *True Story* And
True Confessions

Published by True Renditions, LLC

True Renditions, LLC
105 E. 34th Street, Suite 141
New York, NY 10016

ISBN: 978-1-938877-87-2

Visit us on the web at www.truerenditionsllc.com.

Contents

THE STORM THAT CHANGED OUR WORLD
My husband and I will
never be the same.

It had been snowing steadily for a couple of days. We live way out in the country and our farm looked like a Currier & Ives Christmas card.

As the sun struggled to peek through the dreary sky, it sent down weak rays of light that illuminated the icicles hanging from the eaves of our house. Even the branches of the shrubs that line the driveway were coated with a blanket of snow. I pressed my face against the frosty window and my breath created a warm steam that fogged the glass. Swiping at it with my sweater, I looked out over the landscape hoping to see signs of life.

We're too far out for me to have hoped for a snowplow to come and clear a path up the road from our remote cottage. I hoped that my husband, Derek, would be able to make it home. I listened for the sound of an approaching vehicle, but heard nothing.

Derek and I hadn't exactly parted on good terms that morning and with the weather making driving hazardous, I wondered if he'd even bother coming home. He'd worked late into the night the night before and that evening was going to be no different. I knew that. Derek works for the local electric company and his job requires long hours during emergency situations. I accepted that when I married him and thought nothing of it. Right then, though, I felt alone and a little frightened.

I met Derek on purpose, you might say. Five years before, when my parents died and left me their farm, their old house, and a few livestock, I left my job in the city and moved there. After spending ten years in corporate America working as an executive assistant for the big boss, I was ready for a change. The pressure of my job and the lack of time for friends and family were getting to me. I didn't even have a cat to keep me company in the city. I lived all by myself and had little time to socialize.

When I came home to grieve for my parents, who died suddenly in a car accident, I never went back to my good job or my other life. I became reacquainted with my best friend, Rose, and she told me about this really cute guy who was still single. "He works for Valley Electric," she said, her enthusiasm showing. "If I weren't a happily married woman, I'd go after him myself."

1

At first I was too shy to even think of a reason to speak to him. Still, I'd go into the office once a month to pay my bill and I'd see him. He'd notice me and we'd smile at each other. I suppose it would've gone on like that forever if a limb hadn't fallen on the electric line near my house.

I called the electric company about it and they sent Derek out with another guy to cut the tree back and remove the limb. I stood in the front yard and introduced myself at last. "I'm Mary Ferguson," I said. "I inherited this place from my parents."

Derek climbed down from the ladder and shook my hand. "I'm Derek Allenby. I knew your parents. Sorry to hear about your loss."

"Thank you," I said. "I don't know how I'll manage to run this place by myself, but it sure beats life in the city."

From there we hit it off and Derek asked me out before he jumped back into the company truck and drove away. I told him about my plans to run the farm the way my parents had. I figured I'd raise a few cows, goats, and chickens and plant crops in the spring. "Maybe I'll also supplement my income by growing some herbs and selling gift baskets. I have a green thumb and a knack for putting together flowers, homemade jelly, and cookies in an attractive arrangement. I've already filled several orders with a craft shop and a grocery store in town."

"Sounds like a grand idea!" Derek enthused. "I know you'll be happy here and I'm glad we finally found a way to get to know each other. I've wanted to talk to you, but I couldn't get up the courage. I noticed you the first time you came in to pay your bill."

We dated constantly after that and Derek soon revealed that he made sure his boss sent him to repair my power line because he wanted to talk to me. A year later, were got married. Derek moved out of his apartment in town and we lived a wonderful life out in the country. A few years later, though, the romance was gone and we were sniping at each other all of the time.

It might've started when I didn't get pregnant and the doctor said it was no one's fault. There wasn't a medical reason for it and he said that we should just relax and keep trying. Whatever the reason for the rift between us, our "happily ever after" was evaporating slowly.

A chill shuddered through me as I stood at the window looking at the frozen world outside. I couldn't stop shivering as I went outside and checked on the animals. I made sure the cattle had hay, the goats were fed and watered, and the chickens were clucking happily in their warm henhouse.

I gathered the eggs and fed the chickens early. Then I went back inside and listened to the reassuring sound of the furnace clicking on.

Then suddenly everything shut off. It wasn't dusk yet, so I didn't need candles, but the heat was off and I knew that it wouldn't be back on for quite some time. Because the house is way out in the country, I also knew that we'd be among the last Valley Electric customers to get help. Still, I called the office, anyway.

"This is Mary, Kyra," I said. "Is Derek there?" Kyra is one of the clerks in the office and when she said that he wasn't there I tried not to let the panic show in my voice. "The electricity is out here and I need him to come and see about it as soon as he can."

"There are hundreds of other residents without power," Kyra replied calmly. "You'll have to hold on for a while, but your power will be restored as soon as possible."

She was all business and there I was acting like a silly woman who'd never gone through a crisis before. When I was growing up, the power went out time and time again in the winter. My parents didn't lose their cool then and I wasn't going to now. I told myself that I was a grown woman and I could handle the problem. "Thanks, Kyra," I said before hanging up.

"Just wonderful," I muttered to myself. The old house would turn cold pretty quickly, but we have a fireplace and I could go outside and look for some dry wood. Why I hadn't thought to ask Derek to chop some more before the winter was upon us, I didn't know.

Outside in my boots, jeans, and down coat, I carried an axe with me as I trudged through the snow. Picking up a load of small chunks in my arms that I thought might burn once they dried out, I carried them into the house and set them on the hearth.

My teeth were chattering as I filled the kettle with water and set it on the stove. I realized as I turned the knob that there was no power and therefore I couldn't use the stove. I should've rented a gas tank and piped propane into the house like my parents used to, but I hadn't bothered. And I hadn't thought to buy a kerosene heater, either.

I felt like weeping, but I knew that wouldn't help. It wasn't a tragedy. I'd survive. Where was the spunk and vigor that I'd had when I first came home and fended for myself? Yes, it was great to have a husband, but I wasn't a helpless female. I could make it.

It's funny, I thought, what you take for granted. The clock wasn't telling the correct time and the microwave didn't respond when I placed a cup of soup in there and punched the buttons, forgetting once again that there was no power. The refrigerator wasn't humming and the only things I could find to eat were some crackers and peanut butter. Oh, well.

I thought about all of the food in the freezer and how it would all be ruined if the power didn't return for a couple of days. Once when I was a young child, the electricity went out for three days and I remember my mother crying when she opened the freezer and looked at all of the food we lost.

3

I flopped into a chair and accepted defeat. The wood I'd brought in was slowly forming a puddle on the hearth and even though I wrapped towels around it, there was no way it was going to ignite if I tried to burn it. I didn't have any lighter pine and paper would just make a mess and possibly set the living room on fire. The roof would be safe because of the snow and I knew I'd just have to wrap myself in a blanket and hope for the best.

The night before I'd wanted Derek to watch an old, romantic movie with me, but he fell asleep on the sofa. No doubt it was from boredom. I got up, lit a candle, and found one of my romance novels to keep me company. Wrapping myself in a quilt, I settled down for a long wait. The temperature in the house was dropping rapidly, but I tried to ignore my discomfort.

I turned on the battery-operated radio after straining my eyes to read for more than an hour. The weather report was the last thing I wanted to hear, so I turned to a station playing oldies. At one point I grabbed the remote and pointed it at the TV, forgetting again that there was no power. Picking up the phone to call Derek again, I realized that the line was dead. The snowstorm must've knocked down the telephone lines, too. I hung up in despair.

Listening to the radio, I heard a bleak report about the snow that was continuing to fall. It was bringing down more power lines and causing damage to homes when limbs from large trees broke off and crashed onto their roofs. I worried about our old house for a while, but then decided that I had enough to be concerned about without inventing trouble.

Several hours later, I was elated when the weather report promised no more snow. I looked outside and saw that the flakes weren't falling anymore. It was calm and the wind wasn't whistling through the trees like it had been before.

Alone and cold, I lay down on the sofa wrapped in a cocoon of blankets and quilts and dreamed of a hero like the ones in my romance novels. I wanted a hero who'd arrive just in time to save me from the blizzard and who'd make love to me in my snowbound cabin in the woods. In reality, though, all I wanted in my heart was for Derek to come home and for us to talk and try to put our marriage back on track. I didn't want to argue anymore or feel his disappointment.

Sometimes I longed to feel the warmth of his love enveloping me the way it had before he started finding fault with so many things about me. Derek complained about my indifference to the things that mattered while I buried my nose in romance novels. Money was tight and he complained whenever I spent any of it on nonessentials like books, magazines, and DVDs.

Sometimes I resented him. He thought the farm didn't produce enough income and he wanted me to get a job in town. I'd spent ten years in corporate America and I didn't have any desire to return to that rat race. My gift baskets, garden vegetables, and the cattle I sold at auction paid the household bills. I felt that his salary should cover all of the extras.

Derek didn't want to dine out or go to the movies or do anything except save every penny that we didn't absolutely need to live. He thought I wasn't contributing my fair share, but I wasn't going to change my lifestyle just for him. In my heart I felt that if we broke up, I could survive on my income and I still wouldn't have to return to my old way of life.

Maybe we should've talked more about those things before we got married, I thought. But when we were dating, Derek seemed thrilled with my ideas for keeping the farm afloat. Now he was angry with me over every little thing. And to be honest, I did watch a little too much TV and read a novel every few days, but I got my work done. All of my gift basket orders were filled and my business wasn't too shabby. In a few years I figured it would provide a decent living.

If Derek ever found a dirty dish in the sink, though, he'd get on my case. He'd accuse me of never doing any housework and claim that all I did was lounge around. Even though I took care of the livestock almost all of the time and planted and harvested the vegetables in the spring and summer, I still found time to do my gift baskets. I grew herbs to decorate the baskets along with my homemade cookies and mayhaw jelly. I was no slouch. Derek just thought I shouldn't ever be idle.

True, he worked long hours sometimes, but I'd done the same when I was an executive assistant and I was willing to increase the farm's output if he decided he wanted to quit his job. He could help me out and we'd be able to do all right.

As I lay there mulling over the last few months of bickering and fighting, I felt a fullness low in my belly. I'd missed my period that month, but had put it off on nerves. Now I wondered. I got up and went to the bathroom. On a whim, I decided to use the pregnancy test I kept in the medicine cabinet. I used one often, always hoping, but my hopes were dashed time after time.

A little while later I went back to check and was shocked by the results. The strip had turned blue! I was going to have a baby after all that time!

Will Derek be thrilled or angry? I wondered.

I wondered if I should even tell him. He'd been so out of sorts lately. He might think we couldn't afford a child, but I realized that I was happy. I'd wanted a baby for so long and now I was expecting! I wanted to laugh and shout it to the world. I decided right then and there that if Derek didn't want the baby, he could just move out and I'd raise the child on my own.

Wrapped up again in my blankets after eating a few more peanut butter crackers and drinking a glass of milk for the baby's sake, I fell asleep.

I awoke later on to the sound of an engine shutting off outside. I sprang to my feet and ran to the door.

Derek was trudging up the steps in the dark, his face haggard from lack of rest. After he swung open the door, I flew into his arms and hugged him. "Are you still on duty? The lights have been out for over twelve hours and there's no heat. I'm waiting for some wood to dry so I can build a fire."

I wished right then that I could've greeted him with the house clean, the dishes washed, and myself bathed and smelling of perfume, but it wasn't to be. He was probably too weary to care, anyway.

"I came home to change clothes," he said gruffly.

I wondered if he was still angry with me. I couldn't even remember what we'd argued about that morning. "Do you have to keep working?"

"No rest for the wicked." He quoted from the Bible, a book we've both been familiar with since childhood. That was another thing—we used to attend church together and we'd been slacking off. I remembered my mother saying, "The family that prays together, stays together."

Without another word, he headed straight for the bedroom to change his clothes. I stood around, wondering when we'd be able to talk and whether we'd fight again. Finally, I broke the silence.

"I'm sorry you aren't pleased with me as a wife, Derek. As soon as the power is on, I'll clean the house and make sure all the dishes are washed. I know you work hard and you deserve better than a wife who sits around watching romantic movies and reading romance novels."

He turned and looked at me and his expression was pinched. "Look, I'm sorry that I've been such an ogre lately. I guess I get stressed out at work and I come home and take it out on you."

I moved toward him and he pulled me close and kissed me. "I love you, Mary, just the way you are. You work hard, too, and you deserve a break when you want one. I don't have any right to boss you around and make you feel like you don't measure up, because you do."

"But I thought you wanted me to get a job in town and contribute more to the savings account."

"Forget that," Derek said, hugging me tighter. He drew back and gazed into my eyes. "We came upon a bad accident tonight out on the road. This couple was killed when a tree fell on their car and crushed them to death."

"Oh, no!"

6

After taking a deep breath, Derek continued. "I thought of you when I saw them. I realized that I've been taking you for granted and treating you like I don't love you. I guess I've been putting material things ahead of you, but I'm going to change. I intend to take you out to dinner at least once a week and we'll take in a movie, too. I love you, Mary, and I want to bring romance back into our relationship. I want you to be happy."

"I love you, too, Derek—so much."

He started to leave, but I stopped him. "I have something to tell you and I hope you'll be pleased."

"If it makes you happy, it makes me happy," he said.

"Well . . . I'm pregnant!"

Derek swooped me up in his arms and whooped with joy. Then he set me down gently and placed kisses all over my face. "I'm proud and happy. Nothing could be better than the news you've just given me."

"So, you aren't worried about our finances?"

He shook his head. "We'll make out fine."

Glancing around the room, he frowned. "Are you warm enough? I don't want you to get cold."

I laughed. "I'll get the fire started in just a minute. The wood has dried out."

"Okay, if you're sure," Derek said. "I've got to get back to work, but we'll get up this way in the next few hours."

"Baby and I will be just fine until you get back," I said.

After Derek left, I was able to start the fire after several failed attempts. A sense of accomplishment came over me as the blaze grew stronger and warmed the room. At the same time, the joy inside of me created a warmth that no fire could rival.

Derek and I feel very sorry for the couple who died in that blizzard. Somehow, though, it's changed our lives and brought us back to each other. We'd been taking each other for granted and might've split up if we hadn't realized what we'd lose.

Spring has come and the baby is on the way. We're working hard to add crops and more livestock to the farm. Derek is helping out more now and our love life is the best it's ever been.

The End

A CHRISTMAS BABY
The miracle of having everyone
home for the holidays.

"What is that ringing? Oh, the phone," I mumbled as I reached for the offending instrument.

"Mom, this is Tyson, can you come to the hospital to get David?"

Immediately, I was awake. Tyson and David were my son-in-law and grandson, respectively.

"What is it? Not the baby. It's still November!" My new grandson was due in the middle of December.

"Well, the baby has decided to come a bit early, and we're already at the hospital. I didn't think we had time to stop, but I guess we did." He sounded very tired.

"Oh, my. I'll be there as soon as I can."

The new baby was coming early and our youngest daughter, Toni, was already at Ft. Leonard Wood in basic training with the National Guard. My older daughter, Erica, and I had planned to have a big family Christmas. The new baby would be here and Toni had a break for the holidays. Well, no problem, we would still go on with our Christmas plans. Lots of babies come a little early and everything would be fine.

After I arrived, David decided he would stay, so we all sat down for a rather long wait, especially for a five-year-old child.

Finally, a nurse appeared at the waiting room door holding a blue-wrapped bundle.

"Mr. Freeman, Grandma, we have a fine baby boy."

She held the baby out for inspection.

"He's so little," exclaimed his big brother and reached out to touch him.

His Dad pulled his hand back, but the nurse held the baby toward David.

"You can touch him. After all, he's your little brother."

David touched the baby's tiny fingers, his nose and rubbed his head. The wonder and amazement at such a little creature showed in his big, brown eyes.

The nurse said, "You can come to the nursery and watch him while we get Mrs. Freeman to her room."

We followed the nurse down the hall. There were steps for children to stand on to peep at their new brothers and sisters, so David pressed his nose to the window.

All the babies were under lights, on their backs, with diapers on—except ours. He was naked and on his stomach.

His Dad and I were totally unprepared for what we saw, but David spoke first.

"Grandma, what's that on the baby's back?"

I stared at the perfectly formed baby boy. He was perfect except for a half-dollar sized disfigurement at the base of his spine which had a small pulsating center.

Tyson looked frightened and shaken. We were not expecting this. We were shocked.

A nurse came out of the nursery, and I asked what the strange-looking disfigurement was.

She gave me a medical term, and I asked if it was dangerous.

"It can be," she answered and went on her way.

Later, in Erica's hospital room, Tyson and I kept quiet and let the doctor explain what baby Elliot had. He would have to stay in the nursery in an incubator for a week, then he'd have surgery to close the gaping hole in his spine. It was a form of spina bifida, which to me and my children was a horrifying term.

The next few weeks were filled with cliff-hanging situations. They kept the baby in an incubator except when it was feeding time. Erica made two trips a day to feed him herself, which was a strain. We lived thirty miles from the hospital. He looked so pitiful and pathetic—a tiny, little baby with all this medical equipment attached to him.

We went down for his surgery when he was a week old. The surgeon discussed the problems that might occur. He could close the opening easily, but if fluid had leaked out or an infection had gotten in the opening, the baby could lose the use of his legs and possibly have bowel and urinary tract problems. He may also have to insert a shunt to relieve the pressure of fluids gathering on his brain.

All these medical ifs, ands, and buts hit my daughter hard. Her usually sunny outlook on life crumbled, and she really cried for the first time. I held back the tears for her sake, and we waited and waited.

The whole morning was a nightmare. We were both ready to scream when the doctor appeared. The surgery had gone well. "Now we wait," he said.

"For how long?" Erica wanted to know.

"Until we determine if fluid is collecting on the brain and check his bowel and urinary tract. He seems to have a weaker side that doesn't have quite the reflex it should, but we'll worry about that later. We just hope the fluid does not collect and we can avoid the shunt."

The doctor was kind, but his words were very distressing.

"You're lucky, Mrs. Freeman. It is a rare form of spina bifida.

9

However, he could still develop complications. We're just going to have to wait and see."

I drove home in a haze. How would these children cope with this? Would their insurance hold out? I prayed that the baby would be fine.

The nurses measured his head every day for evidence of fluid retention, but it seemed he was holding his own.

I took off early from my job a few days later and went to the hospital. I wanted to visit my grandson alone. Grandparents were the only people who could visit in the nursery besides parents. Tyson's parents were gone, so my husband and I were his only grandparents.

I stepped into the elevator with mixed feelings. I wanted to see him, and yet I dreaded seeing that tiny, little thing all trussed up in a glass bubble.

I walked to the neonatal unit, remembering my trip to the maternity ward in this same hospital, eighteen years ago.

The nurse led me to Elliot's little glass bed. I was gowned and had washed my hands for the required three minutes. I passed tinier babies, preemies with all sorts of problems. She got me a stool and told me I could put my hands through the little doors and touch him.

He was sleeping amid all the noise of machines and muted voices. He was so little, and yet bigger than most of the babies in the neonatal intensive care unit, and the bandages on his back and the tubes in and out of his head made me catch my breath.

I rubbed his back and his little shaved head. I wondered if his hair would ever come back correctly.

I touched his hand, and it closed around my finger. His legs wiggled and I whispered, "Oh joy, he can move them!"

I sat for a few minutes watching him. He was a part of me, so much like his mother. Her other son was the spitting image of his dad, but this one certainly had her looks. I left the hospital feeling just a little better and wondering if little Elliot would be home soon—it would be another important baby's birthday in two weeks, it was almost Christmas, and I wanted my babies to be home.

More bad news met me when I got home. My daughter had taken seriously ill at basic training. She had a colon problem that would eventually require extensive surgery, and she was being discharged. The problem: a glitch in paper work, lost orders, and other Army regulations made it seem impossible for her to return by Christmas.

Those were the worst two weeks imaginable. I threw myself into redoing her room and helping Erica with her plans. If the kids were not home for Christmas, we would wait until they were to celebrate.

Baby Elliot was doing better. There was no fluid retention, but the doctor said to wait and observe.

The army kept saying that it takes one and a half weeks to process new orders. I was fit to be tied, but what could I do? Two of my children were not here. One was in a sterile, quiet, white hospital neonatal unit, and one was in a forlorn Army base one thousand miles from home.

Two days before Christmas, my daughter called.

"Mama, we can bring the baby home! We're going to get him now!"

I was elated. This baby would not know what it meant, but his family did.

That night, I was still moping around the house when the phone rang rather late.

"Mama," said a tired, little voice. "I'm at the Montgomery airport. Can you pick me up?"

Could I? Her dad and I left like a streak. The first thing Toni wanted to know was if the baby had come home.

Toni's explanation for being home: a caring commanding officer walked her through a new set of orders and put her on a plane home.

We still had Toni's surgery and Elliot's predicted problems to go through, but that Christmas was the best in my fifty-odd years. All my children were with me. That is the height of motherhood: having all your children around you on such an occasion. We would get through the future problems, and I was truly thankful that the other baby, whose birthday we always celebrate on Christmas day, saw it fit to send my babies home to me.

The End

ICE STORM RESOLUTION
Some problems just need
time to work out.

"Mom, the commode's making funny noises."

I glanced up from my work to look at my eight-year-old daughter, Kendra, ready to shoot the messenger. Despite the fact that it was below freezing outside, sweat trickled down my back. Trying not to growl, I said, "When I get this blasted fork out of the garbage disposal, I'll take a look at the commode."

"Donald says you should call Dad."

"I'm not calling your dad."

With a grunt, I yanked on the offending fork. It finally broke free. I held it up for inspection, saw that several prongs were missing, and dove back into the garbage disposal to find them. When I had recovered all three missing prongs, I flipped the switch on the garbage disposal.

It worked!

Grinning with triumph, I looked at Kendra. "See? I fixed the garbage disposal. I can fix the toilet, too."

"But what if you can't? Donald says—"

"What's with this 'Donald says' stuff?" I asked suspiciously. "Normally, you two are fighting like cats and dogs. Even if he repeated the pledge of allegiance verbatim, you'd still argue with him."

Kendra's gaze slid away from mine, like it usually did when she was attempting to lie. "I was just telling you what Donald said," she mumbled before dashing away.

With a weary sigh, I gathered up the tools I'd been using and trudged upstairs to check out the commode.

When it rains, it pours, I thought, remembering my grandmother using the cliché when I was young. I opened the bathroom door and listened. Sure enough, the commode was making a strange noise.

I didn't know a thing about commodes, other than how to flush them, scrub them, and plunge them when they became stopped up; but then again, I hadn't known anything about garbage disposals, either. Removing the lid, I peered inside. I pushed the handle, but it flopped uselessly, cluing me into the fact that the chain wasn't connected to the handle. Doubtful the solution could be that simple, I reconnected the chain anyway.

It worked.

Ha! I thought. Take that Mr. Too-busy-too-fix-it DuPont. Trent DuPont was my husband, and we'd been legally separated for two months. He had his own apartment, and I had every reason to believe he was dating one of his clients.

"Did you fix it?"

I turned around to find Donald, my twelve-year-old son, standing in the bathroom doorway with a hopeful look on his freckled face. He had inherited his red hair and freckles from his father, and it was becoming obvious that he was going to be every bit as good-looking too.

"Yes, I did." I caught a flash of disappointment in his eyes before he summoned an obviously fake smile for my benefit. My heart turned over. Our separation was taking its toll on our kids. I knew that Donald had been hoping I'd have to call Trent. I knew they missed him terribly. They hadn't seen much of him when we'd been together as a family; they saw even less of him now.

"Hey, why don't you and your sister get a big bowl of clean snow so that we can make snow cream?" Snow cream was a mixture of milk, eggs, vanilla flavoring, and snow. My mother used to make it for us when I was growing up. My kids loved it, so we were always eager for the first snowfall.

"Okay."

My son's lack of enthusiasm broke my heart. How would he react if Trent and I got a divorce? I knew that divorce was a definite possibility. Although I knew that I might someday forgive Trent for cheating on me, I didn't think I could ever trust him again, and what was a marriage without trust?

While the kids were outside gathering snow for the snow cream, I remembered that I'd needed to put a load of laundry into the dryer. Before I reached the laundry room, I saw the water seeping out from under the door.

With a cry of dismay, I jerked open the door. The laundry room was flooded, and I could tell by the soapy suds floating on top of the water that the washing machine was the culprit.

"What's next?" I said out loud as I grabbed a mop and began soaking up the water. I was nearly finished when the kids found me.

"What happened, Mom?" Donald asked.

"I don't know yet. I just came in here and there was water all over the place."

"Maybe you should all Dad."

I had time to interrupt him, but I didn't. I felt too guilty. Instead, I said, "I'm going to check it out myself. If I can't fix it, I'll call your dad." Or a plumber, I thought, but didn't say it. Even a busy plumber could probably get to it faster than Trent could or would. "You and your sister can get all the ingredients ready for the snow cream."

"I get to crack the eggs," Kendra stated.

Donald snorted. "You are a cracked egg, egghead."

When they'd gone, I finished mopping and crawled onto the washing machine to peer at the back where I knew the water hoses were connected. They seemed fine, but I noticed the drain hose wasn't inserted in the drain tube. Evidently, the water pressure had caused it pop out of the drain. I popped it back in and got down, beginning to wonder if I had a little house gremlin running around causing mischief.

Or two.

The more I thought about it, the more suspicious I became. I knew that my son was perfectly capable of sabotaging household appliances so that I would have to call his father. Although the possibility exasperated me, it also made my heart constrict. Couldn't Trent see what he was doing to his children? I was fine: I loved having the bed all to myself, never having to worry about sitting down on a wet toilet seat, and never having to explain to the kids—again—that Daddy had to work late.

In fact, the only thing different about Trent living with us and Trent living without us was the occasional sex he and I had, or the occasional dinner.

As I was heading for the kitchen, I glanced out the big picture window in the living room. It was snowing hard. I knew there was a winter storm watch and I bit my lip, wondering just how bad it would get. When Trent and I decided to build our dream home, we'd opted for the country. We'd found four acres of land about five miles from the nearest city. I loved the country. Unfortunately, it took the electric company a lot longer to get to us when we had the occasional power outage, but so far, we'd been pretty lucky.

As if nature had plucked the thought from my head, the electricity went off. It was still daylight, but the heavy cloud coverage made it seem like twilight inside the house. With a heavy sigh, I headed for the basement where I kept our emergency supplies of lanterns, candles, and flashlights. Our house was heavily insulated, so I knew that it would be a few hours before it started getting cold, and I could always build a fire in the fireplace.

When I opened the basement door, I ran head long into Kendra. We both shrieked before we could stop ourselves. Frowning, I looked over her guilty head to my son, who stood close behind his sister with a flashlight.

My kids were supposed to be in the kitchen mixing snow cream, and instead, they had been in the basement—where the breaker box was—when the lights went out. From the looks of their faces, it wasn't going to be hard pulling a confession out of them.

14

Fairly certain now that they had been behind the string of mishaps all day, I didn't have to force myself to be stern. Enough was enough. Besides, it was dangerous to mess with a power box, and Donald knew it. It made me even angrier that he'd gotten his sister involved.

"What were you two doing in the basement?" I demanded, deciding to see if they would try and lie anyway.

Donald tilted a defensive chin, proving that he was a quick thinker. "Looking for our snow shoes."

"Why? You've already gathered the snow for the snow cream." I folded my arms and refrained from tapping my toes. Kendra kept her gaze on the ground. She had yet to master the art of lying.

"We wanted to go back out and play," Donald said, a little desperately.

My gaze traveled to his hands: one was empty, and the other held the flash light. "So where are they?"

"What?"

"The snow shoes." I bit my lip to keep it from twitching. Donald looked as if he'd swallowed one of those snow shoes. He was quick, but he wasn't faster than I was.

"Oh. Well, you see—"

"Never mind, Donald. I know you and your sister pulled the breaker, and I know why you did it. Still, that doesn't make it right. Now you march right back down there and turn it back on."

Looking earnest, Kendra grabbed her brother's shirt and whispered something to him. Donald frowned and shook his head. I noticed that he'd gone pale.

A trickle of unease drifted down my spine. "What is it, Kendra? Donald?"

Kendra hung her head and started to mumble something, but Donald dug an elbow into her back.

"Stop it!" I said sharply. "Kendra, wait for me in the kitchen. Now!" When she left, I pinned a steely eye on my son. "The game's over, Donald. If there's something you need to tell me, now would be a good time."

Donald's earlier bravado deflated like a balloon. His eyes watered as he struggled not to cry. "I didn't mean to."

Patiently, I waited.

"All I did was pull the breaker down, like Dad taught me. But— but something happened. Sparks flew out all over the place." He picked up his t-shirt and pointed to a small hole. "See? One got me right there."

My knees went weak at the thought of how badly they could have been hurt. And like most mothers, my fear fueled my anger. "You could have been killed," I said icily.

15

"I know." He hung his head. One lone tear slid across his freckled cheek.

"You could have gotten your sister killed, too."

His chest hitched. "I'm sorry! I just wanted Dad to come over!"

The mother in me wanted to crumble, pull him in for a hug, and tell him I understood. The parent in me kept my distance. What he'd done was dangerous. "We'll discuss your punishment later. Right now, you can come with me to see if we can figure out what happened." I took his flashlight and stepped past him on the stairs.

"Maybe we should—" he started, but stopped abruptly when I turned back to glare at him. I knew that he'd been about to suggest we call his father. In my opinion, that would be paramount to rewarding him for his wrongful deed.

If it could be fixed, I would fix it myself.

Two hours later, it was beginning to grow cold in the house. As badly as I hated to admit it, what Donald had done to the breaker box was beyond my comprehension.

When I emerged—defeated—from the frigid basement, I could see the suggestion hovering on Donald's lips. Still, he managed to refrain, and I silently congratulated him.

"It's getting cold in here, Mom," Kendra said.

"I know, baby. It's probably going to get a lot colder, too." I glanced at Donald, and then quickly looked away. Two hours in a dark, frigid basement hadn't softened my heart any. "Do you still remember how to build a fire?" I asked him. He nodded, perking up. "Then do that for me, will you?" I turned and headed for the wall phone in the kitchen, the only one that wasn't plugged into an outlet. I knew I was being mean by not telling them I was going to call their dad, but I was still upset with them.

I dialed Trent's cell phone, got his voice mail, and left a brief message, asking him to call me back as soon as he could. I'd taken three steps away from the phone when it rang, startling me. Not expecting Trent so soon, I picked up the phone and said hello.

It was Trent. "You called?"

I tried to focus on the situation at hand and not on what Trent might have been doing when I called him and got his voice mail. He owned his own construction company, and I knew he couldn't have been working in this weather. "Um, yeah. Are you busy?"

There was a surprised pause, then he said, "Um, no. I was just watching the weather channel. They've already closed several interstates because of the blizzard."

His answer gave me pause, because I knew that if Trent could get to our house, there was a good chance he wouldn't be able to leave. He might have to stay the night.

16

I ignored a spear of yearning that bloomed in my chest. "Yeah, it looks bad. Um, I'm calling because our power is out, and I—"

"Are you okay? Are the kids okay? Is it cold in the house? Do you have any firewood?"

He shot the questions at me quickly. He sounded alarmed, as if he cared. I had to swallow a silly lump and remind myself of all the lonely nights I'd spent wishing he would come home early. "We're okay. Yes, it's getting cold, and yes, we've got a little firewood. Donald's starting the fire right now."

"Remind him to open the flue in the fireplace," Trent said quickly.

It irritated me that I hadn't thought of it first. Covering the mouthpiece, I shouted to Donald, "Remember to open the flue!"

"Okay, Mom!" he called back.

"This darn storm," Trent said, recapturing my attention.

"Well . . . we can't blame this one on the storm," I said slowly. "Which is why I called you. Donald pulled the handle on the breaker box."

There was a shocked silence. "Why would he do that?"

For the life of me, I couldn't keep the bitterness out of my reply. "Because he wanted me to think there was something wrong and call you to come fix it."

"And?" Trent's voice had chilled at my tone.

"And his plan didn't go as expected. He said sparks shot out all over the place. I've tried turning it back on, but it looks as if a wire melted on the thick cable leading into the box."

"Don't touch it again," Trent warned sharply.

Stiffly, I said, "I wasn't planning on it." I could have gone on to explain that I'd been worrying about the breaker box for two hours, but I didn't. Trent would have just chided me for fussing over spilled milk, and I wasn't in the mood. Besides, I wasn't a total idiot. I had fixed the garbage disposal, the toilet, and the washer.

"I should be there in thirty minutes." He paused a moment and then added, "make that an hour. It's really coming down out there. I just hope they haven't closed the road to our house."

When we hung up, I stared at the phone with a snarl. Trent had called it "our" house, as if he still lived with us, as if he planned on returning any day now. Didn't he realize how serious our problems were? I had made up my mind. Unless Trent promised to make a lot of changes, our marriage was over.

"Mom? Was that Dad?"

I smoothed the ugly snarl from my lips and replaced it with a smile. I turned to face Donald and Kendra standing in the doorway. "Yes, it was. He's coming to look at the breaker box."

Their whoops of joy slammed into my heart like burning arrows.

The smile froze on my face as I watched them leap into the air and hug each other. As a child of divorced parents, I had vowed that my own children would never have to know that kind of pain. I had failed in that vow. The realization left an ugly feeling in my stomach.

"Can we make him stay for dinner?" Donald pleaded.

"Can he stay the night?" Kendra piped in innocently.

Hedging around Donald's question and completely ignoring Kendra's, I said, "From the looks of things, we're going to be having roasted weenies over an open fire. Your dad hates hot dogs, remember?"

Donald's face flushed as he hopped from one foot to the other in his excitement. "We've got some frozen steaks in the freezer. I could thaw one out and cook it in a skillet over the fire, couldn't I? And if we throw some potatoes in now, they'd be done by then. We did that at camp, and they were good, except for the part that was scorched."

"I could make him some Koolaid," Kendra declared. "He likes grape."

I didn't have the heart to burst their bubbles, so I nodded, cringing as they whooped and danced around the kitchen. As I watched them, fighting tears, I prayed that Trent would notice and appreciate how much his children loved him. I could make it just fine on my own, but they needed him badly.

Telling myself that everything would probably spoil anyway if the power didn't come on soon, I decided to throw together a salad to go with the steak and hot dogs. Ice pinged against the kitchen window as I diced tomatoes and cucumbers. I frowned, trying not to worry. A blizzard was bad enough, but an ice storm could be downright dangerous. Would Trent turn around and go back when he realized it was sleeting? Once upon a time, I could have second-guessed what Trent would do. Not anymore. Not for a while now. We'd lost that special connection couples have with each other.

Forty-five minutes later, the front doorbell rang. I could tell by the whoops and hollers from the kids that it was Trent. Trying to appear casual, I dried my hands and sauntered to the open doorway leading into the living room. Trent was unloading a stack of ice-crusted wood into the nearly empty wood box. He glanced up at me, and his expression warmed.

"I'd better bring some more in so it can dry out. We might need it." He ruffled Donald's hair. "Want to help me, sport? Get your coat and gloves."

"Me too! Me too!" Kendra said, jumping up and down.

I held my breath, hoping that Trent made the right decision.

Trent looked at Kendra and smiled. He reached out and cupped her check. "Sure. But you'd better bundle up. It's freezing out there."

Kendra laughed happily. "Oh, Daddy! As if we didn't know that!"

"Well, aren't you a smarty."

Oblivious to his teasing, Kendra beamed at him. "I am. Mama says so."

Our gazes met briefly, and again it seemed as if Trent's expression warmed several degrees, as if he was glad to see me but was trying not to show it.

After they carried several loads of frozen wood inside, we all trekked down to the dark, cold basement to take a look at the breaker box.

Trent studied it for a long moment and then shook his head. The gaze he aimed at Donald was chiding. "Look's like you did it in, sport. The cable's melted. I could rig it, but I wouldn't feel comfortable doing that, not when we're so far out of town. If there was a fire—" He didn't have to explain. I think even Kendra, who looked scared, understood his meaning.

"What are we going to do?" I asked, beginning to panic. "I doubt we'd get an electrician to come out in this storm."

"You're probably right," Trent agreed. "We'll have to wait the storm out, or try to make it back to town."

"I want to stay here!" Donald said.

Kendra echoed her brother's sentiment.

Clearly Trent was waiting for my vote. Since the alternative was his apartment or a hotel room, I opted to stay. "We have plenty of firewood. If it gets too cold, we can block off the living room instead of trying to heat the whole house." I hesitated, and then added firmly, "We'll be fine. You don't have to worry about us."

Trent jerked his head as if I'd slapped him. "You think I'd leave you guys out here alone in this storm without power?" he asked incredulously.

That was the problem—I didn't know what Trent would do or not do. The reminder kept me stubborn. "Really, we'd be okay. I'm not helpless."

"I never said you were." Trent put an arm around the kids' shoulders. His smile was just a little too bright to be real, but the kids didn't seem to notice. "I'm starving! Got any grub for your old man?"

Deafened by their squeals of excitement, I turned and led the way back upstairs. I could feel Trent watching me. What was he thinking? Feeling? At the top of the stairs, I turned to look down at them as they began to ascend. "I think I'm going to take a hot bath while the water's still hot," I said. I had to get away from them, from the reminder that we weren't a family now. Maybe for a while the kids could pretend, but I couldn't.

It hurt too much.

19

Immersed in bubbles up to my chin, I didn't have to look into my children's hopeful, sad little faces or wonder what was behind Trent's penetrating, warm stare.

Instead, I could think about the good times, before Trent and I became strangers who lived together.

We'd been high school sweethearts from the tenth grade onward. My parents had tried to talk me out of getting married right after graduation, but I was a woman in love. Trent and I wanted to get an early start on a family, build our dream house, and grow old together. My parents wanted me to go to college and have a career first, in case marriage didn't work out.

I remember laughing at my mother, with complete conviction, that Trent and I would be together until one of us died. Couldn't she see that we were soul mates? But I knew what was really bothering my parents. Trent wasn't on the same social scale, as if that mattered these days.

I guess it mattered to them. Daddy was a judge, and my mother was a nurse practitioner. Trent's father was a mechanic, and his mother ran a daycare center from her home. We lived in a two-story house in a rich part of town. Trent's parents still rented, and their neighborhood wasn't exactly great.

It was the classic rich girl, poor boy story, but Trent and I never saw it that way. We loved each other. I'm not saying that Trent wasn't proud, he was, and he proved it by turning my father down when my father offered to make a down payment on our first house. Trent flatly, but politely, told him that we would build our own house and pay for it ourselves.

We had a rocky first year. Trent attempted to start his own construction business, and I got pregnant the first month we were married. We'd planned on starting a family soon, but I don't think either of us thought it would be that soon. We were still living in an apartment, a cramped one bedroom that we had laughingly called our "hovel."

Suddenly, the hovel wasn't funny any longer. We were sharing our bedroom with a screaming baby who cried for three hours every night for the first two months of his life. We loved him, but there were some nights when we were so exhausted that we would have gladly traded him in for a good night's sleep.

Our sex life became almost nonexistent during that time, but when Donald was four months old, the crying suddenly stopped. For the next four nights, we stood and watched him sleep, unable to believe it was over.

Gradually, Trent and I resumed our enjoyable sex life, although we were forced to creep into the living room to make love. By silent agreement, we decided to wait a while before we planned our next child.

Despite the strain on our finances, I stayed home with Donald, just as Trent and I had planned. He never knew that sometimes my mother brought me household supplies and food when he was at work.

By the time Kendra came along four years later, we had moved into a two-bedroom house in the neighborhood where Trent's parents lived. Trent had already begun the blueprints on our dream home, and on occasional weekends, he and I would drive around for hours looking at land for sale. We knew it would be a few years down the road before we could buy, but we would get excited just talking about it.

Finally, when Kendra was three years old, we found the perfect spot for our house. Trent put up his business as collateral, and we got the loan. He planned to start building on the weekends, using his free time so that his business wouldn't suffer. To our humble delight, several of his employees volunteered their time when they could manage it. Trent was a great boss, and it paid off.

The house took a year and a half to build, and another six months to furnish. We furnished one room at a time, painstakingly choosing furniture that we hoped would last a lifetime so that we could create our own family heirlooms.

Suddenly, my bathwater was as cold as my thoughts.

I couldn't pinpoint exactly when Trent began to change, but it seemed to start after we'd been living in our new house for a year or so. He became distant and irritable, and he started working later and later. I knew that he did a lot of inside construction and worked a skeleton crew at night, but our marriage had started to suffer and Trent didn't seem to care.

I was convinced that Trent was falling out of love with me, yet I couldn't bring myself to ask him. I guess I feared the answer more than I feared the possibility.

The bathroom was cold by the time I got out and dressed in warm flannel pajamas. I walked in on a scene in the living room that I knew I would never forget.

Trent and the kids were playing Monopoly by lantern light. I stood in the doorway and watched them for a moment, until Kendra saw me.

"Mom!" she shrieked. "Come play with us! I'm beating the boys."

"She is," Trent grumbled good-naturedly, shooting me a crooked smile. "How many times has she played this?"

"A lot," I said. I wanted to add that we played a board game together every Saturday night and he would know that if he'd ever been home, but I bit my tongue and forced a stiff smile. "She's really good."

"So . . . will you play with us?" Trent asked softly. "After we eat?"

The knot of tension inside me eased a little. "Sure. I thought I smelled roasted hotdogs. Are they ready? I'm starving."

Trent's steak was a little overdone and the potatoes were scorched on the outside and firm on the inside, but nobody seemed to care. Afterward, we played monopoly until Kendra yawned herself to sleep. I brought in a pile of blankets and made a pallet in front of the fire, and Trent moved her to the makeshift bed.

To my surprise—and suspicion—Donald announced he was tired as well, and he crawled beneath the covers alongside his sister. My gaze met Trent's, and I knew that he knew that Donald was attempting to give us some alone time.

I watched the shadows from the firelight dance along the walls and wondered what Trent and I would talk about.

Finally, Trent broke the (oddly) contented silence. "You can have the couch, and I'll bunk on the floor with the kids."

I shrugged to show him that it didn't matter to me one way or the other. I shot a glance at him from the cover of my lashes and caught a flicker of yearning in his eyes. My ears caught fire. How long had it been since he'd last looked at me that way? Six months? A year? Longer?

"Did you talk to Donald about his actions today?" I asked, hoping to get back on safer ground. The setting was too intimate for Trent to be looking at me as if he'd missed me.

"I did," Trent said quietly, as if he had something else on his mind entirely. "He knows he was wrong. I told him it was partly my fault, for not making the time to see him and his sister more often."

His confession startled me into looking at him. It was hard to deny the sincerity in his eyes. "Um, I don't mean to sound accusing, but I agree."

"You know, that's part of our problem," Trent said, astounding me.

My eyes went wide. "What?"

"I said that's part of the problem. You don't tell me what you're feeling. You just get mad and get even."

I couldn't believe what I was hearing! "Are you trying to blame all our marriage problems on me?" I asked in a squeaky, disbelieving voice.

Trent shook his head. "No, no. I know that I'm more than partly to blame for our problems. I was so wrapped up in trying to give you the life you were used to that I forgot what was really important. By the time I realized it, you had asked for a separation."

My jaw hung open. Was it really that simple? Was Trent right? The possibility made me feel defensive. "Are you trying to say that if I had pointed it out to you more often, you would have changed?"

"Sara, you never pointed it out to me at all. You just got angrier and angrier, and colder and colder."

I had to stand for that one. "Oh, come on! Don't sit there and try to convince me that you had no idea why I was mad at you!"

My husband ran a hand through his auburn hair and sighed. "Maybe I did know, but the old Sara would have bawled me out the first time I was late coming home."

"I didn't want to become a nag!" It was the truth.

"So you preferred to be a divorcee, rather than a nag?" Trent challenged.

I clamped down hard on my tongue, glancing at the kids. Kendra was snoring softly, but I had no proof that Donald was asleep. Sitting down beside Trent, I looked him straight in the eye and kept my voice low, so Donald couldn't hear me. "I knew you had to work hard to pay for this house. I knew you were doing it for us, but you just never stopped. It was as if you had forgotten us." I swallowed hard, forcing myself to continue. I was about to tell Trent what had been eating at me for months now. "In fact, I made us a picnic one night and asked your mom to come over and baby-sit the kids. I went to the house you were working on to surprise you, and I saw you sitting in the floor of that new house with another woman, having a picnic with her." Tears stung my eyes at the memory. "You were laughing and you looked so happy."

Trent winced, obviously remembering. "That was Kathy, my client. Her husband had just made partner at his firm but had stood her up for their celebration date in lieu of a surprise party his new partners had thrown. It was all innocent. She needed to talk to someone, and I was hungry and needed a break. I swear that's all that happened."

I looked into his eyes for a long time, finally conceding that he might be telling the truth. "You said . . . you said that I should have said something the first time you worked late. I don't think that's fair. What about you? If you really missed us, why would you work night after night, weekend after weekend, without taking a break to spend time with your family?"

Trent hesitated. He frowned. "I'm not sure I've got an answer for that one, other than it just became a habit. I guess I was driven . . . and a little afraid that I wouldn't be able to stay on top of our bills and your parents would say, 'I told you so.' I couldn't stand the thought of that."

A smiled pulled at my lips. "Now that I can believe. You and that stubborn pride of yours."

"My pride? What about yours?" Trent tapped my chin with his finger, reminding me of the old days. "Instead of telling a guy you miss him, you ask him to move out?"

I blushed and hung my head. "I thought you were having an affair with that woman," I mumbled. I was in shock at the thought of how close I had come to throwing away our future over a misunderstanding.

Trent sounded a little shocked himself as he whispered, "God, I could have lost you." His voice ached. He reached out and cupped my neck, drawing me closer. "If you had any idea how miserable I've been—"

"Me, too." For the first time, I could admit it. My mouth inched closer to his. My insides began to quiver at the thought of his kiss. Trent was the absolute best kisser, among other things, and I had missed him. He was not only my husband and the father of my kids, but he was my best friend.

"Does this mean we can work things out?" he whispered against my mouth. He was teasing me, nuzzling my lips, knowing that he was driving me crazy.

"I think—" My answer was interrupted by Donald's victory shout.

"Yahoo! Did you hear that Kendra? Wake up! Mom and Dad are getting back together!"

Just as I had expected, the sneaky little rascal had not been asleep.

Trent and I slept on our own little makeshift bed the rest of that cold night. Towards dawn, we silently moved to our bedroom and locked the door.

The End

HOLIDAY MAGIC
Will my dream come true?

My friend Malina, called from down the hall, "Sarah, wait up a sec!"

Malina had trained me when I first came to work as a data transcriber for Davies Medical. We also became good friends. Even though she was eventually promoted and moved to a different part of the building, we still remained close.

I turned and smiled. "Hi! How are you?"

"Fine. I'm glad I caught you. I'm going to my parents' house for Christmas Eve dinner, and I thought you might like to join us."

"How thoughtful of you. I really appreciate it, but I'm going home."

"That's super. I thought you said you were staying in town."

"I was, but I really miss my family. I'm going to fly home tomorrow."

"Well, I've got to run," Malina said, glancing at her watch.

"Thanks again for thinking of me," I said, giving Malina a hug. "And say hello to your folks."

"I will."

I guess she didn't want me to be alone for the holiday. Who does? Had I not decided to head home, I would have probably joined her. However, in all honesty, now that I've decided to go home, wild horses couldn't keep me from going. I hadn't seen my family at all this past year. And it had been a rough one. Aside from the fact that I had moved away to be on my own, I had also broken up with my fiancé, Herschel. This would be the first of many holidays I'd be spending without him.

Herschel. I used to say his name with such reverence. We were going to spend our lives together until eternity. That was before I realized how crowded it would be. I can still see the day that turned my entire world inside out as vividly as if it happened yesterday.

We had just finalized our wedding plans the night before. I was so excited and told Malina all about it the next day at work. However, by the end of the morning, my good cheer had all but evaporated, because I began to feel really ill. As soon as I started to get queasy, I knew it was time to leave. I drove home and walked into the apartment. The first thing that greeted me was the unmistakable rhythmic squeaking of my mattress. As I neared the bedroom, I heard a woman moan. I was thrilled that she was having such a great time in my bed with my man. The door was wide open, so I decided to join the party. Herschel

25

saw me first, and he practically threw her off him.

"Sarah! What are you doing here?" he exclaimed.

"Last time I checked, I lived here." Feeling more nauseous by the minute.

"Don't you feel well? You look a little green."

"I'm sick, and seeing this, makes me feel worse."

During this time, the woman, whom I later learned was Herschel's assistant, grabbed her things and slinked out.

Herschel began to apologize, but I wasn't in any mood to hear it.

"I don't care to hear your lies or whatever you want to call them. I'm sure that this wasn't the first time."

"How could you even think that?"

"Because if you cheat on someone once, you'll do it again. It's the first time that's so difficult."

Herschel tried to put his arms around me, but I pushed him away. "Right now, I don't know if it's the bug I picked up, or your unwelcome presence that's making my stomach turn."

"What are you saying?"

I had already taken his ring from my finger. Since this was his apartment, I would have to find another place to live. I was feeling more wretched by the moment, and I needed to be alone.

"I'm saying good-bye. Here's your ring. Now, if you'll excuse me, I have to puke."

I left him standing there speechless as I went into the bathroom and vomited. He was waiting for me when I came out.

"I don't have the strength to talk to you, now," I said as I stripped the bed.

The last thing I wanted to sleep on was a set of soiled bed sheets containing evidence of his indiscretion. Seeing how sick I was, Herschel helped me make the bed. Whether he thought that would win him brownie points mattered little to me at that point. All I wanted to do was lie down and close my eyes so that the spinning in my head would stop.

"We'll talk about this later," he said.

"As soon as I'm feeling better, I'm leaving you."

The word why came tumbling out of his mouth, but he realized how stupid it sounded. He amended it with "I don't want you to leave."

"You certainly have a funny way of showing that," I replied, my eyes closed. "Just go away and let me sleep."

Herschel came home with chicken soup that night, but I couldn't eat it. I just wanted to sleep. The good part about my being so sick was that I didn't think about his infidelity and my decision to leave. That pain would come later when I was feeling better.

Despite Herschel's protests of love and promises never to cheat again, I found the courage to move on. Unfortunately, that resolve would waiver in the following days.

It certainly was a most difficult year, but seeing my parents and older sister and brother would soon cheer me up.

My sister, Rimona, was married to Jerry, a policeman. They had two little girls, ages one and three. My brother, Ian, was married to a lovely woman named Shannon, and had two boys, ages three and five, and a darling baby girl who just turned one. Herschel had become part of my family, and he had gotten along well with them. However, I'd rather be alone than tied to a guy I couldn't trust.

The following morning, I was about to get on the highway leading out of the city when I realized that I had forgotten to bring a cake for my parents. To them, Hanukkah was a holiday for the children, and they didn't want me to bring them gifts. Not wanting to go empty-handed, I turned around. As I drove toward the bakery to get some cookies or a cake, I passed the department store on Main Street, and an idea popped into my head. Instead of a cake, I'd get a holiday basket. Pleased with myself for coming up with such a terrific idea, I looked for a parking spot, and I entered the department store.

I went to the gourmet foods department on four. I chose quickly so I wouldn't miss my plane.

There were many terrific baskets to choose from, but if I didn't want to miss my plane, I'd have to make my decision quickly. I finally selected a basket filled with a variety of cheeses from around the world, crackers, smoked meats, and a bottle of sparkling wine. Turning around quickly, I collided with another person knocking their basket to the floor.

I knelt down to help pick up the scattered items, apologizing and feeling so clumsy, when I turned to face one of the most handsome men I'd ever seen. I couldn't help but notice his deep brown eyes framed by long thick black lashes. When he stood, he towered over me—and I was five eleven.

In a rich baritone, he said, "It's really okay. I'll just grab another." Then he smiled revealing dimples to go with the deep cleft he had in his chin.

I found myself nearly mesmerized by his beautiful, brown eyes. Realizing that I'd been staring made me more embarrassed. After blurting out, "I'm such a klutz at times," I wished him a happy holiday and rushed off to find a cashier. I was doing what I often did best in a tough spot—run.

I wanted to get out of the store as quickly as possible. Locating the sign for the elevator, I hurried over. It was on its way from the third floor. Suddenly, I sensed that I wasn't alone. Turning my head slightly, I realized it was the handsome man with the long hair.

Great, just great. I get another shot at making a fool out of myself, I thought. From the corner of my eyes, I could see he was smiling. I couldn't help but think that he was laughing at me on the inside. He must've thought that I was ditzy by the way I was acting.

Finally, the doors opened and I got on, followed by the mystery man. A moment later, the doors closed and the elevator began its descent. The light began to flicker, and a loud grinding noise could be heard over the music. Then an awful odor, like burning rubber, began to permeate the elevator car. But before I could even react, the elevator car came to a screeching halt between the second and third floors.

"Oh, noooo," I groaned aloud. "Now what?"

"I think we're stuck."

Now there's an astute observation if I ever heard one, I thought. Now I was positive that I was being punished. Why did this have to happen with this guy of all people? I was so absorbed with my own misfortune that I almost didn't hear him say, "There must be an emergency switch or telephone on the control panel."

I watched as he calmly walked over to the panel. "Ah, here it is," he said, pointing to a miniature microphone. A minute later, he was conversing with a service technician who located the problem quickly. That was the good part. Unfortunately, a gear had burned out and a replacement part had to be sent over from a supply house. It would be quite a while. The technician apologized for the delay, but he assured us that as soon as the part was delivered he would get us out of the elevator as quickly as possible.

The man must have noticed how uncomfortable I was to be cooped up in the elevator with him. "Would you feel better if I promised not to bite or do any other nasty stuff?"

I managed a weak smile. He took that as encouragement to continue talking. "My name is Gabriel Green."

"Sarah Stein."

"I guess you live around here."

"Yes. I had intended to bring this basket to my parents' house, but at this rate, it might very well be next year before I get there."

"I was going to visit my parents, too. Funny how we both thought of bringing baskets instead of cake."

"I wanted to be different."

"I did, too," he said as he chuckled. "Where do your parents live?"

"Joliet. Most of my family lives nearby. Where does yours live?"

"Kenwood."

"That's great. You can drive there," I said, glancing at my watch. "I'm going to miss my flight."

"That's too bad. When was the last time you saw your family?"

"Nearly a year ago, I'm afraid. I have a suitcase full of Hanukkah gifts for my nieces and nephews."

"I used to love to light the candles with my dad when I was a little boy."

I would have never guessed that he was Jewish. Funny, but people often said that about me. My father would be thrilled if I brought someone like him home. Herschel had been Lutheran. Though my parents had accepted him, there were always those "what if" questions, like what will your children be?

I reached into my purse for my cell phone and turned it on. I wanted to let my parents know that I'd probably be a little late.

"Can you get a signal?" Gabriel asked.

I looked at him and shook my head and than turned my phone off again.

"I didn't think so. It's the elevator. It's like a tomb."

"Don't remind me."

"Sorry," he said. "We're probably going to be here a while, so why don't you sit down and get more comfortable," he said as he took off his jacket and placed it on the floor.

"Why, thank you. That's so nice of you." I was awed by his generosity.

"I live around here, too, you know."

"Really? Where?"

"The Oak Avenue Apartments."

"That's only two blocks from where I live on Filbert Street."

"It truly is a small world."

I smiled and told him, "My mother uses that expression all the time. Are we related?"

Gabriel chuckled and replied, "It's possible, but I don't think so. What do you do, Sarah?"

"I work for Davies Medical as a data transcriber. And you?"

"I teach drama at the community college."

That would explain his splendid speaking voice. I wouldn't mind sitting in on one of his lectures. I found Gabriel quite nice and enjoyed talking to him. The awkwardness that I had originally felt had quickly disappeared. Being with him helped the time pass more quickly. Had I been alone in the elevator, I might have been climbing the walls at this point, instead. We talked just about everything. I realized that I hadn't felt this much at ease with a man in a long time. The best part was that he seemed to enjoy my company as well.

It took nearly two hours to get the elevator running again. The worst part of the entire ordeal was how hot the elevator became. Other than that drawback, I had a terrific time. And when the elevator doors finally opened on the main floor, I didn't flee.

Instead, Gabriel took my hand in his and said, "It was great meeting you. Sarah. Perhaps we can get together sometime after you return."

"I'd like that very much," I said, really meaning it. "Here's my phone number," I said, jotting it down on a scrap of paper I found in my purse.

I said good-bye to Gabriel, wondering how many times in the past I'd heard men say they'd call and didn't. Somehow, I didn't think that he was one of them. Yet . . .

After giving my mother a call to let her know that I had missed my flight, I turned on to the highway and finally headed to the airport. As I drove, I found myself thinking about Gabriel. He was so different from the men I'd known. Even though he was undoubtedly handsome, he didn't seem affected by it. I could just imagine his classes filled to the capacity by young girls infatuated by him. My thoughts strayed to his shiny brownish black hair tied back with that leather strap. In my mind's eye, I envisioned myself loosening the tie and running my hands through it. I smiled to myself, definitely hoping that he'd call.

I arrived at my parents' house just as dinner was about to be served. The candles had been lit in the menorah, depicting the third night of Hanukkah. It was good seeing my brother, Ian, and sister, Rimona, with their families gathered around the table. After a quick round of hugs and kisses, I joined them. Dad had already carved the turkey, and everything looked delicious as usual. My mom was a wonderful cook, whereas I subscribed to the school of potluck planning. Whatever fell out of the freezer when it was opened was defrosted and cooked. And if you were in luck that day, it wasn't burned beyond recognition!

The main topic of discussion seemed to center around my escapade at the department store. I wondered if a similar conversation was being conducted around the table in Gabriel's parents' house. Of course, there was other news as well. My bother had gotten a new job, and he was thinking of moving to a bigger house that was closer to where he worked. However, the nicest news was that my sister was pregnant, again. I was happy for them both.

Inevitably, the topic turned to my love life—or the lack of one. My older siblings only wanted to see me married and settled down with kids of my own. They got this from my parents, of course. After all, this type of concern was hereditary. I told them about meeting Gabriel in the elevator. That tidbit satisfied their hunger for news, and we were able to move on.

Rimona caught me alone and said, "So you're finally over Herschel?"

I nodded with a sad smile. "It was awful rough, but I could never

30

really trust him again—no matter what he said."

She hugged me. "Things happen for the best. Better to have found out before you were married."

My mother interrupted us. It was time for dessert.

I helped serve the coffee and cake. Proudly, I opened the holiday basket that nearly prevented me from coming. Shannon, my sister-in-law, began to laugh.

"What's so funny?"

"There are two other baskets in the kitchen. We all brought them, tonight."

I had to laugh. Here I was patting myself on the shoulder for being so darned clever, when everyone else had been thinking the same thing. What did it matter, anyway? I was with my family and having a wonderful time. However, it was getting late and the little ones had to go home. So after numerous kisses and thank-you hugs for their gifts, the children were bundled into their coats, and I watched the two families leave.

"Call more often," Rimona yelled out after me.

I nodded and waved. I went back to the kitchen to help my mother clean up.

"You know, I'm glad you'll be spending most of the weekend, Sarah. It will give us time to be together. Your father and I miss you so."

"I miss you and Dad, too, Mom." Smiling, I added, "I know, I'll always be your baby."

She grinned back and hugged me to her ample bosom. "So you did listen when I spoke to you."

"I heard every word."

She laughed and replied, "I'm sure."

I sat in the kitchen and talked to my parents a little while longer before we all went to sleep. Exhausted, I fell asleep in my old bed within moments of hitting the pillow. My dreams were in Technicolor, and they were filled with a tall man with shiny brown hair and gorgeous, deep brown eyes.

I slept late the following day, and I could still felt the warm vibes from the previous evening when I awakened. My parents were already having breakfast when I came down to the kitchen.

"Pull up a chair and join us, princess," Dad said.

That's what he always called me. Rimona was the duchess. Of course, Mom was her highness, the queen.

That day, we spent visiting relatives and before I realized it, it was time to go to the airport. I hated saying good-bye, never really being any good at it. I also hated taking a late night flight, but with the holidays, it was all I could get.

The following morning, what a surprise I got when I opened my door to retrieve the newspaper! Right next to it sat a big holiday basket. On top of the basket lay a long-stemmed, red rose and a note that read: I guess I wasn't too clever after all. Everyone brought holiday baskets. I really enjoyed our conversation in the elevator. Gabriel. His telephone number was written under his name.

I laughed when I read the note. It seemed that everybody bought holiday baskets this year instead of cake. I opened the basket, and I discovered it contained a marvelous variety of cheeses. Suddenly, an idea popped into my head. I hoped this one was cleverer than the last, though. I dialed Gabriel's number.

He answered on the first ring. Had he been waiting for my call?

"Hello, this is Sarah Stein. I found your wonderful basket and was about to whip up a cheese omelet. Would you care to join me?"

"I'll be right there."

That Hanukkah brought Gabriel into my life. We began to date, probably because I made good cheese omelets. However, I doubt if that prompted him to ask me to marry him the following Hanukkah, though. And now, whenever Saturday fell during the eight days of Hanukkah, no matter where we are, we always try to find a store that sells cheese baskets, so I can whip up omelets the following day.

The End

BAH HUMBUG
I had lost the true spirit of Christmas

Bah Humbug! I thought to myself.

The strains of "White Christmas" on my car radio didn't make me smile like it used to. But then again, these days, nothing made me smile.

I never ever thought I'd feel this way. I was the true spirit of Christmas and always had been. I loved everything about the holiday season, from the snow to the shopping that most people dreaded. But not this year. Nope. This year, the decorations had no sparkle, the snow was an annoyance, and I'd yet to do any shopping even though Christmas was less than three weeks away.

This year, the very thought of anything to do with the holiday filled me with dread. Jason's was my ex-fiancé, and it was all his fault. At least, I thought he was my ex-fiancé. I really didn't know. We hadn't broken up, but we also hadn't spoken to one another since Halloween.

The fight had started like most do, I suppose, over something stupid, and it escalated from there. I remember being angry when I slammed into the house and he roared off in his car, but I hadn't thought we would break up over it. The next day, he hadn't called, which made me mad so I didn't call him either. The more he didn't call, the more I didn't call, and soon a few days turned into a week and then longer. I yanked my diamond off and put it on my dressing table. I even told myself I'd mail it back to him, but I couldn't bring myself to make the final break.

I loved Jason, and I thought he loved me. We had fallen in love at first sight and found we had everything in common. Most important to me, we both loved Christmas. That first night, I giggled when he told me his name—Jason Frost. I figured it was some type of sign that I fell for someone with such a seasonal sounding name.

As I walked into the children's center, I tried to shake off my feelings of depression. Volunteering here was the last thing I wanted to do this year, but I'd been helping with their holiday party since I was a teenager. Also, I wasn't about to let them down just because my personal life was a mess.

I normally dressed up as one of Santa's elves, along with some of the other volunteers. This year, I'd heard there was a new Santa since the man who'd been playing the role had finally retired to a warmer climate. I hoped the new guy would be as good as old Mr. Potter.

"Hi Elizabeth. It's so good to see you back again this year." The woman who ran the children's program hugged me warmly as I entered the conference room where the costumes were kept.

"I wouldn't miss it, Kara." I faked the smile I didn't feel as I said hello to the rest of the staff.

"We have another change this year, besides a new Santa." Kara walked across the room to the wall on which the costumes hung in dry cleaner bags. "The girl who was supposed to be Mrs. Santa Claus isn't going to be able to make it, and I don't think the two teenage volunteers should be in that role. I've given them the Santa's elf costumes this year. I hope you don't mind being Mrs. Claus."

Kara wanted me to be Mrs. Santa Claus? I'd never played that part before, but how tough could it be? "Sure, that's not a problem. Hopefully, the costume will fit."

"Actually, there is a bigger problem. They ran out of traditional Mrs. Claus costumes at the shop and they sent me one that, well, I'm not quite sure it's appropriate."

She lifted the cover off the bag and held up the costume. I saw right away what she meant. The skirt was short, very short, and the red top with the fur trim scooped pretty low. I raised my eyebrow and looked at Kara over the top of the outfit. "Did you tell them this was for a kids' Christmas party?" I asked.

She sighed. "Maybe it's not quite so revealing on. Would you just try it? I suppose we could do the party without Mrs. Claus."

I could tell she was disappointed, and I shrugged. "They're little kids, Kara. The oldest in the group is only five. They won't notice my costume; they're only going to be interested in Santa. Let me try it on."

I patted her shoulder to comfort her and slipped out of the room. In the bathroom down the hall, with the costume on, my confidence spiraled down the drain.

"This must have been for a Playboy Mansion Christmas party," I muttered, yanking up the top in the hopes of hiding more of my skin. I didn't put on the red high heels with the fur trim or the red fishnet stockings. This Mrs. Claus was going to wear regular pantyhose and flat black shoes.

I glanced up and down the hall before scooting back to the conference room. Once inside, I blushed as the other staff members' jaws dropped.

"Oh my," Kara said, looking me up and down while shaking her head.

I tugged the fur lined collar up a bit more. "Yeah, it's a little low. But its fine, Kara. And with these black flats the skirt doesn't look nearly as indecent. At least I'm more covered than if I was in a bathing suit."

"I really appreciate you doing this, Elizabeth."

"Just promise me that next year you'll order the costumes further in advance."

"I will," she nodded and continued to look at me. "I will say you look sensational. I don't think I had your figure, even when I was your age."

"Where's the new Santa?" I looked around, noticing all the other garment bags were emptied.

"I've already hidden him in the front closet. If you get up there right now you can get inside before the kids come in."

I nodded, turned, and moved to the doorway. A quick glance confirmed that the hall was empty, and I hurried to the front of the building, grateful I didn't pass any other employees. I could already imagine the younger men on the staff and how their eyes were going to pop out at this costume.

I reached the closet and opened the door, slipping into the darkness.

A person behind me grunted as I backed into him.

"Sorry," I whispered.

"It's OK," he whispered back.

A strange chill went up my spine at that whisper. It was all too familiar. I thought I must have been imagining things because I'd had Jason on my mind earlier.

"Do you know how long before we come out?" he asked.

This time there was no mistake. It was Jason! How the heck did he get in this closet? He was the new Santa? Did he know I'd be here? I tried to remember if I'd ever talked about the children's center. I didn't think I had. We'd shared a lot of dreams and hopes for the future, but I don't remember mentioning my volunteering here at the holidays. And since we'd only met on New Year's Eve, he wasn't with me last Christmas.

Trying to think of how to handle this, I covered my mouth with my hand to disguise my voice. "About ten minutes," I muttered.

"That's not bad. It's just a bit warm in this suit." I felt him shift behind me. The closet was small, and I was directly in front of him.

I felt his hand brush against my backside and I jerked forward. "Sorry," he muttered. "It's really cramped in here."

"That's OK." I muttered again with my hand over my mouth. I didn't think he'd done it on purpose.

"I love that perfume." he said suddenly, and I heard him inhale. "My fiancée used to wear that kind."

I closed my eyes praying he wouldn't somehow figure out who I was. Then again, this might be my chance to find out what he was thinking. Covering my mouth again I said, "Doesn't she still wear it?"

He sighed. "I don't know. She's mad at me."

"That's too bad," I muttered, not knowing what else to say. I wasn't

35

mad at him; he was mad at me. "What did you do?" I decided to ask.

I felt him shift behind me once more. "To be honest, I don't know. We had a fight, like all couples do, but then it just never seemed to end. Pretty soon, we weren't speaking."

"You should have called her," I said, and then, hoping that wasn't too revealing, I added, "unless you're glad to be rid of her."

"No! Not at all. I miss her. I miss her like crazy, but I don't think she loves me anymore."

I felt my eyes fill. Not love him? The big oaf. I love him to pieces. "Why would you think that? You should call her and try to make up. It is Christmas after all."

He sighed again. "She loves Christmas. I never thought I'd meet a woman who loved Christmas as much as I do, but I think she loves it even more. We were perfect for one another."

I fought back the tears. "Maybe she's missing just as much as you're missing her." I suggested."

"I don't know. Sometimes, I think she's better off without me. I'm just a nobody. Maybe she wants more than what I can offer."

"I think you should let her decide that," I said muffling myself once more. My poor, darling Jason! All this time he'd thought that I didn't want him anymore. I couldn't stand it, and I turned around, planning to convince him of my love.

"Maybe this will help." In the dark, small space I reached out and framed his face with my hands, pulling his head down toward me. Immediately, he stiffened and held back. I was confused, and then realized that he thought I was some strange woman in a closet. He was resisting another woman's kiss. I felt my heart burst with love for him.

"Jason, it's me." I giggled and heard him draw a sharp breath. His hands immediately reached for my waist.

"Elizabeth?"

Before I could get the kiss I wanted, there was a knock at the door, which was our cue to come out. Faintly, I could hear the strains of "Here Comes Santa Claus."

"That's our cue, Santa," I whispered. But first, I reached up on tiptoe and brushed my mouth over his. He kissed me back, but before he could pull me close, I whipped around and opened the doorknob. If I didn't leave that closet now, there was no telling how long we'd stay in there. I blinked, blinded by the bright light of the hall. Absently, I tugged at the neckline of my costume and turned to see Jason's jaw drop open.

"That's quite a costume, Mrs. Claus," his voice cracked.

I smiled and linked our fingers together. "Maybe later I'll sit on your lap, Santa," I promised with a wink. His eyes widened as we reached the double doors to the great room where a hundred kids waited.

The party went off without a hitch, and I felt as if I was floating on air. From time to time I'd look up to see Jason staring at me with such love that it was all I could do not to throw myself into his arms right there.

Finally, the party wound down and the last child left. Jason sank back down into the large chair we'd used as Santa's throne. I noticed the wicked gleam in his eye, and I grinned.

He patted his knee. "Come tell Santa what you want for Christmas, Mrs. Claus."

I felt a lot more shy out in the open than I had in the dark closet, but I moved across the room and perched gingerly on his leg. Jason pulled off the fake beard and moustache. "I missed you, Lizzie. I'm sorry for whatever I did to make you mad," he said, stroking my cheek.

"I missed you so much, Jason. I thought you were glad to be rid of me."

"I thought the same. We were so childish."

He pulled me close and kissed me, and I sighed against him. When he pulled back, I looked up at him. "Want to know what I want for Christmas, Santa?" I asked, snuggling deeper into his lap.

He wrapped his arms around me. "Whatever it is, it's yours, as long as I have you back in my arms," he promised.

"I don't want to be engaged anymore."

I felt him jerk as if I'd slapped him, and I pushed away from his chest to look into his eyes. "I want to be married. I want to be Mrs. Frost before Christmas."

One eyebrow rose, but then he smiled. "It is the season of miracles."

We were married in a candlelit ceremony on Christmas Eve, and there has never been a year since when I've thought, Bah Humbug.

The End

A HOLIDAY MIRACLE
What better time of year
to make one last wish happen?

In all my sixteen years as a nurse, I've managed to buck the system a time or two. While I appreciate that the hospital regulations are in place to provide a safe and controlled environment for the betterment of all, there comes a time when common sense and compassion force us to bend a rule or two.

One such occasion confronted me last December, when I had the misfortune of drawing a double shift on the night of Christmas Eve. While I admit that my bedside manner was nothing to rave about, I gritted my teeth and bore the challenge, ever the stodgy trooper.

One particular patient, Miss Harrison, caused me a world of grief, buzzing and making ridiculous demands all day, until I'd worn a smudged path upon the linoleum and wondered if I'd have to invest in a new pair of shoes with my soon-to-be-gotten Christmas gains.

Around four o'clock in the afternoon, Miss Harrison rang for my attention again, and I plodded down the long hall trying to speculate what she would propose this time. Did the pillow need fluffing yet again?

"Ah, there you are dear," the small woman with silver-grey hair croaked out to me as I walked through the doorway to her room. "I'm afraid that I need another favor."

"And what would that be, Miss Harrison?" I must confess my patience waned. Though I took great pity on the woman, who was terminally ill, her needy discontent, compounded with my desire to go home, simply grated on my ability to offer a full repertoire of cheer.

"Oh dear, my daughters, their husbands, and my grandbabies are due to visit this evening, and I'd like to take my supper with all of them."

"Well, supper should be up around five thirty," I replied, "and you should surely be able to dine while they are here."

"No dear, you don't understand. I would like supper brought up for all of them, because it's tradition for us to dine together on Christmas Eve," she said, and her small blue eyes sparkled with the notion.

"Exactly how many meals are we talking about, Miss Harrison?" I tapped my foot impatiently, awaiting the punch line.

"Well, with Carla and her two, Leslie and her five, Beth with three, and the husbands included, oh, what would that make, dear? Maybe fifteen or sixteen?"

And there it was.

"Now Miss Harrison, I can't possibly get the kitchen to agree to bring up that many meals, and there's no way you'll be fitting all those people in your room. Plus, the visitor rule states that there can be no more than four visitors at a time. I can bend the rules a little, but sixteen? Come now," I said, and I shook my head to emphasize the impossibility of her request.

"If I cannot have my family with me to dine on Christmas, dear, I simply will not be eating then," Miss Harrison said, placing her hands together and turning up her nose in the best offer of defiance she could muster.

Miss Harrison and I bantered back and forth for a bit, but there was no changing that stubborn woman's mind. If she could not have her accommodations fixed to suit her, she would do what was within her power to protest, even if would be at the expense of her own health.

Another patient called for help, and I left Miss Harrison, promising to see what I could do for her even though I knew it would not be much. It would take a miracle to get the kitchen staff to cart up sixteen extra meals, and heaven knew how all those folks would be able to squeeze in the hospital room to enjoy them.

And then it occurred to me—what better time of year then Christmas to make a miracle happen? What harm would it do to try to appease a frail, old woman's request to enjoy a small smidge of the holiday with her family? After all, I would be reveling in delicious food, company, and gifts galore in less than eighteen hours. It seemed only fair that a woman, whose whole family cared enough to spend their Christmas Eve in the confines of hospital room, deserved a little extra holiday cheer.

After tending to my other patients, I finagled the kitchen staff to whip up the extra meals and agree to deliver them to Miss Harrison's room lickety-split. Then I proceeded to con the maintenance crew and an orderly on duty into helping me find extra chairs and tables from the family room so we could set them up inside and outside of Miss Harrison's room.

Just as the last chair was set down, Miss Harrison's crew began to arrive, adorned with matching red bows and holiday smiles. They carried gifts in to Miss Harrison's room and the exclamations of joy and love trickled down the hall, filling the air with enough harmony to challenge the beautiful strings of a world class symphony orchestra. Their voices produced the best strain of Christmas music my worn ears had ever heard.

The kitchen staff arrived with a mound of meals and the family readily passed them out. Everyone gathered as close together as possible, and those stuck outside the doorway, simply plopped down on the linoleum to enjoy their supper.

I crossed my arms and watched the foray on the camera view, smiling and feeling mighty good about the small favor I paid, all the while knowing I'd suffer the repercussions of my actions when I returned to work later in the week.

Miss Harrison's family began milling around the floor, and I watched in amazement, discovering that they had brought small teddy bears to deliver to all the other patients. Their good will and Christmas magic spread like wildfire, brightening the whole floor to the luminosity of the Christmas star itself.

Even hours later, after they left and the plates and chairs were taken away, the glow upon our unit lingered, and the joyous spirit still resonated through each patient.

Miss Harrison thanked us all, over and over again, as we cleaned up her room. After we left, she didn't buzz the call button anymore. The reprieve lasted the remainder of the evening. When I checked in on her during rounds, she lay sleeping serenely with the look of an angel about her.

I left that night with the smiles of Miss Harrison and her relations burning through my brain, knowing I'd never forget the tenderness and good nature of that loving family. As I hurried home, I knew this Christmas would be a memorable one for me, as I came to be reminded of the true meaning of the holiday that night.

Miss Harrison died in her sleep on Christmas morning as I sat around the Christmas tree opening presents and embracing the warmth of my family. The nurse on duty that day told me that they found her lying peacefully in her bed with a smile etched on her tiny features.

After hearing the news, I had a peace about me too, knowing that I granted Miss Harrison one last Christmas wish. At work, I took my lashings and paid the price for the misdeed, but it hardly mattered. For the first time in sixteen years, I truly understood what it meant to be selfless.

The End

A Holiday Romance With
Charity At Its Heart:
SNOWBOUND!
We fell in love saving lives

"**Y**ou better get out of here and get ready to go to the party, Christian," Dad said as he poked his head into my office, interrupting the work I was concentrating on. I really wanted to get the stuff finished and out of the way.

"Yeah," I answered him halfheartedly. "Just a minute."

"Christian, you aren't still working on that Norelli account, are you?" Dad asked. "I thought you'd have it finished by now. Well, no matter—just close it down and come on home and get ready and I'll see you at the party in about an hour. Gotta keep the employees happy, you know!" he added with a grin. Then he was out the door, his tall frame moving toward the elevator, headed home.

I sat there, struggling to make the account do what it was supposed to do. Why was it so easy for others to do this work when for me, it was such a chore?

I had never liked the job. But I didn't have much choice; as the only son of Stanford Lattimer, owner of Lattimer Industries, I was expected to work there—to "learn the ropes"—and to someday step into his shoes.

I shuddered at the thought. Even graduating from college hadn't helped me feel prepared for eventually taking over the business.

Turning off my computer, I left the office and walked wearily through the large computer center with its individual cubicles where people sat all day programming data into high-tech equipment. Right then the place was empty; everyone had left early to get ready for the annual Christmas party. It was really quiet—a welcome respite from the ongoing hum of talk and chatter and endlessly ringing phones.

I was just reaching to push the elevator button when someone behind me called, "Hey, hold the elevator for me!"

I glanced around to see Holly Marshall hurrying toward me. She was struggling to shove her arms into her coat and trying to manage an oversized purse that kept getting in the way.

"Take it easy," I told her as I chuckled at her efforts. "Here—let me help you." I held the back of her coat steady while she pushed her arms into the sleeves. "There. How's that?"

"Better. Thanks." She grinned as she adjusted the purse on her shoulder—a purse that was big enough to hold an entire wardrobe. I never have been able to figure out why women tote around such big purses. Mom does the same thing and so does my sister, Whitney. Once Whitney tried to explain it to me and only made it sound more ridiculous.

I pushed the elevator button, the door slid open, and Holly and I stepped inside. "You ready for the party?" she asked as I felt the car start to move.

"Are you?" I countered.

Holly was the only girl who worked there who actually talked to me. The others sort of kept their distance, or else they flirted outright with me—something I can't stand. I knew the flirty ones saw me through the dollar signs in their eyes. The quiet ones seemed uneasy around me. To be honest, I had difficulty talking to all of them; I guess I've just never been the talkative, outgoing kind—unlike my dad and my sister. You can't get Whitney to shut up at times. Me, well—lots of times I just don't know what to say.

When I didn't respond she repeated, "Are you going to the Christmas party?" Then she laughed. "Well, since it's your family who's giving the party—yes—I'd guess you're going."

"Want to know the truth?" I asked.

"Sure."

"I can't stand these parties. They're boring, noisy . . ."

"But the company does this every year—they rent the Commodore Room at the Regal Hotel, pay for a fantastically sumptuous buffet dinner, and hand out neat door prizes." She shrugged. "It's a tradition, I guess."

"That doesn't make me like it," I told her.

She studied me. "You mean that, don't you? You really don't like to go to these shindigs, do you?" Before I could admit it, she spoke up. "Well, that makes two of us, then. I don't like them, either. I mean, I appreciate the company doing this for their employees but, like you said . . . booooring!"

Suddenly we were both laughing—standing there as the elevator went down to the lobby—and we were laughing as though she'd said something hilarious. We were still laughing when the doors slid open and we stepped out into the lobby. I was glad Dad wasn't around; he doesn't approve of us Lattimers being too chummy with the workers.

I looked at Holly. She looked at me. At the same time, we both said, "Booooring!"

"Let's not go." I surprised myself when I said it. "Let's just forget the party."

"Really?"

"Sure. Let's go do something else."

"Aren't you afraid your dad will fire you if you miss the company party?"

I grinned. "Hardly. I already own a good amount of stock in the company and I'm Dad's only son, so I guess my job is somewhat secure. At least I hope it is."

I pushed the wide glass door open and we walked out into the chill winter air. "I have an idea," I told her as I watched snowflakes fall from the darkening sky. "Let's run away. You don't want to go to the party and neither do I, so let's 'not go' together."

"Are you serious?"

"Yep."

"But what will we——"

"Come with me," I said as I took her arm and headed toward my car parked in a reserved spot near the front entrance. It was one time when I appreciated the perks of being the boss's son: I had an excellent parking space.

The next thing I knew we were sitting in a small diner on the edge of town in a not-very-good neighborhood. Most of the buildings around there were in various stages of deterioration and the people who lived in them seemed a lot like the buildings. Dad would never visit that section of town but I frequented it because that worn-out diner served the best chili in the state.

Holly and I sat together in a booth near the back. Steaming bowls of pungent, red-brown chili were placed in front of us and I watched the expression on Holly's face when she took her first taste. I grinned as she nodded.

"Yep, you're right—it's the best!"

We concentrated on devouring the warm, tasty chili and eating thick slices of homemade cornbread. As we were finishing our second bowls, I asked her, "Now, isn't this better than anything being served at the Christmas party?"

"The party!" she yipped. "I totally forgot the party! Your dad is going to kill us both!"

"Don't worry about it," I assured her. "He'll be so busy playing the role of 'gracious host' that he won't have time to miss us."

And so we sat and talked and shared so many things—our mutual love of music and books, her interest in gardening, my interest in sci-fi movies. It felt so right, so comfortable, being there with her. I'd seen her at work so often, but I hadn't paid that much attention to her. Not until that day.

Now I looked at Holly sitting across the table from me. It was as though I was seeing her for the very first time. She's pretty in a gentle sort of way—dark hair combed back from her round face, dark eyes that had hints of gold in them when she laughed or looked thoughtful.

Her voice was soft and sort of musical as she told me more about herself. She's small—like my mother. She isn't boisterous like a lot of the girls at the office are. There's a gentleness about her and yet, there's also a strength about her. She teased me, she laughed with me, and she listened intently to the things I said. She was listening to me—not to the son of Stanford Lattimer.

Why hadn't I noticed Holly before? To think that for the past year she'd been working out there in that computer room day after day . . . and this was the first time I really saw her. Maybe it would be a good Christmas, after all.

We were enjoying our second cup of coffee when the door opened, ushering in a blast of cold air and also a young lady dressed in a worn, blue uniform. The "official" hat she had was soaking wet. She carried a coffee can with a plastic lid. A handmade sign that sagged limply around the container read: HELP US HELP OTHERS! The Dover Street Mission thanks you.

She moved about the room, stopping at each booth, inviting people to contribute something to the mission. Only a few people dropped a few coins into the slit in the plastic top of the coffee can.

There was a weariness to her shoulders as she turned toward our booth. "Would you like to contribute to those less fortunate?" she asked as she held out the can. I could tell she'd said those same words a million times and had been rejected a million times more. Something about her—her determination; her threadbare, cast-off uniform; the way her blonde hair straggled wetly beneath her hat . . . it got to me.

"I'll give you something," I told her. "But first you must do something for me."

She looked momentarily taken aback. "What?"

"Please, sit down." When she hesitated I got up, moved around behind her, and pulled out an extra chair and gently pushed her into it. Then I took my seat across from Holly. "When's the last time you ate?" I asked.

She shrugged.

"That's what I thought," I said as I summoned the waitress and asked her to bring us another bowl of chili. And more cornbread. And more hot coffee.

After the young lady had devoured the chili, cornbread, and coffee, she sat back in her chair and looked at me and then at Holly. "Sorry. I know it's rude, but I didn't realize how hungry I was . . ."

Holly chuckled warmly. "And you didn't realize how great the chili is! Don't worry—I did the same thing just moments ago. The minute I started on the chili I kept at it . . . there was no way to stop me!" She giggled. The young lady giggled, too.

44

"This is so kind of you." She looked from Holly to me. "I'm Liza Dolittle, by the way. I work at the Dover Street Mission."

"Glad to meet you, Liza. I'm Holly. And this gentleman is Christian."

"Do you come here often, Liza?" I asked her.

"No, this is the first time I've been in here, actually. But with Christmas just two weeks away and our funds so low—well, I decided to move beyond the territory I usually cover, which is closer to the Mission. That's how I ended up in here."

"You walked here?" Holly asked, surprised. "That's quite a distance. And the weather is so bad."

"Well, Miss Liza, you aren't walking back," I told her firmly. "I'll drive you back. Holly and I will see that you get back to the mission safe and sound—and without having to slosh through snowdrifts."

That's how Holly and I ended up at the Dover Street Mission.

I couldn't believe how run-down the place was. The entire neighborhood was in a state of rapid decay. I had a weird feeling as I drove up in front of the little storefront mission; for a second, I was almost afraid to get out.

But Liza insisted that we come inside. I could see that attempts had been made to create a welcoming atmosphere in a very dismal setting. A few old, wooden pews faced a low platform on which stood a rickety sort of pulpit and a piano that must've been salvaged from a junkyard. Still, although the furnishings were very humble, they gleamed with polish, and above the generalized musty smell, I could detect the faint scent of the same furniture polish the maid uses at our house.

Liza gave us a tour of the mission. She showed us the kitchen area where several tired-looking picnic tables had been laid with a tablecloth and place settings, ready to serve those who'd soon come in for a hot meal. Through a door near the antiquated refrigerator lay the small room Liza shared with another woman, Barb, who helped her run the mission.

Liza offered Holly and me slices of apple cake she'd baked earlier that day. "I try to keep something like this on hand for anyone who comes in any hour of the day or night," she explained as she poured us mugs of mulled cider from a Crock-Pot.

"This is wonderful," Holly enthused. "You baked this yourself?"

"I sure did. I bake, I clean, I teach classes . . . whatever's needed."

"How do you and Barb do it all?" I asked. "And where is Barb now?"

"She's at her grandmother's this evening. Gran is really ill, and wanted me to come and pray with her. But Barb decided to go there by herself so I could go out and try to raise more contributions."

"Are you a minister?" Holly asked.

45

"Yep. I'm a minister . . . and this is where I minister." She chuckled at her own little joke.

"Do you play that piano out there?" Holly pointed back out to the main room.

"Sure. I have to. There's no one else to do it."

"Will you play something for us now?" I asked.

"Now?" Liza hesitated, then nodded. "Okay. If you want me to."

She led the way back to the main room, sat down on the piano bench and ran her slender fingers over the keys. I was surprised by the quality of the tone that came from the old piano. At one time, it must've been a truly marvelous instrument. In fact, it still was—when Liza's hands touched the yellowed keys.

"Want to hear some Christmas carols?" she suggested.

The three of us spent an hour there together, singing all the Christmas songs I've known since childhood. We soon realized that our voices blended very well and we even attempted some three-part harmonies.

As Liza played and we sang, the run-down mission took on a certain charm and tranquility. I looked at Holly's face as she stood there, singing the old songs; she was totally enjoying the moment. And I was totally enjoying her.

Then I looked at Liza as she moved her work-worn hands over the keys and lifted her soprano voice to lead us in the songs. I could hardly sing because of the lump in my throat.

When we finally ran out of songs I decided that Holly and I should leave. As it was, I feared we'd overstayed our welcome.

Picking up our coats from the back pew, we started for the door. When I opened it, I saw that during the past hour or so, a blizzard had moved in on us. Snow was falling furiously, turning the dingy-looking street into a white path through a winter wonderland on which the few feeble streetlights cast a weak amber glow.

Closing the door, I turned back to face Holly and Liza. "I think we're snowbound."

"Really?" Holly questioned. "You have to be kidding me."

"See for yourself."

Pulling aside the curtain that hung at the front window, Holly looked out and admitted, "Yep. We're snowbound. There's no way we're getting out of here."

Liza laughed. Her reaction surprised me. What was so funny about us being snowbound in that dismal neighborhood? My home was clear across town. I realized that snowplows were surely already struggling to move mountains of snow out of the way—the people who lived in the tony Hillcrest Historical District wouldn't be inconvenienced by an overabundance of snow. But in the mission neighborhood—well, I knew that snowplows rarely cleared the area in a timely fashion.

"What's funny, Liza?" Holly asked.

"Now is when the action begins," she told us. "When the weather gets really bad, the people who're homeless or live in wretched tenement apartments with little or no heat, well—they all come here. At least here, they know they can be warm and get some food."

Liza was right. Before long, over a dozen people had come to the door and Liza greeted each of them warmly, inviting them in out of the stormy night.

To me, instantly, the place was wall-to-wall confusion—people milling freely about the place, talking with each other. Someone played the piano, pounding out a ragtime song. Three women sat in a back pew, chattering away. Then several kids started playing tag between the pews. Liza put a stop to that by bringing out a large box filled with discarded chunks of wood—different sizes and shapes—just stuff she'd picked up in her travels throughout the area. The children started laying the chunks of wood on the pews, making roadways, tunnels, towers—whatever their imaginations could think up. They didn't have computer games or high-tech toys but they certainly enjoyed playing make-believe with little bits of lumber. Two men went to the kitchen and sat at one of the picnic tables and played checkers, keeping score to see who could win the most games.

I could see then that they'd all been through this before because everyone seemed to know what to do to entertain themselves in spite of there being no TV and no store-bought toys.

I didn't feel comfortable around the men—and I think they felt uneasy having me there in the mission. I didn't know them and they didn't know me; I was an "outsider" and they knew it. I finally went into the kitchen where Holly was helping Liza make ham sandwiches and I could smell a pot of coffee brewing on the back of the old stove.

"What can I do to help?" I asked.

"See that shovel over there?" Liza pointed to a battered snow shovel leaning against the back door. "If you want to help, you can go outside and shovel a path to the back door and also one to the front door. That way, it'll be easier and safer for people to get in here."

So I went out and shoveled snow at both the front and back entrances of the mission. I was almost finished at the front door when I realized it'd been hours since I'd last spoken to Dad. As it was, he had no idea where I was and despite the hubbub of the Christmas party, I knew that as time passed and I didn't put in an appearance at the annual event, he'd start to worry—and then in time he'd get frantic. And Mom, well—she'd be hysterical if she thought I was M.I.A. during an Ohio blizzard.

Luckily, I had my cell phone in my coat pocket and after leaning the shovel against the front doorframe, I tramped over to my car to make sure it was still all right and also to talk privately on the phone. But a cell phone doesn't help much if the battery is dead. As it turned out, I couldn't call Dad.

I went back inside to the kitchen and asked Liza if she had a phone. She pointed to one hanging on the wall next to a cupboard and I managed to get through to the Regal Hotel where the party was being held . . . only to be informed that everyone had been sent home on account of the blizzard.

When I called home, Whitney answered. "Christian! Where are you? Mom and Dad have been worried sick! You never went to the party! No one knows where you are! The party was cut short because of the storm! It's terrible outside! A blizzard! We're going to be snowbound! Where are you, Christian? Are you okay?"

I had to grin as I listened to my sister go on and on. Good old Whitney. "If you'll close your mouth for a minute, I'll tell you. I'm fine. Safe and sound. I'm at a mission, actually."

"You're on a mission? What kind of a mission can you be on when we're in the middle of a blizzard? What are you talking about, Christian? You'd better get home, Christian."

"Whitney, shut it. Listen to me. I'm at a mission—the Dover Street Mission, to be precise. I'm okay. I'm—"

The line went dead.

I checked the wall phone and I could hear a dial tone, so I figured the line at home must've gone down. Well, at least they'd heard from me; they knew I was okay.

By the time we'd fed everyone sandwiches and cups of coffee and hot chocolate for the kids, everyone was exhausted. Someone brought out a stack of blankets from a supply closet and soon people were laying down—some on the pews, some on the slightly raised floor of the stage—a couple of men even lay down on top of the picnic tables and pulled blankets over themselves and soon the place settled down for the night.

Liza moved quietly among the people—her "guests," as she referred to them—checking to make sure that everyone was as comfortable as possible, given the circumstances. Holly and I walked over to the front window and stood side by side looking out at the night. The snow had finally stopped but nothing looked as it had when we'd arrived a few hours earlier. The dismal landscape outside had been transformed into a winter wonderland. All the trash that was scattered along the curb and lying in the gutters didn't matter at that moment—the beauty of the snow hid it all.

I reached for Holly, pulled her close. I felt as though she and I were intruders there; we weren't really a part of that "community."

Actually, most of the people had pretty much ignored Holly and me. Maybe they didn't have much—but they had each other. And in times of difficulty they held onto each other.

I felt a shiver go through Holly and knew the cold air seeping in around the window chilled her. I wrapped my arms around her to ward off the cold but in doing so, I realized that holding her close to me, feeling her soft hair brush against my face, catching a whiff of her perfume . . . it all brought back into focus the things I was beginning to feel and think when we were sitting in the diner. We'd gone there to "run away" from the Christmas party, but in running away from the party, I wondered if we'd actually run to each other.

I turned slightly so I could look back into the room where I saw people sleeping on wooden pews, saw folks wrapped up in blankets lying near the pulpit or the piano. I heard a child crying, heard a mother's voice saying soothing words, and then the crying stopped.

Then I realized someone else was crying. Holly's head was resting on my shoulder and tears were running down her cheeks as a slight shudder went through her body.

"What is it?" I asked her softly. Instantly, I was stunned by how her tears cut into my heart. I didn't even know why she was crying, but just the fact that she was caused me pain.

Holly pulled away from my embrace. Glancing around the room sadly, she said, "These people . . . how horrible. People shouldn't have to live like this. They should have warm homes, food, and a place to put their children to bed at night in comfort. This is so wrong . . . so horribly wrong . . ."

"You're right," I agreed softly as I wrapped my arm around her slender shoulder. "No one should have to live like these people do. But the important thing is that in spite of the storm outside, they're warm and safe in here. I guess that's why they call it a 'mission.' All this is Liza's doing. She's the one who makes them feel so at home here."

Holly nodded. "You're right. She's amazing."

As we stood there so close together I was even more drawn to Holly, even more aware of her "specialness" . . . and of the moment. I looked across the room to where Liza was sitting in a pew, holding a little girl close, rocking gently back and forth to comfort the child. A woman lay on the pew, a faded blanket wrapped around her sleeping form.

I looked at Liza's face in the glow of the few lights she'd left on. I saw peacefulness, a look of total assurance. This was what she was meant to do—to minister to these people. And she did it all with such grace and dignity. A part of me envied her; she'd found what she wanted to do with her life and she'd pursued that goal. It'd brought her to this pathetic mission, but it'd also brought her fulfillment, a real sense of purpose to her life. She had so much more than I did; she had peace and a feeling of being who she was truly meant to be.

Holly shifted slightly against my shoulder. I glanced down at her; maybe I, too, had finally found my purpose in life . . .

Suddenly the quiet was shattered by a scream—

"Fire!"

Instantly, everyone was awake. Three men raced from the kitchen shouting, "Get out! Everyone out! There's a fire in the kitchen!"

Mass confusion filled the room. People were racing for the door, crowding against each other in their efforts to get out. Holly pulled away from my side and rushed toward an elderly woman who'd stumbled beneath the rush of people. Grabbing the old woman's arm, Holly picked up a blanket that had been tossed onto a pew and wrapped it around the woman's bony shoulders and half-carried her to the door. I saw them both go out into the night.

I could smell the smoke but I saw no flames. And I didn't see Liza. I raced to the kitchen and as I stepped through the door I saw red flames inching toward the ceiling, curling fiery fingers along the wooden framework of the cupboards. Through a billowing cloud of smoke I saw Liza reaching for the phone on the wall, trying to call for help. Before she could reach it, a part of the cupboard gave way and started to fall.

Instinctively, I hurled myself at her. Somehow I managed to get to her before the enflamed cupboard door did. I shoved her to one side with one hand, and with the other, I sent the burning door flying across the room. Then I reached down to pick up Liza, who'd been pushed to the floor.

For a moment, I thought she was dead. She didn't move; she seemed lifeless, and a feeling of horror crashed down on me.

Liza! My mind and heart screamed the word. But a part of me knew I had to remain calm and deal with the danger that surrounded us. So I lifted Liza's lifeless body into my arms and, still holding her, I moved to the wall, reached for the phone, and quickly dialed 9-1-1. The second I heard someone pick up on the line I yelled, "Fire! The Dover Street Mission! Send help!" Before I could say more, the hungry flames reached the phone line and I lost contact with the outside world. I only hoped and prayed that they'd understood my cry for help.

Carrying Liza like a rag doll, I moved toward the door, but by then, the entire wooden frame was engulfed in flames. Suddenly, I realized that we were trapped—I couldn't risk going through that door toward the main room, which was our only route of escape. Because the entire back wall of the kitchen was on fire, I couldn't go out through

50

the back door, either. But I knew we couldn't stay in the kitchen; the heat from the blaze was rapidly making it impossible to breathe.

I held Liza against my chest, hoping to protect her from breathing in any more smoke and fumes than was inevitable. "Lord, help me!" I prayed aloud as I headed toward the door once more. Then, knowing full well that I was taking a major risk, I leapt with Liza in my arms and hurled us through the flaming doorframe. I made sure that I held on tightly to Liza, trying to shield her body from the flames with my own.

Then I was racing through the now-emptied main room of the mission. The shock of the blast of cold winter air that hit me as I stepped out into the night almost sucked the breath out of my lungs but I still held Liza as close to me as possible. I was no longer shielding her from the flames and smoke but I was trying to protect her from the bitter cold of the winter night.

People who'd escaped the mission were running down the street, scrambling over mountains of snow to get away from the engulfed structure. Some huddled across the street at the entrance to an abandoned store. For an eternal moment I stood there, holding Liza in my arms, trying to focus my attention, trying to determine what to do next. My car was parked in front of the mission and I considered opening the door and placing Liza on the backseat where she would at least be out of the cold air. But then I realized that if the burning building collapsed, it might fall right onto my car.

As it was, several people were sitting on the roof of the car, staring in frightened fascination at the fire, which by then was creeping along the exterior sides of the mission. There was a time when I would've been angry that they were perched on my expensive car. Suddenly, though, my only concern was the fact that they were in danger.

"Get away from the car!" I screamed. "It could explode!"

They quickly scrambled away from the vehicle, scattering to stand in several vacated doorways across the street.

The next moments are a blur in my memory. I saw Holly across the street, her arm around the old lady she'd helped outside who was now wrapped in the blanket Holly had picked up. Realizing she was safe, I felt a part of my heart relax slightly.

There were sirens screaming through the night—fire trucks, ambulances—their flashing red lights casting blood-colored splatters of rotating light on the now-trampled, soot-blackened snow. Then someone took Liza from me, placed her in an ambulance, and moments later I watched it drive off, wailing through the night as it headed for the hospital. Several others were also taken to the emergency room and the quick actions of the firemen prevented my car from catching fire or exploding. But there was no way to save the already dilapidated, fire-blasted mission.

As the drama of the fire subsided somewhat, the local people seemed to disappear into darkened doorways. Then once again, Holly and I were alone. Somehow, I managed to drive us to the hospital. We had to see how Liza was faring and check on the few "guests" who'd also been taken there. Fortunately, we were told that no one had been seriously injured. By the next day, most of them had been released from the hospital and walked out the door and out of our lives.

The next few days were difficult for Liza. She'd inhaled so much smoke and there was a burn on her left arm, which was also broken. My parents and Whitney were at the hospital almost as much as I was. They'd come there when they'd been told that that was where I was, fearing the worst and then relatively relieved to find out that I was there on Liza's behalf. Mom and Dad took an instant liking to Liza and Dad arranged to handle all of her medical expenses. Whitney and Liza "connected" the moment they met; it was like they were long-lost sisters.

The destruction of the Dover Street Mission made the front page of the newspaper, but after a few days it was old news—replaced by more festive news items referring to the rapidly approaching Christmas holiday.

I returned to work; Holly returned to work. We tried to resume our old routine, but people at work now looked at us as a couple. I noticed that some of the women seemed to shun Holly. I saw the hurt look in her eyes when they excluded her from their "girl talk" during coffee breaks or in the lunchroom. She said nothing, but I could tell she was feeling ostracized because she was now considered "the boss's son's girl." Neither Holly nor I looked at it that way, but I had to admit to myself that what we'd been through at the mission, the impact of facing life and death together—it had created an indelible bond between us. I took her to dinner a couple of times; we went to the cinema to see a holiday movie. I took her to my home and we spent an evening with Mom and Dad and Whitney, just watching a video and eating popcorn in the den. Nothing fancy—just homey stuff.

After Liza was released from the hospital she had no place to go—no home, no mission. The director of the regional branch of her denomination arranged for her to stay at a nearby boardinghouse temporarily while she healed from her injuries. Before I realized it, the holidays were over and we were into a new year. Then Liza started working at a local counseling center. With her extensive background in missionary work and her natural abilities, she was a real asset to them.

I don't know how he did it, but Dad quickly arranged for the demolition of not only the remainder of the Dover Street Mission, but he also bought up the entire ramshackle block. The newspapers didn't print the story of how he intended to raze the empty buildings and build a low-income housing facility. Dad carried his plans even further by arranging to turn an empty warehouse into a branch of Lattimer Industries. The new Dover Street Lattimer Distribution Center would serve as an outlet for many of Dad's products and it also brought employment to the people of that area. Dad assigned me to oversee the operations. The work was markedly different from what I'd been doing before and I quickly found that I really enjoyed it.

Dad told Liza that he was renovating the abandoned church that stood a few blocks away from the original mission building. Soon Liza was using the Dover Street Chapel as a new version of the original mission; she conducted church services there, taught nutrition classes to the women of the area, and even opened a daycare center for the mothers who were now employed by the Dover Street Lattimer Distribution Center.

By that point, Holly and I were seeing each other on a continuing basis. I felt comfortable around her, not the way I'd felt with the other girls who worked for Dad's company. I knew she cared for me but she didn't push the issue; I was sure that in time, I would ask her to marry me. But right then, well—something kept me from taking that final step. I couldn't understand it, but I was hesitant.

Because my new job was located in the same neighborhood as the chapel, I found myself going over there often to check on Liza and make sure things were going alright for her. After the daily hustle and bustle of work I found a serenity and peacefulness at the chapel that I didn't find anywhere else. I helped Liza with chores around the place; together, we painted one of the small rooms and turned it into a Sunday school room. Another room we decorated as a senior citizen meeting place and yet another we set aside especially for the teenagers who'd started to gravitate to the chapel as a general meeting place after school.

The more I helped Liza with the chapel, the more I got to know her. I learned that she had no family to speak of; rather, the church was her "family." She loved everyone who came through its doors no matter what hour of the day or night or whatever their need might be. I hadn't realized that organizing work such as Liza was involved in required so much time and attention and detail, but she took it all in stride; in fact, she really seemed to enjoy every aspect of it from the cooking, cleaning, and teaching to helping the teenagers with their homework.

Before I realized it an entire summer had gone by and we were heading toward the holiday season again. Then Thanksgiving Day came and went and Christmas was on its heels. I was still going places and doing things with Holly, but not as often as I had before. The sparkle that had once been a part of our relationship seemed to have faded somewhat and often, I was tied up with things at work or with helping Liza with some ongoing project at the chapel.

Then I began to hear that Holly had gone to a movie with Frank, one of the company drivers, or had been seen at the mall with him. Several times when I drove past her place on my way to work I saw Frank's car parked out front.

At first, it bothered me. I guess I was jealous. But things were so hectic at work and I was so involved with helping Liza put the finishing touches on the chapel so she could have it looking nice for the upcoming Christmas service she was planning and, well—I just didn't have time for much of anything—including jealousy.

Then once again it was time for the company's annual Christmas party. This time it was to be a combined celebration for the employees of Lattimer Industries and the new workers over at the Dover Street Lattimer Distribution Center. Again, Dad reminded me not to be late for the party. He told me that it was my "responsibility" to be there— to mingle with the employees and show "goodwill" and a "holiday spirit."

I thought back to the same time last year. I remembered being in the elevator with Holly and both of us saying, "Booooring!" We'd "run away" from the party to an old diner, had bowls of chili, talked, and got to know each other. I'd felt so comfortable, so at ease with her. I recalled being with her at the mission, discovering what a special person she is. At that time, I knew that I was falling in love with her. Now, we'd survived the fire—and we'd survived the office gossip that followed.

Several days before the party I was in my office when my phone rang. When I answered it, Holly was on the line.

"Christian, can we meet someplace? Maybe get a cup of coffee? I'd like to talk to you."

There was something in her voice—a tone I hadn't heard before. "Sure," I told her. "We can meet. Where? Are you okay?"

"Remember that little diner where we went for chili? I'll be there in half an hour." With that, she hung up.

I arrived at the diner a few minutes early and ordered cups of coffee. When Holly walked in, I could see the tenseness in her posture.

She sat opposite me—just sat there, looking at me. Were there tears in her eyes? I didn't know what this was all about so I didn't know what to say to her.

"Christian, I chose this place because, well, this is where it all began . . . where we came a year ago, where we 'found' each other . . ."

She hesitated, but something told me to say nothing—to just let her say whatever it was in her own way, in her own time.

She took a sip of her coffee. "I found something very special here, Christian," she said softly. "I found you. You changed my life. You made me see myself in a different way. I'd always felt like I was less than the other girls—not as pretty, not as outgoing. But you accepted me just as I was. You were my friend. And then you became the love of my life."

"Holly, I—"

She held up her hand to stop me from saying anything more. "Let me finish. The fire—the terror of the flames, of seeing people come so close to death . . . it made me reevaluate my life, Christian. I've said nothing to you because I wasn't sure what direction I was going in. But now . . . now, I've made a decision."

"What kind of decision?"

"I'm going away, Christian. I've always wanted to be a nurse or work in the medical field in some way but I never thought I was good enough. But this past year, you've made me see that I can do things—that I can set goals for myself, reach for them—and actually attain them. Just like Liza did when she became a minister, just like she did working at the mission—and now at the chapel. And you—taking on the job of running the distribution center. I'm sure it hasn't been easy for you, but you are doing it. And if you and Liza can take up challenges and accomplish things, well, then—I can, too."

Her face looked different then. She was more relaxed suddenly, and there was a hint of a smile on her lips and I could see the tiny glints of gold in her brown eyes again. I could tell she was determined—wonderfully determined and inspired.

"You're going away? Where?"

"I'll be attending medical school close to Chicago. I start right after the first of the year. I've already given notice at work; tomorrow is my last day on the job."

I was stunned by what she was telling me. Suddenly, Holly was going to be going out of my life; I could sense that she wasn't only moving away from our town—she was also moving away from me.

A pain seemed to start in my heart then and quickly make its way into my mind. Holly was leaving. I didn't want her to go and yet, I knew it was something she had to do. And I was proud of her for taking that step, for reaching for her dreams.

The Christmas party was a week later. Holly wasn't there because she'd already left town by then.

I guess I never realized how much she meant to me until she was gone, but I also knew that she was doing what was best for her.

I'd never taken anyone to the party before, but that year I had Liza by my side. She looked beautiful and I was proud to be her escort.

I was also proud to have her by my side three months later when I made her my wife.

Maybe I knew from the moment I met Liza that she was the one for me. Maybe that's why I was so hesitant about taking my relationship with Holly any further.

I continue to run the Dover Street Lattimer Distribution Center and Liza continues her work at the chapel. Several years have passed and Liza and I now have a son and a daughter. Mom and Dad are grandparents and my sister is now Aunt Whitney—and she still talks nonstop. I wouldn't change her for the world.

Holly completed her medical training and returned to town and now works at a public health clinic close to the Dover Street Chapel. Her husband, Dr. Tim Holloway, is in charge of the clinic.

I saw Holly a few days ago at the mall. We had a cup of coffee together, had a chance to catch up on news. She seems very happy, secure in the choices she's made. I'm very happy for her. I'm also very proud of her. She is still my special friend . . . and she always will be. To this day, I never pass the little diner without thinking of how a bowl of chili led me to perfect happiness at Christmastime.

The End

I SAVED SANTA
And it was the best Christmas ever.

It was three days before Christmas and I was driving home through a heavy snowstorm. I wasn't looking forward to Christmas this year—that is, until I saw Santa Claus standing by the side of the road.

At first, I couldn't believe my eyes as I stared at his red suit, black boots, white hair, and beard. It was him all right, and he was waving at me.

The road was a sheet of ice under the snow, and it took me a few moments to stop my pickup truck.

Santa walked up to my vehicle as I rolled down my window.

"Is something wrong?" I asked him.

"I wonder if you could help me. My car slid off the road."

I got out of my truck and looked over to where he was pointing. A small SUV had slid off the road into the ditch. The swirling snow had nearly covered the skid marks.

Santa shook his head. "I knew I should have brought the sled. Rudolph would never have let this happen. I tried to drive back out of the ditch, but the car is stuck. The only reason I bought this car was because it has four-wheel drive. I thought that meant it wouldn't slide on the ice."

"Everything slides on the ice, no matter how many wheels you have driving," I explained.

"Can you pull me out?"

"Ordinarily I could, but I'm afraid I can't do it now. I can't get enough traction on this ice, and I would end up in the ditch with you. You'll have to call a tow truck. Do you have a cell phone?"

He shook his head. "I wouldn't know who to call even if I did. I'm a long way from the North Pole."

"It's okay. I've got a cell phone, and there's only one tow truck company in the area. I'll call them for you."

When I tried the number, the line was busy, and by the time I got through, I was told that it would be hours before a tow truck could get there. According to the woman I spoke to, people were off the road everywhere.

I explained this to Santa. "Can I give you a ride somewhere?"

"Yes, if you wouldn't mind. But first, I need to put some stuff in the back of your pickup. It's a good thing you have a camper shell."

I walked down into the ditch with him, and we hauled three large bags out of his SUV and put them into my truck.

"What is all this stuff?" I asked.

"These are bags of Christmas presents I'm delivering for charity. I was supposed to make three stops tonight. The first is to the county children's home. That's where I need you to take me."

Santa climbed into my truck and struggled to fasten his seat belt over his padded suit. I stared at his face in the fading daylight, but with the long hair and beard, I couldn't tell what he looked like.

"You don't know how much I appreciate this," he told me as I put the truck into gear. "I never learned to drive on the ice."

"Really? I thought there would be a lot of ice at the North Pole."

He sighed. "As if you couldn't guess, I'm not the real Santa. I'm just one of his helpers. The real Santa Claus is sick this evening, and I offered to cover for him."

"That's really nice of you. So I take it you're not from around here."

"Well, I live here now, but I was brought up in south Texas. It almost never snows there."

"What brought you to the Colorado Rockies?"

"I moved here to take a job, and I've loved it ever since I got here. The first time I saw the snow on the mountains, I thought it was the most beautiful thing I had ever seen. Of course, I'll have to have more practice driving in the snow. What about you? What's your name and how did you come to be here?"

"I've lived in this area all my life. I'm Brenda Salinger, and my parents own a ranch at the foot of Eagle Mountain. I'm a medical receptionist at the clinic, and I was on my way home when I saw you standing there. How long had you been stuck before I arrived?"

"About a half an hour. Luckily, this Santa suit is warm. I don't know what I would have done."

"You wouldn't have been stranded for much longer. Someone would have driven by eventually. By the way, you didn't tell me your name."

He glanced over at me and a grin peeked out from under his beard. "Just for tonight, you can call me Santa."

I laughed and went along with the joke. "Okay, Santa. What about Mrs. Claus?"

"So far, there is no Mrs. Claus. I guess I haven't met her yet."

The county children's home was close to the center of New Kingston, the town where I lived. Due to the snowstorm, there was very little traffic on the streets, and I pulled up right in front of the building. The home housed both orphans and children who had been taken into protective custody.

My passenger climbed out of my truck and slung the largest of the three bags over his shoulder. The real Santa Claus couldn't have done it better.

"Come in with me for a few minutes until I can get someone to take the other two bags out of your truck," he said.

I followed him to the huge front door, which swung open when we approached. A man introduced himself as the assistant director, and we followed him into a huge room. A Christmas tree had been placed at one end of the room, and children of all shapes and sizes waited near the tree. When Santa walked in the room, they cheered.

"Ho, ho, ho," Santa bellowed, and the children surrounded him.

They all began to talk at once.

"We thought you'd never come," one boy said.

"Did you bring me a present?" another boy asked.

"I love you, Santa," a little girl told him.

"And I love you too," he said warmly. "I brought presents for all of you. I'm sorry I'm late, but I had a little trouble with my sleigh. So my helper, Brenda, brought me here."

I had been standing near the wall at one end of the room, and when Santa nodded in my direction, several of the children came over to thank me.

"You're welcome," I told them over and over.

Santa asked the children to sit down, and he handed out the presents.

Most of the children remembered to thank him, and one little girl said they had milk and cookies for him. "We have some for your helper too," she added looking at me.

I hesitated. "I really should go."

"Come on, Brenda," Santa urged. "You can stay for a few cookies. It would mean so much to the kids."

"Stay, stay," they chorused until I agreed.

"Tell us about the North Pole, Santa," someone requested.

"Well, it's very cold up there, and it has been snowing every day," he said between cookies. "This time of year, the sun doesn't come up at all, but the elves keep the lights burning in the workshop round the clock to make sure everything is ready for Christmas."

"What about the sleigh?" one boy wanted to know. "Will you have it ready by Christmas Eve, or will Brenda have to drive you around?"

Santa stroked his white beard. "As much fun as it would be for Brenda to drive me, the sleigh will be ready."

One of the girls turned to me. "Have you ever ridden in a sleigh, Brenda?"

"I've ridden in a sleigh, but I've never ridden in Santa's sleigh. The one I rode in was pulled by a team of horses. They just trotted through the snow on the ground. But the reindeer that pull Santa's sleigh can fly."

59

"Maybe he'll take you for a ride in his sleigh sometime," she said.

"I don't know. I'm afraid of heights, and those reindeer fly very high when they're in a hurry."

While I was talking with the children, Santa left the group, and when he returned, he took me aside.

His eyes caught mine. "I've just discovered that no one is available to drive me for the rest of the evening, nor is there a car here I can borrow. I still have two more stops to make. Is there any way you could take me? I would be willing to pay for your gas and your time. I wouldn't ask if it wasn't an emergency."

I looked around at all the children playing with the toys he had brought. "Of course I'll take you. You don't need to pay me."

"But I don't want to trespass on your evening without giving you something in return."

"It's okay. I didn't have any plans, and as for getting something in return, the smiles on the faces of the children are all I need."

"Thank you, Brenda. I hope that in the future you'll let me do something special for you."

After leaving the children's home, I drove slowly through the snow. Santa asked about my family and what they were doing for the holiday.

"I thought Santa knew everything," I teased him. "Remember the words of the song? 'He sees you when you're sleeping. He knows when you're awake.'"

"That's true," he conceded, "but I already told you that I'm not the real Santa. I'm just doing this to help him out."

"In that case, my parents are in Montana taking care of my dad's sister, and my brother is in the Marines, stationed on the east coast. None of them will be home for Christmas."

"What about your boyfriend?"

"I don't have one." It wasn't exactly the truth, but I didn't want to bore a man I'd just met with the details of my terrible relationship.

"So you'll be spending Christmas by yourself?"

"Not exactly. I'll be taking care of several cows, my mother's mare, and my dog Scout."

Our next stop was a homeless shelter in a restored warehouse down by the railroad yards. There were only a few people staying at the shelter, but they seemed as happy to see Santa as the children at the home. The kids clamored for his attention, while the adults hung back and watched them.

Everyone there had the same lost look in their eyes, but that look disappeared from the children's faces when Santa handed out the presents.

One little girl, who had unwrapped a doll, ran over to Santa and threw her arms around his black boots. As he bent down to her, she began to cry.

"Oh Santa," she sobbed. "I was so afraid you wouldn't find me here."

He gently stroked her hair. "Don't you know that wherever you go I'll find you?"

An older boy standing nearby gave Santa a challenging look. "How can you say that? You don't know where she's going to go."

"I can say that because I'm Santa," he insisted. "I see you when you're sleeping. I know when you're awake."

As I watched him with the children, I couldn't help thinking about my boyfriend Brendan. He was a sales representative for a drug company, and I had met him when he came into the clinic. The doctor he'd been scheduled to meet with had been tied up with a patient, so Brendan passed the time talking to me. Before he left the clinic that day, he asked me out.

At first, I was thrilled to have a date with a witty and successful man, but after I thought about it, I decided that Brendan must have a girlfriend in every doctor's office in Colorado. He would probably try to get me into bed on the first date.

As it turned out, he didn't try to get me into bed at all. Instead, he took me to a nice restaurant and we had a great conversation. He had a good sense of humor, or so I thought at first. As time went on, however, I learned that Brendan's witty conversation was the result of jokes and anecdotes he had memorized in order to charm the doctors into prescribing the drugs he represented. The real Brendan was anything but witty. Impatient and rude, he only cared about what he wanted. Unfortunately, after I figured this out, I kept on dating him.

He had made plans to go to the Bahamas for Christmas, and he'd wanted me to go with him. "I've made the reservations online, and I got a deal on our tickets. We'll be playing in the ocean while the snow piles up here."

I had explained that I couldn't go. "I promised my parents that I would take care of the ranch while they were staying with Aunt Stacy."

"You can hire somebody else to take care of the ranch," Brendan had insisted.

"No, I can't. My dad would worry himself sick if he thought I left his cows and Mom's horse with someone he didn't trust."

"So find someone he trusts."

"He trusts me." No matter how I tried to explain it, Brendan refused to accept the fact that I couldn't go.

"Whatever, Brenda," he finally said. "I hope you don't think I'm going to stay here just because you can't go. I hope you have a Merry

Christmas with your cows and your horse."

Just as he'd threatened, he left without me. He'd been gone for three days so far, and I hadn't heard from him.

I didn't miss him, though. Even at his most charming, Brendan would never have agreed to put on a Santa suit and pass out gifts to children.

Once again, after Santa had distributed the presents, the people at the homeless shelter offered us milk and cookies.

After answering questions about the North Pole, the reindeer, and the elves, Santa told everyone how I had rescued him and saved Christmas. Several of the children came up and hugged me.

"Where to now?" I asked as we got back into my truck and pulled away from the homeless shelter.

"Well, as of now, we're done with delivering presents to children. I got this Santa gig because one of the men I work with who usually plays Santa came down with the flu, and I promised I would deliver the presents to the children's home and the shelter. This last stop is all my idea. We're going to Bright Horizon." He gave me the address.

"Isn't that a nursing home?"

"They prefer to call it a 'retirement center.'"

"How do you know that?"

He shrugged. "Because I'm Santa."

"You just explained that you were filling in for one of your coworkers," I pointed out.

"I know that people don't usually think of a home for the elderly as a stop on Santa's route, but old folks need love too. A lot of them don't have any families, and you'd be surprised at the number of elderly people whose families never visit them."

"You seem to be a Santa who thinks of everything and everyone."

He nodded. "I like to try and brighten the lives of old people because I was raised by my great-grandmother."

"Your great-grandmother?"

"Yes. Both my mom and my grandma were killed in a car accident when I was little. My grandpa had died, and I never knew my dad. My great-grandma had to go to court to get custody of me. At first, the state refused to let her have me. The social workers thought she was too old to take care of a three-year-old boy. But she got a good lawyer, and instead of growing up in an orphanage or a foster home, I had a great childhood with someone who loved me."

"Is she still alive?" I asked.

He shook his head. "She died last year. She was ninety-six."

The snow was still falling, and I had to concentrate on the road. Still, I couldn't help being amazed by this man who had lost the only family he had, and instead of sitting around feeling sorry for himself, he had volunteered to dress up in a Santa suit and help make the holiday merry for others.

I wished I knew what he looked like, but other than noticing that he had blue eyes and was very tall, the padded suit hid everything else about him.

The people at the nursing home were singing Christmas carols when we arrived, but they stopped when Santa knocked on the door. He carried the last bag into the room.

"Ho, ho, ho. Merry Christmas," he said.

Just as they had at the last two places we'd been, the elderly people came up and gathered around Santa. Several of the men clapped him on the back, and a couple of the women hugged him.

"This is Brenda," he introduced me. "She rescued me when my car slid into a ditch."

"We thought you'd be here earlier," one man said. "We've already had dinner, but we saved some meat loaf. Maybe you and Brenda would like to have a sandwich."

"That would be great," Santa agreed. "All we've had to eat this evening is cookies." He set his sack down on the floor and opened it. "I tried to get everything you like. Jim, I brought you peanut brittle, and Anne, I got those chocolate-covered cherries you like. Norm, here's your salt-water taffy, and Elaine, chocolate truffles for you."

As I watched him hand out boxes of candy, it dawned on me that he knew these people, and they knew him.

A woman walked up beside me. "You're Brenda Salinger. I haven't seen you since you were seven. You were in my second-grade class. Do you remember me?"

She was a little stooped and her hair had turned white, but she had been my favorite teacher in elementary school. "Mrs. Bernhard? Of course I remember you. You used to read us stories every afternoon. How have you been?"

"I can't complain. I lost my Ronald a few years back, and then I moved in here. It's like being in a big family. There's always something going on. Come on, let's go into the dining room where we can talk while you eat your sandwich."

She led me to a table where the man who had offered to make the sandwiches set a plate in front of me. On it, he had put a sandwich, some cheesy potatoes, and some sliced fruit. He set a cup of punch down beside the plate.

Mrs. Bernhard introduced him. "Stan, this is Brenda. She was one of my second-grade students. Brenda, Stan Moran is the manager of this place, not that a bunch of old fogies like us need managing."

Stan nodded at me, and the overhead light reflected on his bald head. "So you were one of her kids. She told me she ruled her class with an iron fist and everyone was scared to death to sass her."

Mrs. Bernhard winked, and I laughed at the thought of the second graders being afraid of her, but I joined in on the joke.

"She had a big paddle on the wall that she called her 'Board of Education,'" I informed him.

Stan snickered. "Now I know you're pulling my leg. She'd never be able to hit anyone. Well, Brenda, it's nice to meet you. Santa will be joining you in a minute. I'll go and get his plate."

Mrs. Bernhard asked where I was working, and I told her about my job at the clinic. "I thought everyone came into the clinic, but I've never seen you in there."

"That's because there's a doctor on staff here," she explained, "and if we need a hospital, we go over to Wilson City. Brenda, how is your brother? He was in my class a couple of years before you were."

"He's in the Marines. He won't be home this Christmas."

She nodded. "I'm sure you'll be missing him."

"I'm afraid that I'll be missing everyone this Christmas. My mom and dad are in Montana, and they won't be home either."

Mrs. Bernhard patted my hand. "Brenda, you don't have to be alone on Christmas. You're welcome to join us. On Christmas Eve, we build a roaring fire in the gathering room, drink hot chocolate, and sing carols. And on Christmas Day, we have a feast. We would love for you to come."

"Thank you," I told her as Santa slipped into the chair beside me.

"Now what are you two talking about?" he asked.

"We're just catching up," Mrs. Bernhard told him.

"I heard you say that you had both Brenda and her brother in your second-grade class." He glanced at me. "Now, Brenda, tell Santa about your favorite Christmas, the best one you've ever had."

Just for a moment, I felt like Santa had put me on the spot. I didn't like to talk about myself that much, but Mrs. Bernhard was looking at me expectantly, and I thought it would be very rude not to answer Santa's question.

"When I was nine and my brother was eleven, Dad hired Mr. Morgan to bring over his team and his sleigh and take our whole family for a sleigh ride on Christmas Eve. He took us for a ride through the forest, and I'll never forget how much fun it was."

"I remember Mr. Morgan," my teacher commented. "He used to give hay rides in the summer and sleigh rides in the winter. I think his son does it now." She turned to Santa. "Tell us about your best Christmas."

"It was when I was sixteen. A few days before Christmas, my great-grandma had a heart attack while I was at school. One of our neighbors found her and called an ambulance. I stayed in the waiting room of the hospital until the doctors said she would be all right. That was on Christmas Eve."

"What a wonderful Christmas story," Mrs. Bernhard commented. "Remember that you're welcome to join us here for the holidays if you'd like."

"Did you get some hay for the reindeer?" he joked. "They'll be hungry by the time we're done."

I carried our dishes into the kitchen after we'd finished eating, and Santa went to make a phone call. When he returned, he announced that the tow truck company could pull out his car now.

"If you wouldn't mind taking me back there, I'd appreciate it," he said.

I thanked everyone for dinner and put on my coat before walking out to my truck. The snow had stopped falling, and here and there, stars peeked through the clouds.

Santa sighed loudly. "Do you smell that crisp Colorado air? That's why I moved here."

"You know, you're a great Santa Claus," I told him. "Wherever he is, the real Santa must be proud to have a helper like you."

"And you," he added. "Are you sure I can't reimburse you for your fuel or your time?"

I shook my head. "It felt special just to be included tonight. Who would have thought I would run into my second-grade teacher?"

The tow truck was already there when we got back to Santa's car.

"Brenda, you've been an angel," he told me, and before I realized what was happening, he leaned across the truck seat and kissed me. "Merry Christmas," he whispered.

As I drove away, I realized that I had forgotten to find out his name.

It was the strangest thing. Ever since I had learned my parents wouldn't be home for the holidays, I hadn't felt any Christmas spirit. I hadn't even bothered to put up any decorations around the house. But as I drove home that night, I began to sing Christmas carols, and as I pulled into the driveway, I felt a sort of peace that came from knowing that I had helped make Christmas better for others.

My collie ran out to greet me as I got out of my truck.

"I'm sorry I'm so late, Scout," I told her. "I met Santa tonight."

She bounced along beside me while I threw some hay to the cattle and fed the mare.

"Come on," I said to my dog. "Let's go in and you can have your dinner." Scout took off toward the house. I was still thirty yards away when she launched herself through the dog door.

The next morning, there were only a few people at the clinic. Most of my coworkers had taken the day off to get ready for the holiday, and I only had to work a couple of hours. Snow crews had been plowing the highways, and the roads were clear. However, more snow was predicted to fall during the next few days.

My job was slow that morning, and as I sat at my desk, I had plenty of time to think about the man I'd met the night before. I wondered whether he'd gotten home safely. I wondered who he was and what he was doing at that moment. Mostly, I wondered what he looked like and if I would ever see him again.

I reminded myself that I didn't know anything about him, but I felt like I knew a lot. I remembered how he'd spoken to the little girl who had feared Santa wouldn't find her at the homeless shelter. I had never seen his face, but I had seen inside his heart. I wished he would have asked me out. Maybe after Christmas I would call Mrs. Bernhard and ask if she knew his name.

When I got back home from work that day, I was glad that I was home for Christmas, even if I was going to be alone. I would rather be home alone than in the Bahamas with Brendan. I wouldn't have been happy there—I wasn't happy with Brendan anywhere. Right then, I made up my mind that if Brendan hadn't already dumped me when he left, I would break up with him as soon as he got back.

Christmas wouldn't be Christmas without a tree, so I went out to the storeroom and dug out the box that held the artificial tree my family always put up in the living room.

It might seem unusual that a family that lived on a ranch covered with blue spruce would use an artificial tree for Christmas. That was my fault. When I was about six, my dad announced that he was going out to chop down the Christmas tree. I threw a fit and insisted that murdering a tree for Christmas was a mean thing to do. To quiet me down, Mom finally promised that we would get a plastic tree and Dad would never kill a tree for Christmas again.

Scout watched as I assembled the tree and strung the lights on it.

"I would string popcorn for a garland too, but when I wasn't looking, you would eat it," I told her.

The tree lent a warm glow to the room, and so did the fire I built in the fireplace. I spent the evening reading a book while Scout snoozed on the hearth rug. I must have fallen asleep in my chair, because I dreamed that Santa Claus was watching over me.

I woke up thinking about him, and as I got ready for bed, I remembered that he'd said he hadn't met Mrs. Claus. If I found out who he was, maybe I would give him a call.

The next day was Christmas Eve, and my parents telephoned from Montana.

"It's snowing here," Dad announced.

"It's snowing here too. It must have been falling all night, because we have several inches of new snow."

"Are you going to spend Christmas with Brendan?" Mom asked.

"He had to go out of town." I hadn't told them anything about the Bahamas trip.

"Then I guess you'll be spending the day with Betty's family," she went on.

Betty was my best friend, and she'd invited me for Christmas at her home, but I had declined her invitation. I knew her mother would want to hear all the details about Brendan going to the Bahamas without me, and I didn't want to talk about it.

"No, Mom. I decided to spend a quiet Christmas at home." Before she could protest, I changed the subject. "You'll never guess who I saw the other day—Mrs. Bernhard, my second grade teacher. She lives at that retirement home on the north highway over toward Wilson City."

"I remember her. Tom was in her class too. She was a nice lady. Where did you run into her?"

"It's a long story, Mom. I'll tell you when you get home."

"Speaking of home," Dad interrupted. "We'll probably be back during the first week of January. We just called to tell you we love you and to have a Merry Christmas."

"Oh, and if you look on the top shelf of the linen closet behind the blankets, you'll find your Christmas present," Mom added.

"You got me a present? When did you have time to do that?"

Dad laughed. "You know your mother. She always gets an early start on Christmas. She hid your present there in September."

"That was so nice. Thank you. I love you both. Merry Christmas."

In the top of the linen closet, I found a box wrapped in gold paper. At first, I thought I wouldn't open it until the next morning, and I put it under the tree, but then I couldn't wait, and I opened it. Inside the box, I found a digital camera, the very camera I had been thinking about buying.

About half an hour later, my brother called. "Merry Christmas. How's the weather there?"

"It's snowing. There are a couple of feet of snow on the ground, and it's about thirty degrees. What's the weather like in North Carolina?"

"Well, right now it's raining and there's a cold wind, but it's supposed to clear up this afternoon. It's usually nice here, but it's not home. I miss my family, and I miss Colorado. I sent you a sweater for Christmas, but I didn't get around to mailing it until yesterday." Tom was the opposite of Mom.

"Did you get the present I sent you?" I had sent him a mystery novel.

"Are you kidding? I'm halfway through it. I couldn't wait until Christmas. I love you. Hug Scout for me."

"I love you too," I told him before I hung up.

I wondered whether Brendan would call from the Bahamas, but he didn't. I wondered about Santa Claus too. How was he spending his Christmas Eve? And I wondered whether Mrs. Bernhard and her friends were gathered around the piano at the retirement center singing Christmas carols.

Scout plowed through the snow beside me as I walked down to throw hay to the cows and feed the mare. I was just about to walk back to the house when Scout started barking and ran out of the barn. When I stepped outside to find out what she was barking at, I saw her looking at the road. I couldn't see anything through the falling snow, but when I managed to quiet Scout's barking, I heard something.

Bells. Sleigh bells. I stared toward the sound. Before my eyes, two huge gray horses materialized out of the snowstorm, pulling a large sleigh. A man in dark clothing held the reins, and on the seat beside him sat another man dressed in a red Santa suit. The sleigh turned into the driveway and pulled up beside the barn.

"Ho, ho, ho, Brenda. Merry Christmas." Santa jumped out of the sleigh and walked up to me. "This is Peter Morgan. His dad was the one who drove the sleigh on your favorite Christmas ever."

I looked up at the man in the driver's seat. "Hello, Peter. I'm Brenda Salinger."

He nodded and said hello.

I turned to Santa. "What's with the suit? I thought you had delivered all your presents."

"Not quite. I have one more, a present for you."

"You didn't have to—" I stopped as he put a small red box in my hand.

"You don't have to open it until tomorrow if you don't want to, but I'd love it if you would open it now."

I opened the box and found a necklace inside—a tiny angel on a slim gold chain.

"An angel for an angel," Santa said.

"It's beautiful," I murmured.

"So are you, and by the way, my real name is Tyler Franklin and I would really like to take you for a sleigh ride."

"Well, Tyler Franklin, it's nice to finally know your name. I'd love a sleigh ride."

A smile peeked out of his beard. "Good. Make sure you're wearing warm clothes. And would you mind if I came inside your house and changed out of the Santa suit? I only wore it because I was afraid you wouldn't recognize me without it."

I was already wearing warm clothes, so all I had to do was put on the necklace while Tyler disappeared into the bathroom to change out of the Santa suit.

When he came out, I saw a tall, lanky man with dark curly hair and a wide smile.

I hugged Scout, promised I'd be back later, and followed Tyler out to the sleigh.

"Where are we going?" I asked as he helped me into the back seat and slid in beside me.

"Oh, I know of a Christmas party at a place where they serve great meatloaf sandwiches."

Peter picked up the reins, and the horses trotted off through the forest. The snow whispered all around us as we snuggled under a blanket in the back of the sleigh.

"I couldn't stop thinking about you," Tyler confessed. "You're very special, Brenda, and I hope you'll give me a chance to get to know you better."

It was a magical ride through a blue spruce forest, with the man I would later marry. I didn't even notice when the sleigh stopped in front of Bright Horizon, because at that moment, I was kissing Santa Claus.

The End

BLOWN AWAY
What would happen to our holiday?

My two children and I shivered in the hallway as the wind howled around our house. I'd heard that the safest place to be during a storm was in the center of the house, away from all windows. I sure hoped that was right because it sounded awful outside.

"I'm scared, Mommy," my daughter, Ashley, cried.

"We'll be fine, honey," I said, although I was just as scared as she was.

"Manny said a real bad hurricane is coming," my son, Jared, said. "He said it could blow down houses—just like the wolf blew down the pigs' houses."

In the semidarkness, I forced myself to smile at him. "Manny is a great storyteller, isn't he?"

Jared's eyes widened as he studied my face. I tried very hard to act like this was no big deal, but the last news I'd heard was that the storm was heading straight for us. It was supposed to hit north of us, but at the last minute, it changed direction. Now, it was coming right at our coastal town.

I wished I'd accepted my ex-husband's parents' offer of letting the kids come to their house. They hadn't offered to let me stay there, of course, since my ex had his girlfriend there, too. I would have had to ride out the storm without my kids, so I selfishly said we'd be just fine. They'd tried to talk me into it, but I'd been stubborn.

Squeezing my eyes shut, I turned away from Ashley and Jared and said a silent prayer for our safety. Even if the house got torn up, I only wanted my family to come out of it unharmed.

Then it happened. The wind had no sooner picked up when I heard the roof being ripped from the walls.

"Mommy!" Ashley shrieked. "Are we gonna die?"

"Just hold on to me, sweetie," I said, my throat constricting.

I've never been as frightened as I was during the next hour, while the storm ravaged our tiny cottage that I'd scrimped and saved for after my divorce. I felt like my life was being ripped from its seams, and I was being punished for something I didn't yet understand.

When it was over, an eerie calm fell over us. Slowly, my iron-grip loosened on my children, and I glanced around. A huge chunk of wood was balancing precariously over us, held up by walls that leaned on either side of the hallway. I could tell, even from my vantage point, that my house was not stable. I needed to get the children out of there.

"C'mon, kids, let's go see the damage," I said. By now, there was no way I could sugar coat anything or make it seem like no big deal. My children were smart enough to know better.

"Mommy!" Ashley said as we looked around at our things mixed with stuff from the neighborhood that lay scattered over the lawns down the street. "Everything's all messed up."

"There's nothing left," Jared said in awe. He turned to me. Worry furrowed his brow. "What are we gonna do?"

I opened my mouth, but I quickly closed it. I didn't have any answers for him.

One of the neighbors came out of her house next door, shaken but apparently unscathed. "Carmen, are you okay?" she asked.

"Sure, I'm fine," I said with my lips, but she knew I wasn't.

"Looks like most all the houses on the street are goners," she said. "We should have gone to the shelter when we had time."

I nodded.

My neighbor was old enough to be my mom, and she often helped out by sitting with the kids when I had to go somewhere. She edged closer to us, and she gently touched each of my children on the shoulders. I could tell that small gesture was more comforting than words could be at the moment.

"I reckon we'll have to find a place to live for a while," she said. "At least until the insurance comes through. With all this damage, it might be a while before the adjusters get around to assessing things."

In the meantime, where would I live? All sorts of things crossed my mind. My parents had died shortly after I got out of school. The only grandparents my children had were my ex-husband's parents, and I didn't want them to go there. Although they loved Ashley and Jared, their idea of watching my spirited four-year-old and six-year-old was not the same as mine. They always gave in to whims, and they didn't believe in any form of discipline, which was probably why their son never took responsibility for anything—including his own family.

We spent the day walking around the yard in a daze. For a storm that hit very late during hurricane season, this one sure packed a mighty punch. I'd mistakenly thought that we were out of the woods by this time of year. Now I had to sort through the biggest mess ever. At least, I had a decent job now. I knew that with all this mess and destruction, finding an apartment would be a challenge, but I was willing to take anything since it was temporary. Being a survivor of what I'd thought was much worse; I figured I'd do just fine.

Later in the day, a large truck arrived at the end of the street. My road was impassable, so a crew of men got out and walked toward the few people who'd insisted on staying home. I saw the grave expressions on their faces.

71

One of the men came up to me and nodded toward the kids. "Those your children?"

"Yes," I replied.

"There's a shelter set up in the Church of the Transfiguration's basement for families with small children," he said. "We can take you there in the truck."

I looked over at my neighbor who mouthed, "Go on. I'll be fine."

I was in a daze as we drove past the biggest mess I'd ever seen in my life. Houses, businesses, and streets were torn up, with large trees uprooted and lying across the road. Several times, the truck had to find alternate ways past the debris, bumping up on curbs and driving on lawns.

By the time we got to the church shelter, I was shell-shocked. My entire town looked like a war zone. My children were silent as we were shuttled into a room filled with weary parents and crying children.

"There's food over there," one of the workers said. "Keep a close eye on your children." Then, he left me standing with Ashley and Jared.

I paused for a moment to take it all in, and I gently nudged my kids. "C'mon, let's go get something to eat."

"I'm not hungry," Ashley said. Her little body was rigid.

"I am," Jared said, as he tried to take off without me.

I reached out and yanked him back. "Oh no you don't, buddy boy," I said. "You're sticking with us. We'll go over there, together."

I had to pick up Ashley and carry her because she was frozen in place. I certainly understood. This whole scenario was overwhelming, and I was on sensory overload. I could only imagine how my children felt.

Jared took care of himself, grabbing a plate and holding it out so the women on the other side of the table could fill it. I got a plate for Ashley, and one for myself. Although I wasn't hungry, I wanted Ashley to eat, so I figured I needed to set an example for her.

We found a place at one of the long tables and huddled together to choke down our food. I'd managed to get Ashley to eat three bites before Jared piped up. "Mommy, if we can't go back home for Christmas, how will Santa Claus know where to find us?"

My heart sank. The late storm had taken everyone in South Carolina by surprise. Normally, the worst of the storm season had long since passed. Fortunately, I'd put some toys and clothes on layaway at the local discount store, so at least my kids would have that. I was thankful I hadn't gone ahead and brought them home because almost everything in my house had been destroyed.

"Don't worry, sweetie," I told him as I forced a smile. "Santa is a very smart man. He'll find us wherever we are."

"Are we gonna stay here?" Ashley asked, her eyes wide with fear.

I gulped. "I—I don't know where we'll be," I had to admitted.

Her little face puckered up in a pout. "I don't like it here. It's yucky."

Jared took a quick look around. "I think it's cool. There's a bunch of kids to play with."

He was right about there being a bunch of kids. The place was crawling with them. However, most of them didn't appear in the mood to play. They all had the same fearful expressions Ashley had. Jared was the only one who seemed delighted by the situation.

"Mommy, can I go see if that boy over there wants to race?" he asked, pointing to the edge of the room where a boy about his size stood with an exhausted-looking woman.

"No, not right now, Jared. Let's get a better idea of what's going on."

After we finished eating, I led the children to the dishpan where we deposited our plates and glasses. Then I made my way over to some uniformed people standing guard at the edge of the room.

"What are we going to do?" I asked.

One of the uniformed women shrugged. "Beats me. We're waiting for information, too. Not many houses still standing, and there aren't any hotels for miles."

It was obvious I wouldn't get anything from her—at least not yet. So I led the kids over to a small area of the room where we could talk. I knelt down, pulled both of my children to me.

"I don't know what's going to happen today or tomorrow, but I do know one thing. As long as we're together, we'll be fine," I said.

Ashley started sniffling as tears trickled down her cheek.

For the first time, Jared didn't appear to be having fun. He swallowed hard. I could tell he was fighting tears, too.

That night, we were given pallets, blankets, and small pillows. The kind people from the church said we could stay in their basement until suitable housing was found for us. We still didn't know what was going on outside the church doors.

The next morning, I got up, took the children by the hand, and ventured outside. The instant I took a good look and saw the mess around us, I felt a wave of nausea flood my body. It was even worse than I thought. The church was the only structure standing for what seemed like miles. Houses had been broken apart and lay like matchsticks across lawns and roads. The church steeple had been knocked over and broken into three parts.

The next several days went by in a blur. Trucks took families to their homes—or what was left of their homes—to see if anything could be salvaged. I found my small plastic box of pictures and a few items that meant something to me. My old minivan had been flipped upside down in the driveway, so there was no way I'd be driving that anytime soon.

Over the next week, people gradually found places to stay—with relatives who were willing to take them in and friends who lived outside the storm range. My kids and I weren't as fortunate. We had no place to go. What made matters worse was that the place where I worked had been destroyed as well, and the corporate headquarters in another state wasn't sure they'd rebuild. After this storm, they worried that insurance rates would go up, and they couldn't afford to do business in this area.

With the small amount of severance pay they direct deposited into my account, I wasn't about to blow it on an expensive hotel room, which was all that was left in town. Nearly a third of the people in town needed to collect unemployment compensation, so we were told it would be a while for them to bring people in from other parts of the state to process the claims. The whole situation was a complete mess.

I accepted the generosity of the church people and stayed in their basement, where they'd erected partitions so the remaining families could have a little privacy. We even took turns cooking the food that the members of the church had brought in. If it weren't for them, I don't know what we would have done.

After a couple of weeks, there were still three families left in the church shelter. The generous people who attended church there told us to stay as long as we needed. My pride hurt, but I didn't have any choice.

Jared made friends with a little boy from another neighborhood that had gotten hit pretty badly. They played outside on the playground after school each day. Since Jared's school had lost the roof and nearly an entire wing of classrooms, he was bused to another elementary school miles away, which concerned me. I was just thankful they put his new friend in the same school as him.

Ashley delighted in hanging out with some of the kids who came to the church nursery. She called herself a "teacher's helper," and she proved to be just that. The woman who was in charge said Ashley was the best-behaved four-year-old she'd ever met. Her daughter was a year younger than Ashley, so they played together, with Ashley taking the lead. She enjoyed feeling like a big sister for a change.

Each day that passed brought Christmas a little closer. The store where I'd purchased my children's gifts had been demolished, so there was no hope of getting the things out of layaway. Of course, I'd lost my receipt, so I didn't think we'd ever see any of the items I'd put a deposit on.

I made friends with one of the churchwomen, and I cried on her shoulder. She was very sweet as she told me God was in control and that things would work out like they were supposed to. Then she led me in prayer.

I didn't want to let the children know there wasn't much chance of them getting much of anything for Christmas and certainly not anything they'd painstakingly put on their list. They were so trusting, so they assumed Santa would come through for them.

One afternoon, I asked them to sit down so we could talk. Taking each of their tiny hands, I looked into Ashley's eyes, then Jared's.

"What, Mommy?" Ashley asked. "Have we been bad?"

"No, of course not," I replied, my heart aching for my children. "It's just that . . . " I felt so choked up I couldn't speak, at first.

"Are you sick?" Jared asked, his eyes wide with worry.

"No, I'm not sick."

He blew out a sigh of relief. "Good. I was worried you were gonna tell us you were about to die."

"No," I said. "At least I don't think so, anytime soon."

"What do you wanna talk to us about?" he pressed.

I swallowed hard and forced a slight smile. "You know those Christmas lists I asked you to make?"

Jared nodded. Ashley just looked at me, waiting.

"Well, Santa's very busy helping people in town get back on their feet, so—"

"Is he bringing us a house for Christmas?" Jared asked, interrupting me.

"Um, well . . ." I was at a complete loss for the right words to say.

"Mommy!" Ashley squealed. "Santa's bringing us a house? That's better than all the toys in the world."

"I'm sorry, honey," I said. "Santa really can't do that—not when all these other people are suffering so much."

Jared scrunched his nose. "What's Santa doing, then?"

My mind drew a blank momentarily; then an answer popped into my head. "Here we are, eating wonderful food in this fabulous church. We're surrounded by people who love God. There are some people out there who don't have anything. They have to live in tents."

"What if another storm comes?" Jared asked.

"Will the wind blow their tent away?" Ashley added.

How could I tell my children what I was trying to say without making them worry even more?

"Let's hope not," I replied. "What I'm trying to say is that everyone's doing the best they can to make things good again, but it'll take a while."

"After Christmas?" Jared asked.

"I'm afraid so, honey."

Jared frowned, then nodded. "I understand. I don't even want those dumb old toys anymore. All I want is our house back."

A tear trickled down Ashley's cheek and her chin trembled. I felt like a failure as a mother, although I knew none of this was my fault. But that didn't make our situation any easier. This whole group living thing was taking its toll on us.

Finally, Jared stood up, took his little sister by the hand. "We'll be just fine," he announced. "I won't let anything happen to either one of you. Maybe I'll even build us a new house."

Now, I felt like bursting into tears. My son was trying hard to be a man. I was very proud of him.

That night, I lay on my cot thinking about how only a few days before the storm, my children and I sat down to a wonderful Thanksgiving dinner with the woman next door and her grown son. We said our blessing without really thinking about the words. The day after Thanksgiving, I hit the sales, and put my kids' Christmas gifts on layaway, thinking I had all my shopping done.

We managed to avoid the subject of Christmas, again. However, now I had no choice but to think about it. It was less than a week away.

Then, one day, while Ashley was helping clean up the nursery classroom, Blythe, the woman in charge, called me over to the side. "I was wondering if you'd like to come to my house for Christmas."

I blinked. Was she offering charity? Suddenly, I felt defensive.

"I—I'm not sure," I stuttered, since my already deflated pride had just taken another hit. "I don't think so."

"Carmen would love it so much. You know, she adores Ashley." Her expression was one of gentleness and concern and not at all condescending. "That would mean all the world to her."

"But I couldn't—" I began.

"Please," she said, quickly. "You don't have to make a decision, now; tell me tomorrow."

I sighed. "I'll think about it."

She reached out and squeezed my shoulder. "Okay. Just remember there are people who really care about you. Besides, we feel like you're part of our family, now. It helps us when you let us help you."

"Thanks, Blythe. I appreciate it."

I expected her to return to what she was doing, but she didn't. She just stood there and looked at me. So I hesitated.

"Carmen, God knows what He's doing," she said softly. "He's not going to let you continue to suffer. What happened to you could have happened to any of us."

I wanted to scream: Why did He let it happen to me? But I didn't. I fought the urge to show my bitterness that had built up and been pushed back for the past several weeks.

"Know why I think He let this happen?" she continued.

"No, why?" I asked as I folded my arms over my chest.

"I think He wanted you and your little girl to come into my life. My husband and I have had such a difficult time for the past year, and you've shown me a strength I can only aspire to. This would be good for all of us."

When I walked away from her, those words echoed in my head. She wanted my strength? Didn't she realize I was ready to crumble at any moment? Did she not see the fragile nerves I had to hold in check every single waking moment? Had I been that good at hiding what was really going on?

As if in answer to all my questions, I felt a subtle peace fall over me. It wasn't an earth-moving moment, or anything anyone else would have seen. But I felt it.

For the first time in my life, I'd been put in the position of having to rely completely on other people. Even when my husband was still with us, I was self-sufficient. I didn't need anyone. I had my kids, and I could take care of us without any help from another person.

I shut my eyes and said a prayer for guidance. Was this God's way of letting me know I couldn't continue to plod through life alone—not allowing anyone else the pleasure of being there for my children and me?

Later that evening, after soup and sandwiches, I huddled with my children in our little space. "How would you like to celebrate Christmas with Carmen?" I asked, looking at Ashley.

Jared tugged on my arm. "But Carmen is just a baby," he said.

"Yes, she's a little girl, but you do realize she has a big brother, right?"

"She does?" He tilted his head to one side as he scrunched his eyebrows together.

"Yes, but I'm not sure how old he is," I replied. "I think he might be in second or third grade."

"Her brother is a big, huge giant," Ashley said.

I laughed. To my little Ashley, any kid taller than her brother was a big, huge giant.

"Yes, he is a big boy. I've only seen him a couple of times, but he seems pretty nice."

"That would be way cool, Mom," Jared said. "But how will Santa Claus find us there?"

"I'm not sure, Jared," I replied. "I guess we just have to trust and believe he will."

Jared thought it over for a minute. "Even if he doesn't find us, I guess it doesn't matter. Without a house, what good are the toys, anyway?"

"I'm sure Santa will bring you something you like," I said.

I'd gotten a little bit of money from the bank to get a couple of things for the kids. I didn't want them to suffer for something they couldn't control. They were just kids.

When I told Blythe we were taking her up on her offer, she acted like I'd given her the best gift in the world. Her eyes lit up, and she hugged me.

"This will be the best Christmas ever!" she said. "Just wait until I tell Jason and Dack."

"Jason and Dack?" I said.

"Jason's my husband, and Dack's my son. He's sort of a lonely boy because he can't play sports, and the other guys . . . well, they leave him out."

"Oh," I said. "I'm sorry to hear that."

"It's been rough," she said. "He had some health problems since he was born. We've learned to cope."

"I'll add him to my prayer list," I offered.

Tears sprang to her eyes. "That's the nicest thing you can do."

"I'd like to do more."

"Trust me. Sometimes, the only solution to a problem is prayer. When Dack was diagnosed with autism, we were told he might not live a normal life. Jason blamed himself, and he's never quit struggling. The power of prayer got us through those difficult early days. We felt like we were out of the woods, but then Dack started having seizures that sent us to the emergency room too many times to count."

"I'm so sorry to hear that," I said. "How old is he?"

"Eight," she replied. "And it's been a very long eight years. Jason and I hadn't planned to have any more children, so when Carmen came along, we were completely caught off guard."

"Carmen is a precious little girl," I said.

"Yes, she certainly is. And she's been a real blessing because when she came into our home, Dack started responding. He took one look at her and fell in love with his little sister. The doctor said it was a miracle—a true testament to the fact that children have the power to heal without medicine."

I instinctively reached out and pulled her into a hug. I felt her tense muscles relax as she patted me on the back.

"Thanks, Carmen. You're a kind woman. I don't want to sound mean or anything, but I'm glad you came here. Until you came, I never felt like I could really open up to anyone. People are afraid of Dack—even my husband."

"I don't understand that," I said, shaking my head. I'd seen Dack, and he was a quiet boy. "Dack is just a child. All children are different."

78

"That's so true," she said, as a grin spread across her tear-streaked face. "I think we can be very good friends."

"Me too," I agreed.

Now, I had no doubt why I'd had my house ripped from me. Blythe and I needed each other. I needed physical help, and she needed someone to listen. Come to think of it, I'd noticed other women in the church walk a wide berth around her. I didn't think anything of it at the time because I'd known people who were hard to be around. Now, I realized it was because many people didn't know how to talk to someone who had as much difficulty in their lives as her.

I wasn't quite sure what to say to my children about Dack. I'd seen him, and there didn't appear to be anything wrong with him. Dack wasn't sick, and I had no idea how to explain autism to a four-year-old and a six-year-old. Maybe if I didn't say anything, they wouldn't know. I decided to use the silent approach.

On Christmas Eve, I had a small bag that had been donated and packed with clothes I'd managed to find in the remains of my house. Blythe had brought the new items I'd bought to her house to hide them for me. My kids were excited, even though it was obvious they wouldn't have as much this year as before. I guess it was the season and all the festivities we had to look forward to. Plus, it would be a nice change of pace to be in someone's home, too.

Blythe came by midafternoon. She had a twinkle in her eye that looked awfully suspicious.

"What's up?" I asked. "You look happy about something."

"Oh, I am happy," she replied.

"Care to tell me about it?"

She giggled. "You'll find out soon enough."

"Come on," I begged. "You can tell me."

"No I can't," she said, shaking her head. "It's a surprise."

That made me a little nervous. I never liked surprises. Even good surprises rattled me. However, I could see that there was no way I'd get any information out of her because she was obviously having too much fun with her little secret.

I was amazed at how clear the streets were as we drove through town to get to her house. Last time I'd gone out, when one of the elders had taken me shopping for Christmas presents, there were still tree branches and limbs scattered over the roads, and personal belongings of victims had been strewn across lawns. Now, with the exception of the skeletal remains of a few buildings, most of the town looked somewhat normal.

Her roof had obviously had some patches—there were several sections where the colors had faded and others that looked new. But she was still fortunate to still have a house. I had nothing.

My kids eagerly scrambled out of her car and ran up her front porch steps, where her children stood. Little Carmen smiled around the thumb in her mouth as Ashley embraced her. Dack looked at Jared, then turned around and headed inside. Jared followed. I looked at Blythe to see her reaction, but she just smiled at me and gestured toward her house.

"I hope you don't mind, but I'm letting Ashley sleep in Carmen's room and Jared in Dack's. You'll have the guest room to yourself."

"Mind?" I said with giddiness. "Not only do I not mind, but I'm totally thrilled. Do you realize how long it's been since I've slept in a room all by myself? For more than three weeks, I've awakened with kids piled on top of me."

"I want you to have a good time while you're here. Jason has to go out of town on a business trip, and he suggested you stay here until after New Year's."

"That would be great," I said. I'd left my pride behind a long time ago. To have a regular bed and be surrounded by sturdy walls and privacy would be utter paradise.

The children played while I helped Blythe get the Christmas Eve dinner prepared. She commented about how nice it was to have Ashley around to keep Carmen from being underfoot in the kitchen. I understood because I'd once dealt with that with my own children. Being in her home seemed like the most natural thing in the world.

After dinner, it took us several hours to get the kids to go to sleep. They were wired from excitement, so Blythe reminded them that morning would come sooner if they went to bed.

As soon as we were sure they were sleeping, Blythe crooked her finger and motioned for me to follow her. I did. We went out to her double-car garage, where there was a huge tarp over a bunch of lumps.

"Help me with this, okay?" she said, as she lifted one corner.

I grabbed the other side, thinking this was where she hid her children's gifts. Fortunately, I'd warned my children they'd be watching Carmen and Dack open gifts, and they wouldn't get much because of our circumstances. In spite of the fact that they seemed okay with it, I still felt bad.

The instant we had the tarp off the things, my eyes bugged. "I can't believe this. A lot of this is what I put on layaway for my kids."

"That's what this is," she said with a wicked grin.

"What are you talking about?" I asked.

"This is yours."

"But how—" I began, before her husband, Jason, appeared at the garage door.

"The store had all their layaway records in the computer system at their corporate headquarters. One of the women from the church overheard you telling someone you'd just put some stuff on layaway," Jason said. "Blythe called to see if they had the records on file, and they did."

"But I thought it got destroyed," I argued as my pulse raced. I was excited, but I couldn't afford the balance on all this stuff.

"They have other stores." Jason and Blythe did one of the glance exchanges while I caught a breath. "And your account was marked paid in full."

"I can't believe all this," I said as I fell to my knees. As much as accepting charity bothered me, at least, my kids wouldn't have to suffer.

"We told them you'd be here for Christmas, so they had everything delivered yesterday afternoon," Blythe said. "And they threw in a few things for my kids, too. I thought that was nice. In fact, they've donated quite a bit of merchandise to our town."

I glanced over at Blythe just in time to see her wink at her husband, wearing one of her goofy grins. Something else was going on, but I knew better than to try to pry it out of her. She was too good at keeping secrets, and I knew, by now, she would never talk.

We brought all the things inside, put tags on them, and placed them around and under her tree. Then we stood back and had a cup of hot cocoa as we admired the beauty of the room that was illuminated only by Christmas tree lights and candles on the mantle. A peace settled over me, and I knew right then that everything would be fine—especially since I knew Blythe and Jason. They were good folks, as were all the other people at the church. Their kindness and generosity without making me feel like I owed them anything showed me that there actually were people who lived their faith.

"Go on to bed, now," Blythe whispered after a few minutes. "We have a big day planned tomorrow." Again, she and Jason looked at each other and smiled.

Later on, I lay in bed, staring at the ceiling, as tears trickled down my cheeks. Although my children would get some of the things they wanted, we had no place to keep them. I felt sadness that I wouldn't have a home for quite a while. The insurance company was dragging their feet, and they said it would be months before they'd be able to settle. Besides, my home was under-insured, which meant some of what I'd lost wasn't covered. In the meantime, I had to rely on other people's goodwill. But at least, my kids didn't seem to be suffering too much. They just took it all in stride by now, even though they still talked about how much they missed having their own rooms.

The next morning, I was awakened by joyful shrieking. I got up and threw on my clothes, then went to where all the action was. When I arrived in the living room, I saw the kids rummaging through their loot. All four of them wore huge smiles.

"Mom, this is so cool!" Jared said. "I think this is the best Christmas in the whole world."

Ashley tenderly held her new doll and glanced over at her little friend. "Look, Mommy, Santa brought Carmen a baby doll just like mine."

Carmen held the doll up for my inspection. She had her other thumb in her mouth, and she was smiling once again.

Blythe chuckled. "Carmen really looks up to Ashley. I'm glad they're such good friends."

When I turned around, Dack and Jared were quietly watching a small toy train as it went around and around on the tracks. I'd noticed how they'd quietly become friends. Jared seemed to instinctively understand some things about Dack, and he was fine with it.

Another thing I'd noticed was that my children seemed satisfied with a fraction of what they'd requested. They're such wonderful children.

Blythe called everyone into the kitchen, where Jason stood at the stove, wearing an apron and holding a spatula. "Pancakes, anyone?" he asked.

"Carmen and I are going to go for a little drive while you feed the kids," Blythe told her husband.

"Have fun," he said. "We'll be fine, here."

"Where are we going?" I asked.

"You'll see," she said as she nudged me out of the kitchen. "Get your coat and let's go."

On the way to her car, Blythe nudged me. "This is the most fun I've seen Jason have in quite a while. He loves kids."

We were five minutes into our drive when I turned to her and said, "This is the way to where my house used to be."

"That's where we're going," she said.

My heart sank. I was having such a pleasant Christmas. I really didn't want to see the mess the hurricane had left. But I couldn't say anything to Blythe after all she'd done for me.

As if she could read my mind, she reached over and placed her hand over mine. "Trust me, Carmen, everything will be just fine. Everyone in the church is praying for you and the other families who still haven't found a place to live."

I swallowed hard and nodded. When I was able to talk without crying, I said, "I think it's really nice that there were three families willing to take all of us in."

"It's more than that," Blythe said as she rounded the last turn to my house. "Not only are we glad we've been able to help you, we feel like this horrible disaster has brought our church closer together and allowed us to live our faith. I'm really thankful for that."

Now, I couldn't control the tears. They'd begun streaming down my face in rivers.

"Look," Blythe said as she pointed to the end of the street.

I glanced up and blinked. I couldn't believe my eyes. All the debris had been cleared away, a foundation had been poured, and wooden studs had been erected where my house used to be.

"But the insurance—" I began, before she interrupted me.

"They were taking way too long, so we got some people from church to come over and get everything cleaned up. You'll be happy to know a few things were saved. We put them in a storage unit until we get you and your family squared away. The insurance company said they'd reimburse us for materials if we give them the receipts."

"This is so sweet," I said.

"It'll still be a while before we get the house finished," she said, apologetically.

"Yes, I understand that. I'm just so thankful for all the church has done for me."

She opened her mouth to say something, but she quickly closed it. I knew, though, that she was going to talk about Christmas and how the church was doing what they felt Jesus would want them to do. I had no doubt I'd experienced Christian love in the biggest way, and I was too thankful to turn any of it down. Plus, I vowed to join that church and give back because I knew it was the right thing to do.

"Do you want to get out and walk around?" she asked.

I looked out the window and shivered. "No, I think I'd like to get back to the kids, now."

"Me, too," she said as she pulled into the driveway to turn around.

Jason was sitting in the big overstuffed chair watching the kids when we walked in. He pointed to the tree. "You overlooked something, Carmen. Santa left you an envelope."

I looked at Blythe, and she shrugged. Slowly, I walked over to the tree and plucked the envelope from the branch. When I opened it, I saw a gift certificate from the store where I'd had my kids' things on layaway—and it was enough to cover totally redecorating my place.

"What is it, Mommy?" Ashley asked, as she came to me.

I hugged her and replied, "It's good, old-fashioned Christian love, sweetheart." When she hugged my leg, I locked gazes with Blythe and mouthed, "Thank you."

What had started out a disaster had turned into the best Christmas of my life. No matter what happens in the future, I know that with kindness and focus on being true to my newfound faith, anything in this life can be overcome.

The End

THE LAST CHRISTMAS
It was a time for remembering and hoping.

Last Christmas, my wife Nettie and I had special cause for celebration: we were winning a fight against terrible odds. Despite all our previous Christmas celebrations together, I was to learn that, for all the presents we bought each other to show our love, the one that I valued the most embodied the very essence of the season and the very reason we had spent the last twenty-seven years together.

For months, Nettie had suffered fatigue, night sweats, and insomnia, which was especially unusual for her. Our primary physician had long passed such symptoms off as Polymyalgia Rheumatica or PMR, a catchall term for many ("poly") painful muscles ("myalgia"). Although the symptoms can also include weight loss and a slight fever, Nettie was experiencing neither. Then, in early November, a blood test showed a strangely high "sed" rate (the normal rate in women under fifty years old is less than twenty, over fifty is less than thirty, and Nettie's was one hundred and fifteen), more common for inflammatory ailments like arthritis, tuberculosis, Hodgkin's disease, and sometimes other lymphomas. This suggested that her body was fighting a mysterious infection.

So at last, our doctor allowed a referral to a more sympathetic rheumatoid-arthritis specialist. Her first step: ordering a series of tests, beginning with a bone marrow biopsy. On November seventeenth, three days before our twenty-seventh wedding anniversary, and two weeks before I was to join Nettie in early retirement, the diagnosis came through—Nettie had an often fatal cancer of the blood known as acute myelogenous leukemia (AML).

By the first day of a "mild" chemo treatment on December eleventh, Nettie had already improved. We had eliminated her intake of refined sugars as best we could, using natural foods like organic meats, grains, fruit, nuts, and rice milk. That helped her lose five pounds, bringing her down to the slim one hundred and sixteen pounds she had been when we first married in 1976. More importantly, the diet reduced her leucoblasts (the cancer cells) from 78 percent to 66 percent—still dangerously high—and increased her neutrophils (healthy germ-fighting white blood cells) from five hundred to seven hundred—still dangerously low. A week later, once the chemo took effect, the leucoblasts dropped to 46 percent and the neutrophils rose to eight hundred.

So, we entered the Christmas season with considerable hope that, despite the inconvenience of driving into downtown Portland on Christmas and New Year's Day for blood tests, we would be allowed to appreciate our many holiday rituals.

Because of these tests, and out of fear of exposing her to more infections from crowds, we hadn't finished all our shopping yet. We'd gotten out in November to pick up the Christmas tree that Nettie had wanted. We'd even put up the tree right after Thanksgiving for our traditional Christmas card photos, waiting a week to decorate in hopes that Nettie would be able to help. However, she proved to be too tired, so I did most of it on my own.

Despite the crowds, we had to finish shopping at the mall. So, on Sunday, December twenty-first, Nettie, again unusually tired, waited for me at the food court while I went out to get the last gifts she'd hinted that she'd wanted before we knew about the leukemia.

Unable to make up my mind, I chose two pairs of what she called "good time" shoes, classy yet alluring evening sandals she had admired. We hoped she could wear them on New Year's Eve. She had also mentioned a cashmere scarf, hat, and glove set, so I picked up the only complete set available, though it was regrettably black.

By time I got back to her and took her home, she was so tired that she napped for three hours, a long time even for her.

With Christmas Eve imminent, though, she experienced renewed energy, managing to bake sugar cookies even though she couldn't have any herself. She made up the frosting, but we never got around to decorating the cookies, something that had always been a two-person ritual. Instead, we frosted them individually as we ate them.

That night, we unwrapped our "big presents." She'd honored an unwitting "theme" in what she bought for me: everything would keep me warm and safe or help us have fun later together. Her gifts included a new burgundy parka, a ladder that would make it easier to fix our house's Christmas lights, a Courvoisier brandy set we planned to share during the season (though I joked I was more of an eighteen-dollar cognac kind of guy), the anniversary edition of Trivial Pursuit (always my favorite game), and a special turntable edition of Scrabble, her favorite.

She seemed to have done so much more for me with her gifts. Because of what might be our precarious future, I wanted her to know, through my presents, just how much I loved her. I think, though, she was disappointed in the scarf set. She had originally wanted pink, but the store had sold out of that color early on. Still, the "good time" shoes pleased her. She especially liked the less expensive gold pair. As a prelude to our planned New Year's Eve outing, she tried them out later that evening. I can vouch that they promised a "good time" indeed!

But the most touching thing she gave me was what we always started Christmas Eve with: our cards.

Mine featured a red heart on a black cover and ended with this printed sentiment:

And so, for Christmas,
I'm giving you a promise
 as a part of my gift—
A promise to love you even more
and make you even happier—
To make all our days together
 days to remember always, to cherish
as the priceless treasures they are . . .
This promise is my special gift for you,
a gift to keep forever.

Then in my own scrawling handwriting, I added,

As if I haven't already made such a promise to you many times over—even more so now that we're retired. I never thought we'd get to this place in our lives. I'm certain we'll overcome this obstacle because we were meant to get this far—and beyond. I love you, honey, and I look forward to all our Christmases to come.

Despite my having been a wordsmith all my life, Nettie easily bested my comments with what her gold-embossed holly leaf card contained. We had always made it a practice to write something personal in our Christmas cards—not just to each other but on those we mailed out. That always made them mean more. Hers announced, To My Husband, My Friend, My Love. Inside it continued:

You're the man I adore,
the partner I can share everything with,
the friend who understands me so well,
the lover who captures my heart . . .
I'm the luckiest woman
in the world—
because I have you.
Merry Christmas with All My Love

Then she added in her much more elegant script:

I'm your new full-time job.

I'm just so happy that we are together in our beautiful home during this holiday season. I have so much to be thankful for, and you are at the top of that list. Once we get over this bump, we will have a great retirement. I love having you home full-time, relaxed, and with fewer headaches. No matter what we do, it's always more fun together.

Love,
Nettie XXXOOO

The tension headaches she mentioned had plagued me throughout the twenty-eight years that I'd worked at a job I'd never really liked. Since I'd retired with her, I hadn't suffered one headache.

On Christmas Day, rather than making a traditional German meal, her grandmother's legacy that now seemed too much work, Nettie busied herself by making gnocchi, my Italian family's holiday tradition. As usual, she kneaded the dough while I cut the ropes she had rolled out into bit-size pieces, ridging them with the tines of a fork. The gnocchi, along with my organic buffalo meatballs and low-fat homemade spaghetti sauce, made up our traditional Christmas meal. We couldn't have been happier.

The Friday after Christmas Day, the oncologist's nurse followed up with good news. Although the neutrophils had vanished altogether—Nettie now had no healthy white blood cells to fight infections—her cancer cells had dropped to a remarkable 24 percent

That same day, Nettie's close friend, Valerie, arrived from Los Angeles with her husband, Sandy, to spend the weekend visiting us. Valerie and Nettie had stayed best friends since my twentieth high school reunion in 1983, when they had allied themselves in mutual boredom as classmate spouses. We had made many trips down there, and I'd also surprised Nettie on her fiftieth birthday when I'd flown Valerie here to Oregon. An ex-nurse, Valerie understood the seriousness of Nettie's leukemia.

Valerie and Sandy insisted on taking us out to the nicest place to eat in my hometown. At the restaurant, where Nettie and I had also celebrated our twenty-seventh anniversary, we both talked excitedly with Valerie and Sandy about the trips we would soon take—to Europe or maybe even back to our beloved Kauai—once we knocked this leukemia into remission.

Then, on Sunday morning December twenty-eighth, the day Valerie and Sandy flew back to California, Nettie awoke with words that stopped my heart.

"I have," she said, "the start of a sore throat."

For a week, we kept the infection at bay with a small dosage of amoxicillin, which we later increased. However, because of a series of events, including a rare, heavy snowstorm that kept us from picking up her antibiotics or even bringing her into the emergency room,

Nettie ended up in the hospital for four days. She rallied afterward while on the antibiotics, painkillers, and steroids. However, afraid to go back on the chemo that, along with the leukemia, had brought on a sore throat that hurt so badly she couldn't swallow her own saliva, she eventually gave up these pills, too.

Nettie tried naturopathic means instead, including an exotic frankincense massage I lovingly administered to her spine for two weeks. Nothing helped. By February fifth, her cancer cells had skyrocketed to 96 percent. On February eighth, I called for hospice care.

Nettie was lucid until the morning of February eleventh, when I helped her to the bathroom at five in the morning and we both told each other, "I love you, honey." Then, she fell asleep and lapsed into a coma that deepened until, at three that afternoon while I sat helplessly by with a raging headache, she softly passed away.

The "presents" I cherish most? Putting up the tree, making Christmas dinner together, and those loving words she wrote: "I have so much to be thankful for, and you are at the top of that list." Me, too, honey.

Those heartfelt sentiments, along with her hopeful courage, made me want that season we spent together to last forever—the last Christmas with my wife, my best friend, my love. In my mind, at least, it has.

The End

KEEPING UP APPEARANCES
His love helped me past my deception.

It's bad enough that every year for my whole life, I've been coming to Aunt Iola's for Hanukkah dinner, which made twenty-one brisket and latke meals, to be exact. Although, I can't remember anything before the year my cousin Gerard sat on my shiny new Barbie car, cracking the wheels in half.

But that year, I was the only one at the kids' table over ten years old, and I was forced to play another game of Driedle with Freckles and Jojo. Gerard conveniently took a job three thousand miles away in New York City. He'd called earlier saying he wished he could be here. But I figured, if he wished he could be here, he would've been here.

It's my philosophy that we make time for the things that really matter.

Which is why making time to come to yet another dinner had me a little ticked off. I thought Aunt Iola's party was going to be on the last night of Hanukkah, instead of the second. I had plans to go to a snowboarding club meeting that night with some of the tellers from work.

Instead, I sat spinning the top and betting with chocolate coins, wrapped in gold foil. The only thing that saved me from eating a dozen pretend dollars was the surprise guest who showed up as I spun the Dreidle with a perfect flick of my thumb and forefinger.

I immediately knew my spin earned me the whole pot. I didn't know until a few weeks later, that our guest, Morris Carroll, would make my whole life spin away from where I thought it was headed.

"You got a gimmel, Janelle!" Freckles shouted. "You get to take the whole pot."

Freckles was the smartest seven-year old I know. She's pretty sweet, just like her mom—my Aunt Di. But her mom's not here, tonight. This year, it's her dad's turn to have her for the holiday. And this year, he's brought along some sweet young thing named Rosalee.

I had talked to her earlier, and I felt sort of sorry for her. She's not Jewish, doesn't understand anything about this holiday, and she doesn't seem too excited to be here.

I could relate to her on that last point. Don't get me wrong. I didn't mind being Jewish. I just don't make a big deal out of it. The last time I felt involved was while I was studying for my Bat Mitzvah. Part of it was really boring. But then, I remember the proud looks on my grandparents' faces as I practiced for them, and well, nothing since has ever made me feel so good inside.

And I love my family. When Mom and Aunt Iola got together, they were always laughing—which put everyone in a good mood.

But without my cousin, that night just wasn't the same.

"Yep. You get to take the whole thing."

The deep voice came from over my shoulder. I turned my head and looked up.

And that's when I immediately wished I had worn my black miniskirt and silver tank top, instead of ratty jeans and T-shirt with our bank logo plastered on the front. Of course, I would have dressed nicer if I hadn't been on the way to the meeting when Mom called to remind me about it that night.

"Who are you?" Freckles asked, saving me from having to say anything.

Because, I couldn't have. My voice had landed on my tongue, and was being held captive against my upper teeth.

"I'm Morris," he said, crouching down between Jojo and me. "Can I play?"

He folded his long legs beneath himself, and sat cross-legged on the carpet. Our arms were practically touching. Well, the hair on my arms was touching his shirt, since it had sprung out as if I were near some electrical current.

I moved a few inches away and nodded. My heart was beating like an out-of-control metronome.

Morris's sky blue eyes looked right into mine. He smiled as he picked up the Dreidle.

"What are we playing for?"

"These." Jojo held up a handful of gold covered chocolates. "Here, take some."

"That's my cousin, Janelle," Freckles said, pointing at me. "I'm really Liza, but everyone calls me Freckles, because of course, you can see why. That's my brother, Jojo. He's only five."

"And a half," Jojo added.

"Nice to meet you all," Morris said, twisting the Dreidle between his long fingers.

I nodded like a complete idiot. What was wrong with me? I've been around hot-looking guys before, and they hadn't acted that bizarre.

We each put two chocolate coins into the pot. I took a few quick breaths and glanced over at Morris.

He raised his eyebrows at me before giving the Driedle a spin. I couldn't have turned any redder. I felt myself blushing from my toes to my cheeks.

"Shin," Freckles called out.

Did I mention, that not only is she smart, she was our narrator.

Whatever we played, Freckles was the self-appointed, play-by-play announcer.

I had the feeling that at any minute, she was going to announce what was happening to my body parts. Janelle's heart was thumping its way to her stomach. Her palms were getting sweaty, and her breathing was quick. She was feeling a bit queasy, and was heading for the back porch.

I needed air. After standing outside for a few minutes, wondering why Aunt Iola liked plastic plants over the real thing, I came back inside.

At least she liked "real" food. Nothing processed or canned for my aunt. The house always smelled like onions and hot oil and brisket. Earthy. Comfortable. Familiar.

My stomach actually growled as I walked through the kitchen. When that happened in a book, I always thought it was such a fake thing. But Aunt Iola's cooking really did get to me. Either that, or all my senses were on high alert since Morris had arrived.

"Do you kids know what these symbols mean?"

Morris held up the Driedle as I sat back down.

"Well, duh," Freckles said, grabbing the Driedle out of Morris's hand. "Nun means do nothing. Gimmel means take it all. Hay means take half. And Shin means to add to the pot."

She straightened out her back, and then grinned at Morris.

"Yes, but do you know that these letters stand for Hebrew words: NES GADOL HAYAH SHAM?"

"Okay." Freckles opened her palms and stared at Morris. "So?"

Morris winked at me before answering, "Which means 'a great miracle happened there.'"

For a second, I thought Freckles might cry. But then, she jumped up, and spoke.

"Yeah. I know that. We learned it in Sunday school. For the drops of oil that burned for eight days and nights, right? Did you know that's what they meant, Janelle?"

I didn't know. And honestly, I didn't really care. I don't give much thought to being Jewish.

And I didn't date Jewish guys. Except for when I was a senior and spent a few weeks with Mort Leiberman.

I was almost hoping that Morris wasn't Jewish. But I knew he was. And a lot more into it than me.

He seemed genuinely upset that we hadn't lit the menorah at sundown. We had exchanged gifts before he had arrived. But we had forgotten to light the candles.

It didn't bother me at all. What bothered me were these feelings I had for him. This jumpiness inside me that begged to just know him better. But that was also making it so hard for me to say anything halfway intelligent.

I'd been in the same room as Morris for over an hour and still hadn't said anything more than, "Okay. Your turn. Time for dinner."

It was definitely time for me to say something meaningful. Especially since Aunt Iola sat us down next to each other at the kids' table with Freckles and Jojo. I figure I'll be at this table until I have my own kids, which could be sometime in the next century.

We passed the food around, our fingers touching with each plate. Brisket platter. Warm sensation up my arm. Latke plate. A sizzle between my thighs. Carrot dish. A tingle as our fingers touched. Applesauce. Green beans. I wanted to keep passing the food.

"What do you do for a living, Janelle?" Morris asked, just as I took a bite of latke.

I shoved the potato pancake into the corner of my mouth.

"She works in a bank," Freckles said.

Okay. Enough. I can talk for myself.

"Yeah, like she said. I'm a teller. But just for now. How about you? What do you do?"

"I'm a music teacher," he answered. "For the Chesterfield school district. And I have a band."

"Cool!" Freckles said. "A rock band?"

Morris shook his head.

"Well, not exactly. I write kids' music."

Freckles was disappointed, but I was fascinated. And also a bit envious. I'd been thinking of going back to school to become a teacher.

"Where do you play?" I asked.

"At the temple preschool, and for the youth group. I'm a leader there two nights a week," he added.

Okay, I thought. Jewish youth leader. Jewish music. He probably kept a kosher house. So different from me. It's just a physical thing; and after he leaves tonight, I'll never see him again and that will be just fine, because really . . . we probably don't have anything in common.

And right at that thought, Morris asked me if I ever snowboarded, and then our conversation opened like a dam, and we talked right through coffee and Aunt Iola's special nut cake.

Finally, Aunt Iola called everyone over for the lighting of the menorah. I stayed in back with my parents, Uncle Mo and Rosalee, and these friends of my aunts whose names I never remember.

Morris was up closer with Freckles and Jojo. I looked at the slight bump in his nose and decided it was perfect for his face. It went with his angular jaw and kissable lips.

In our family, we took turns lighting the candles. Since it was only the second night, there was just the Shamash and two other candles.

Aunt Iola lit the Shamash, and handed it to Jojo—who then used the Shamash to light the first candle. He handed the Shamash to Freckles who lit the candle to the left of the one Jojo had lit.

Aunt Iola set the Shamash back in its holder.

"Baruch ata Adonai elohanu melech ha olam asher kiddishanu b'mitzvotav v'tzivanu l'hadlik ner shel Hanukkah," Morris recited the prayer, and the rest of us mumbled along with him.

Aunt Iola started to say something when he was done, but he went on to a second prayer. We usually just said one prayer, and sometimes, didn't get all the Hebrew words right.

I was mesmerized by Morris's smooth voice, and was anxious to hear him sing—even if it was just a kids' song.

I didn't have to wait long. Right after the last prayer, he started singing and within minutes, everyone was singing along with him.

"The candles are burning bright. One for each night."

"Janelle, do you want to sit outside?" Morris asked after everyone had left except my family.

My mom was helping Aunt Iola clean up, and my dad was watching CNN. We walked out back and sat on my aunt's swinging chair.

"It was really nice of your aunt to invite me," Morris said. "Our moms are good friends, and my folks are out of town tonight."

"My aunt's great," I said.

"And Freckles and Jojo are too much," Morris said with a laugh.

"Yeah, they are."

"That's what I love about my job. The kids I get to reach. And as a youth leader, I can really instill Judaism and all it stands for. So many kids today just don't get enough religious training, you know."

"You're right," I said. I didn't really care one way or the other.

"We have such a strong history. It kind of irks me that so many people don't understand Hanukkah, and think it's just our version of Christmas, with the gifts and everything."

"Yeah, but getting presents for eight nights is fun," I said. Now, I usually just get money from my parents and gift certificates from my aunt.

"Do you know why?"

I didn't say anything. I prayed he didn't drill me on the meaning of Hanukkah. I used to know all of that stuff. For a second, I wished I could remember. Because, honestly, when I was younger, I looked forward to Sunday school. The teachers made the stories fun and meaningful.

And being with Gerard made it one of the best days of the week. Why had I forgotten so much?

93

"What do you tell your kids?" I asked. A memory of sitting in a circle listening to our rabbi flashed across my mind. "Do you sing a song about it?"

"Sort of. I make it simple." He gave the swing a push with his feet. "I explain to them about the Jewish calendar, and how it's based on thirteen months, and that Hanukkah is always on the 25th of Kislev—which makes it a different day every year on our regular calendar."

"That always gets me confused," I said.

"It does?"

"No, not really."

That was the beginning of my lies.

"And then I tell them in poems and rhymes about how the Jews weren't allowed to practice Judaism, how they were ruled by the Greeks until 165 B.C. when Judas Maccabee started the Jewish rebellion and reclaimed the temple. Also, how when they lit the candle to rededicate the temple, the bottle of oil miraculously burned for eight days—instead of just one."

As he reached for my hand, I realized that I was smiling. Morris was telling me things I really wanted to hear. Things I had forgotten about, but that were important to me.

I didn't want to pretend that it didn't matter anymore. I always worked on Good Friday, so the other tellers could go to church. But when it came to the high holidays, I would just shrug and say I wasn't really a practicing Jew. But why? Was it because I really didn't care? Or was it because I was the only Jewish employee at the bank? Listening to Morris was bringing me back to my true self.

"What temple do you belong to?"

My heart felt like it was gasping for air.

"Beth Hillel."

My second lie. My parents were members of the temple, but not I.

"Reform, huh?"

"Yeah."

"With Rabbi Jacobs. How is he?"

"He's good."

Lie number three. I've never heard any of his sermons.

"We belong to Valley Shalom. Conservative, but my grandparents were orthodox."

"Mine, too."

That was not a lie.

And I wasn't lying when I gave him my number and told him I'd love to go out next Friday night. I didn't realize it was the last night of Hanukkah, and that it was also Shabbat, and that I would be in the eye of all my lies.

I even lied to the girls at the bank. I told them I was seeing a guy

94

in a band. I didn't tell them it was called Morrie's Mopheads, and that their biggest hit was "Oh Shalom, Shalom."

I did tell Gerard, though, when he called. He just laughed, and said he knew I'd fall for someone Jewish.

"How could you not?" he asked. "It's who you are."

And if anyone knew me well, it was my cousin.

Throughout the week, Morris and I talked on the phone—every night, to be exact. He called me around nine, and we talked for at least an hour.

I told him how I really hated working in the bank. He said he loved teaching. I said I didn't like living at home. Morris said his apartment was great, and he got along fine with his roommate. I complained about the service at the Mexican restaurant near the bank. He told me how he had great lunches at this little café near his temple.

I was beginning to see a pattern. I wondered if he saw it, too.

When did I get so negative? And why was he so positive? Was it because of his belief in God?

Every time religion came up, I pretended it was an important part of my life. I don't even know why I was acting like this. I mean, I did like him. I did want to see him, again. But I knew I should be myself. And with everything else we talked about, I was honest. He was getting to know the real me with one minor alteration. Religion.

"So, Friday, at my parents. Can you meet me there?" Morris asked. "I have to come straight from a meeting at school."

"Sure," I said, stretching out on my bed.

"You sure your parents aren't going to be upset?" Morris asked.

"About what?"

"You won't be having Shabbat dinner with them."

"What? Are you . . ." I caught myself. "No, they'll be fine."

"I haven't missed a Shabbat dinner in years," Morris said. "And being the last night of Hanukkah, it is a special night."

"It is."

And I meant it. An unexplained excitement bubbled up inside me, making it hard to sit still. As I folded my laundry, I tried to tell myself it was because of Morris, because of the way he touched me. But I knew deep down in that place where I keep my secret thoughts, that it was something more.

The minute I walked into the Carroll house, I realized my mistake. And I knew it was too late to do anything about it.

My jean skirt was too short. My blouse too low. My lipstick too red. The wine I handed to Morris's mom was all wrong.

The worst part was that unlike at Aunt Iola's, I had taken over an hour to get ready. I had remembered that Shabbat dinner meant I should dress nicely, but as I stood there, feeling completely out

95

of place, I realized that nothing in my closet would have been appropriate.

"Come on in. I'm Paula, Morris's mom," she said, looking me up and down with nothing short of daggers and amazement. This is whom my son is so excited about?

I walked into a spacious living room. I smelled something cooking. Chicken, maybe, or lamb. Nothing that made my stomach rumble like my aunt's cooking.

"Morris is running a little late," Paula said. "Make yourself comfortable."

Right. Like that was even an option. I sat down on their leather couch, trying to make my skirt cover my knees.

"That's a really nice menorah," I said.

That was about the only truth I told for the next ten minutes.

"So, Morris tells me you belong to Beth Hillel."

Paula sat down on a chair across from me, and crossed her legs beneath her floor length skirt.

"Yeah." I nodded, biting on the inside of my cheek.

"Sometimes, I wish I had a daughter. Do you and your mom do a lot of things with the sisterhood?" Paula leaned forward.

"Yeah," I said, softly. Suddenly, it felt awful to be lying. I just couldn't do it, anymore. I wanted to turn the clock back, just five minutes when I had commented on the menorah. That didn't seem like too much to ask.

And then, I could start over by telling the truth this time.

"Your parents didn't mind you coming here, tonight?"

I kept my head down and tugged on the edge of my skirt. The grandfather clock across the room ticked way too loud and way too slow.

"Hi."

Morris rushed into the room. And there went my heart, again. He was so darn handsome. What had I gotten myself into?

Paula immediately left the room, and a second later, she called Morris into the kitchen.

I sat there alone, wondering if I should just climb out the window and disappear forever. What I wouldn't have given for magical powers at that moment.

I was standing up reaching for my purse, when Morris came back into the room.

"My mom says you won't talk to her. Which sounds weird to me because you talk so freely on the phone. What's up with that?"

He went on before I had time to answer.

"My mom's not a hard person to talk to. She's just like your aunt."

"I. . . ."

I chewed on the inside of my cheek.

Morris stared at me with his gorgeous eyes, not making it any easier for me to say the words which were forming a traffic jam in my throat.

"Morris . . ."

His name came out all choppy. I took a step backward and avoided looking into his eyes. Instead, I stared at the menorah across the living room. "We don't have Shabbat dinners. I don't even remember what they mean. I don't belong to a temple. I've been lying to you. A lot."

"Why?" he asked.

Why? I thought. Because of the way your hand feels against my skin. Because everything about you is so perfect. Because I'm just a mixed up girl.

"I don't know," I said.

"Are you even Jewish?" he asked, biting down on his lower lip.

"Yes. I'm not lying about that."

He nodded his head for a moment.

"I was even bat mitzvahed," I said.

"No joke?"

He smiled at me.

"I'm not lying about that, I swear."

"So why were you lying?"

"Because I really like you, and I wanted to be someone you would like. And I know how important religion is to you," I said, truthfully.

It felt good to finally be honest with him. If he didn't want to date me, well then, so what? It was better than lying.

But it didn't feel better. I ached for his arms to hold me.

"It must have been important to you, too. When you were younger," Morris said.

I shrugged.

"Not really. I did it mostly for my grandparents and for the money."

"No one suffers through all those prayers, just for the money."

I thought back to those hundreds of nights poring over the prayers, learning my Torah portion. He was right. Part of me did enjoy it. A large part.

"You are right about my religion. I don't date non-Jewish girls, ever. And the ones I do go out with are usually conservative or even orthodox."

He was moving closer to me. My heart was throwing a tantrum inside my chest. Get it over with; tell me to leave, I thought.

Morris put his hands on my shoulders.

"Shabbat is a night to remember and observe," he said. "That's why we light two candles."

I bit down on my lip and just stared at him.

97

"You're already remembering how you felt when you were thirteen. And I think you really liked it."

I nodded. I tried not to cry, but the tears came, anyway.

"I do like being Jewish. I'm just not that involved. I mean, I always thought it didn't matter, but I think it does. I couldn't bear not to teach my children about Moses and Passover and Purim."

"Children?"

Morris smiled.

I giggled.

"You know what I mean."

"I think I do."

He leaned forward and pressed his lips against mine.

A half an hour later, after we'd kissed and talked and kissed, we stood with his parents and lit the menorah. I watched all eight candles and the Shamash burning, throwing long, flickering shadows against the wall. The last night of Hanukkah was always my favorite, and I loved to watch the candles until they disappeared.

Morris led me to the couch, and we sat holding hands as his father read from the Torah. A calm, peaceful feeling settled over me.

I could feel my present feelings starting to fade, replaced by traits from the old Janelle, and the Janelle I hoped to be.

I think Morris felt it too, because I could feel his heart beating in rhythm with mine!

The End

THE GIFT OF THE STORM
It started as a blizzard . . .
and transformed my evening into
a winter wonderland.

The snowstorm wasn't entirely unexpected, though many people had bet that it wasn't going to hit us at all. Indeed, if they bet money, they lost a lot to those who bet it was going to turn out to be one of the biggest snowstorms we'd seen in years.

I awaited the first flurries with trepidation. My children were visiting their father for his part of the Christmas holiday and were expected home later that evening—Christmas Eve—so that I could have them for the entire day on Christmas.

With the impending storm, I could only hope that Carson would bring them home early. Instead, as one inch of snow grew to three and then four, I started hoping that he wouldn't chance bringing them home in such bad weather.

It was an hour past the time they were to be home, and as I looked out at the snow that had accumulated to over six inches, I resigned myself to spending my first Christmas alone. I knew that it was better than Carson trying to drive in that weather. His Lexus was ill equipped for the conditions, even if he had been experienced at driving in that kind of weather—which he wasn't.

That was one of the many differences Carson and I shared during the last difficult months of our marriage—a marriage that had gone downhill ever since that day almost two years before when we moved into the farmhouse that I'd inherited from my grandfather.

We'd agreed to give living there a try and see how we adjusted to the move. I'd adjusted to the move quite well. Even the boys seemed perfectly content living there instead of in the row house in town where the only yard we had was little more than a space where you could park your car.

Carson spent nearly every day reminding me that it was only a temporary arrangement. He wasn't at all happy living in what he called "the wilderness."

In actuality, his "wilderness" was my beloved country home, some fifteen miles from the town where we'd been living.

I tried to be understanding about Carson's feelings. In truth, that fifteen miles was in the opposite direction of the hour's drive he made into the city each day to work. Considering the fifteen extra miles were on winding back roads, it added an additional thirty minutes of travel time to his trip to and from work each day.

And, of course, there was the fact that Carson had only just started a new job with a prestigious advertising agency in the city. He worked as an account executive, which amounted to his working more with the numbers than with the people, as he'd done at his previous job. He told me that the higher pay more than made up for moving to the less creative side of the business.

He had it figured that in no time we'd be able to move out of the small row house we were renting and into a home of our very own. And that's just what we did when we moved to Grandpa's farm, but what Carson had in mind was a move closer to the city instead of farther away.

He grew increasingly irritable, which he blamed on the time he spent driving each day. Yet, I felt certain that it was more the fact that he didn't seem happy with his new job.

He wanted me to sell the farm and move to the city. I wanted him to consider a job closer to the farm. We were at a stalemate. That is, until he announced that he was taking an apartment in the city to save him the commute each day. He said he'd come home for weekends and other special occasions in between.

If he thought that was going to change my mind, he was wrong. I knew that eventually he'd come to the realization that this work wasn't what he wanted to do. I mean, ever since we met in college he'd always said that he looked forward to working directly with companies and developing advertising campaigns that would make their businesses thrive.

"Someday I'll take a small business that's just starting out and I'll turn it into a Fortune 500 company," he'd say.

And I believed that if anyone could do that, it would be Carson. He was good. When he first started working after college he'd talk to me and share many of his ideas and strategies. He was creative and insightful.

Some of my friends used to tease me when I told them about our dates, saying that he didn't sound like much of a romantic. But they didn't see the fire in Carson when he talked about his work. They didn't see the depths of his passions.

And when he wasn't talking about work, those passions were focused on me. There had never been a doubt in my mind that he loved me. Even after fourteen years of marriage and two sons, his eyes still held the same spark of passion when he looked at me.

But the spark slowly dwindled after he got that new job. It was barely visible after we moved to the farm, and it was totally extinguished after he started living in the city.

His trips home on the weekends became less and less frequent; he insisted that work was keeping him tied to the city. Then he started missing those promised special occasions when he'd said he'd be home—like our anniversary.

I remember that night all too well. Late that night, after giving up all hope that he'd be home, I called his apartment to wish him a happy anniversary. A husky-voiced woman answered the phone. I hung up quickly without ever leaving a message after verifing that it was his number.

It was another week before I spoke to Carson, though I knew he'd called and spoken to the boys several times. Each time I'd been out running errands for the new business I was starting.

"Busy lady these days," Carson said when I picked up the phone.

"Yes, well, you should know how that is," I said sarcastically.

"Is that supposed to be some kind of dig?"

"Take it however you like," I replied coldly. "Now, will you tell me why you're calling so I can get back to what I was doing?"

"Actually, I was calling to apologize for missing our anniversary," he said. "Did the boys tell you I called before?"

"Yes," I replied, squeezing the phone and knowing that he was lucky it wasn't his throat.

"I was so bogged down with things here at work that it totally slipped my mind," he started. "I called to see if we could do something special this weekend."

"Save the gas and the money," I replied. "You can use the time for something or someone else."

"Wait a minute. What's that supposed to mean?"

"I think it should be pretty clear," I replied.

"Look, Ellen, I think we need to talk. I'm coming home this weekend."

"I don't think that's a good idea," I said bitterly. "I'm going to be pretty busy. We've got a lot of orders coming in."

"You mean with that little craft club thing you belong to?"

I sighed, hating the condescending way he always spoke about my business. "It's a craft co-op. At least it was. It's now a profit-making company. My company."

"When did all this take place?"

"While you were busy with your own affairs." I accented the last word, but it didn't seem to faze him.

"So, you're saying that you don't want me to come home, is that it?"

"Carson, just do what you want," I replied. "Just don't expect me to sit around waiting. I've got my own life to live."

"I see. Then I suppose it's hardly worth my coming back to see you."

But you still have two sons! I wanted to cry out the words, not wanting them to be hurt by what was happening between their father and me. Tears threatened. I never thought I'd see the day when I'd have to remind Carson that he had two sons who loved him. No matter what else, he'd always been a good father.

"Well, I'll be home soon, anyway. I'd like to see the boys."

I sighed in relief at that. "I'll make sure they know you're coming," I replied. "So don't let them down."

"Since when—"

"I really have to go now," I interrupted before he could argue further. "Good-bye, Carson."

And that was that. When Carson came home that weekend, I had all his things packed and sitting by our bedroom door. He got the point. Without a word about it, he loaded them into his car.

So there I was several months later, on Christmas Eve, planning to spend the holiday alone. I'd finished up all the last details on the holiday orders and sent the last shipments via overnight shipping the day before. I'd spent the entire day preparing for when my sons would arrive home, hoping and praying that the storm would change direction or that Carson would bring the boys home early.

Neither had happened.

Funny how I usually found solace in the place that had been my grandparents' home. It had been a haven during my most difficult times—like after my parents were killed. I was hardly much older then than my sons were now.

My grandparents opened their home and their hearts. Grandma put me to work with her in the kitchen and around the house, and we made the crafts she so loved together. And when that didn't seem like enough, she'd send me out to the barn to help Grandpa with the sheep. There was always something to do, and keeping busy helped keep my mind off of what I didn't have. Grandma and Grandpa's love kept me focused on the things I did have.

I decided to busy myself that night. Baking cookies would certainly be better than sitting there and pitying myself. And I'd been so busy that year with my new business that the only cookies I'd helped bake were the ones we sold in our gift packages.

I pulled out the flour, sugar, butter, and nuts. Oh, and chocolate chips, I thought as I grabbed two bags of them from the shelf. There's nothing like chocolate when the emotions are raging.

Yes, I remembered eating plenty of Grandma's chocolate-chip cookies during my last visit, just before her stroke. It was right after our baby died. That was the second time we'd nearly had another child. The first time I had a miscarriage at three months; the last time I carried the baby nearly full term.

Tears filled my eyes at the memory and the memory of the love that my grandmother doled out with just enough understanding. She knew how much I'd longed for those babies. They were the little girls I'd always wanted.

She knew I felt guilty about that, too. It wasn't as though I wasn't happy enough with my sons—I was. I loved both Michael and Derek so very much. I'd never trade either of them for any other child. But there was a part of me that always remembered how wonderful it felt to be a daughter. There's a special bond between mother and daughter. I'd had it with my own mom and she'd had it with hers. I'd had it with Grandma, too. I wanted to share that same bond with my own daughter, but it wasn't to be.

Grandma and her chocolate-chip cookies helped me through the depression that followed until I could finally face that fact.

Then, after Grandma died, I'd come back as often as I could to make those same cookies for Grandpa. Tears would fill his brown eyes whenever he stole his first bite and I knew that he was remembering Grandma.

They'd loved one another so much. When he died it was almost difficult to be sad because I knew that he was finally home with his Marjorie.

I was just pulling the first tray of baked cookies out of the oven when I thought I saw headlights in the driveway. A few minutes later I heard shouts and laughter.

I rushed to the window and saw an unfamiliar SUV parked in the driveway. Then I watched with anticipation as my sons made their way up the walk, shouting and throwing snowballs as they made their way to the door. They stomped their feet halfheartedly and then greeted me with laughter.

"Wow! You should've been with us, Mom," Derek said. "We were sliding all over the place!"

"It wasn't that bad," his older brother said. "Would never have made it with the car, though."

"Yes, it's good that I finally took someone's advice and got a four-wheel drive," Carson said as he entered behind our sons. He was carrying a huge box and he set it down by the door.

"You traded your Lexus," I said in disbelief.

"No, I just left my toy at home," he said sarcastically, reminding me of how I'd referred to the extravagant vehicle he purchased right after we split up. "They've predicted a bad winter and I knew that if I wanted to see these guys, I'd have to get something that could handle the snow."

"There are some times when you still shouldn't be out," I replied. "Like tonight."

"I realized that when we reached the point of no return," Carson said. "Besides, I didn't think you'd like being alone for the holiday."

"Cookies!" the boys shouted as they discovered the ones I'd just taken out of the oven. At the rate they were going, I knew they'd quickly have those eaten and be ready for the next batch.

"If you'd like some cookies, you'd better hurry before they eat them all," I offered.

"Tempting as they are, I'd better be on my way before the roads get any worse."

"You can't go back out in this storm," I said, realizing just how dangerous the trip would be even in a four-wheel-drive vehicle. "Like you said, you already passed the point of no return—unless you have other plans." It was at sudden moments like those that I remembered the sultry voice of the woman who'd answered his phone on our anniversary.

"No. No plans for tonight. Or tomorrow," he replied.

"Then I insist you stay." It's the least I can do, I told myself. It was Christmas. I couldn't put out the father of my sons. "You can use the sofa bed in the living room."

"Thanks," Carson said. "From what I remember, the boys think it's a cool place to sleep because the TV is in the same room."

I laughed, remembering our visits while my grandparents were still alive. Yes, the boys never complained—until their grandfather pulled the plug on the television set. "And I promise not to pull the plug on the TV," I joked.

"If this storm keeps up, you might not have to," Carson replied. "Remember the blizzard of ninety-six?"

Oh, yes, I remembered it all too well. I felt my body temperature rise just thinking about it. It was right after my grandmother died. I'd been on an emotional seesaw—missing her terribly and worrying about my grandfather. Making love was the last thing on my mind.

Yet, late that night when the house grew cool from the power failure, in our sleep, Carson and I pressed our bodies close seeking warmth from the cold. We woke up slowly and pleasantly, and before long, the temperature in our room was rising. We didn't even realize the power had gone out until our sons came into the room complaining that they were cold.

Grandpa must have realized at about the same time, because the next thing we heard was his voice from the hallway telling us that he was going to go light the kerosene heater in the kitchen. If any of us wanted to get warm, we could meet him down there.

To our relief, the boys rushed after Grandpa, giving Carson and I the chance to put on some clothes. We were thankful that the boys hadn't crawled between the blankets and caught us naked.

When we eventually moved to the house, we kept the same room, turning my grandparents' room into one for the boys. The only difference was that we put a lock on our door so we wouldn't have any surprise interruptions when we were getting romantic.

Only there weren't as many of those times after we moved here, I remembered. It was that thought that brought me back to the present just in time to keep the next batch of cookies in the oven from burning.

Carson was watching me, his eyes thoughtful as though he, too, was thinking the same things. "Ellen, I want to thank you for letting me stay tonight," he said as I removed the cookies from the tray. "There's no place I'd rather be tonight."

"Any port in a storm," I said brightly, but the joke fell flat.

"What's that supposed to mean?"

I shrugged. "Just that there's a storm outside," I said. "I'm sure there are other things you'd rather be doing besides being trapped here by the weather."

"Actually, there aren't," he said. "Christmas alone isn't something I was looking forward to."

"Alone?" I repeated skeptically.

"Yes, alone," he said.

"I'd have thought you'd have plans for the holiday. Parties. Dinner invitations. Guests of your own." I don't know why I persisted, except perhaps to finally get him to tell me about the other woman in his life. We'd never discussed her before. In fact, I'd never ever admitted to him that I knew about her.

"Holidays are for family," he replied. "Especially Christmas."

I felt tears sting my eyes. I might've almost felt sorry for him if I hadn't known about his companion. Or companions. After all, the woman who answered the phone that night could've been one of several female companions.

"Ellen, there's something I've been wanting to talk about," he started. "Maybe now is the time."

He was going to confess. I stiffened, waiting.

"Are there more cookies ready?" Michael asked as he returned to the kitchen, his brother following at his heels.

"Just took some out of the oven," I replied, glancing at Carson.

"Later," he said, grabbing a cookie for himself before the boys took them all.

"Okay, guys—you don't have to be hogs," I scolded. "Leave some for your father and me. I have more in the oven, though I think you've had enough."

My reprimand caused a chorus of groans, but at least they didn't argue. They each took a handful of cookies and headed back into the living room.

"They would've missed your cookies if we hadn't made it back," Carson said. "I don't have anything nearly as delicious at my place."

"They would've survived till they got home."

"I don't know. I'm sure they wouldn't have been too thrilled with Spam for Christmas dinner."

"Just a different form of what I'm serving: ham."

"Very different," Carson said. "I have to say, I hope the roads aren't cleared too early so that maybe I can have some, too."

"Of course you can join us. I didn't think otherwise."

"You wouldn't have asked me if it weren't for the storm."

"Carson, I would've assumed you had other plans."

"Then you would've assumed incorrectly."

I didn't know why he was persisting along this vein. It was almost as though he were trying to get me to feel sorry for him for being alone on the holiday. It might have worked if I hadn't known that he didn't have to be alone.

"Ellen, can we talk, please?"

I sighed. "I think we should wait till the boys go to bed."

He nodded. "That's probably best."

Of course, without the incentive of Santa—both boys were far too old to believe in the jolly gift giver—neither of them was too anxious to go to bed early that night. It was obvious that they were taking every advantage of every moment that they had their father under their roof.

I decided to go into my office and check for orders even though I knew that if anyone had placed an order that late, they certainly had to realize that they wouldn't receive it for Christmas. Still, we were offering a New Year's Eve party tray that would be shipped on time for that holiday. There still could be orders for that.

And even if there weren't any orders, there was plenty of year-end work that needed to be done. And preparations for the following year. Valentine's Day would be our next big promotion.

As it always does when I work on the computer, time passed quickly. I wasn't even aware that the sounds from the living room had quieted until I realized that Carson was standing in the doorway, watching me.

"The boys finally went to bed," he said. "I thought you might want to go say good night."

Yes, it had been our ritual since they were babies. I'd always go to their room to say good night to my sons, listen to their prayers, and wish them a pleasant night's sleep. I didn't look forward to the day when they'd feel too old for me to continue, but I knew that day was coming.

I forced that thought from my mind as I headed upstairs to their room. I didn't want to think of them growing up, of their someday leaving home, or of my being alone.

When I returned downstairs I found Carson in my office, seated at my computer. "I hope you don't mind," he said. "I was curious about your business. The boys have talked a lot about it. I hope you don't mind."

I shrugged. "No, maybe you can see what's happened to my little craft club." I knew I was being sarcastic, but I was only echoing what he'd said so often.

"Well, I can see it's a lot more than that," he replied. "It looks like you've done quite a job here. You got a lot of orders for your first season. You obviously aren't doing this all from home."

"At first, while we were still a craft co-op, we did a lot of the work from our homes," I explained. "But once I got the idea to try my hand at e-commerce, I knew we'd have to have a main focal point, so I managed to get a small business loan and purchased the old Third and Chestnut Street building downtown. It's not big, but it serves its purpose. It provides a storage and distribution area. The only real work I had to do on the place was to modernize one area for our kitchen. We package much of our merchandise from that location."

"I see that you purchase many of the craft articles directly from the various people who were in the co-op," Carson said. "Smart move."

"Keeps my employees to a minimum," I said. "Which actually totals three if you count me."

Carson nodded. "I'd like to learn more about what you're doing—but later. Right now, I want us to have a long, overdue talk." He got up from the chair and crossed the room to stand in front of me. "Why don't we go in the other room where it's more comfortable? Maybe I can open a bottle of wine or mix us a drink."

I opted for the wine since I still had a few bottles put away from when we were still together. Occasionally, on a weekend, we'd open one and sip it while watching a movie on TV. It seemed like so long ago. Things had changed a lot since then.

I sipped the wine waiting for Carson to start, certain he was about to tell me that he wanted to file for divorce. I was surprised that he hadn't already done it. Then again, maybe he didn't have to. Maybe the woman with the husky voice was just a fling. Nothing serious. Still, I couldn't blame him for wanting to get on with his life.

"Your mind is going a mile a minute," Carson said, interrupting my thoughts. "I see that hasn't changed."

I stiffened.

"Don't get all defensive on me, Ellen," he said. "I didn't say it to start a fight. It's just something I had to get used to about you. Maybe I never completely did. Your brain just goes a mile a minute from one thing to the next, seeing things in ways I never thought of seeing them, and projecting outcomes I never imagined possible. It's probably that ability that's made your business a success," he continued. "You can juggle so many tasks."

"Thank you, I think." I smiled, trying to take no offense. Actually, he was expressing himself more carefully than he had when we were together. He used to seem frustrated by the way my mind works. Sometimes he'd yell at me to slow down so he could catch up.

"I, on the other hand, have always had to maintain my focus on one thing at a time, giving it my full attention," Carson said. "I think that may be where I went wrong."

"Wrong?"

"Yes, wrong with us, Ellen. I was trying so hard to be a success at my job that I couldn't handle all the changes at home—moving, the added pressures of commuting, and the changes in you."

"I wasn't aware that I was changing."

"Maybe expanding is a better way of putting it," Carson said. "Growing. Where family was always important to you, you were also beginning to expand your horizons."

"I joined the craft co-op. I did a couple of craft shows and flea markets," I said. "I don't think that exactly qualifies as expanding my horizons. What was I supposed to do? Spend all my time waiting till you decided to come home?"

"Let's not fight," Carson said. "I know I was wrong. That's what I'm trying to tell you."

"Wrong about what?" I had to persist. I wanted to get it all out in the open. I wanted him to understand why I had to change and why I had to find a new place for myself. It was because I knew the place I'd had for nearly fifteen years was slowly disappearing.

I hate change. At least some changes. I had to make adjustments to myself, to my life. As I'd had to do when my parents died and I went to live with my grandparents. Things I loved kept going away. My grandparents. My babies.

Then there were other changes and adjustments to my life, like when I married and when I became a mother. Yet, it seemed that even they were temporary.

My husband had grown distant. My sons were growing up. Where would I be if I didn't change? If I didn't insulate myself? One word could answer that: alone.

"I was wrong to take the apartment," Carson said. "Hell, I was wrong to take the new job. You were right—it's not what I want to do."

"So what are you saying, Carson?"

He put down his glass and ran his fingers through his hair. "I'm saying that I'm floundering like a fish in a toilet. I know it's not where

I belong, and half the time I feel like my life is about ready to go down the drain."

I could almost have laughed at his analogy if I hadn't known he was so serious. Poor Carson was sounding as panicked about his life as I'd been about mine.

I reached out and cupped his cheek. "Life keeps changing so quickly. I know it's not easy," I said softly. "It's adapt and survive."

"I'm afraid I don't adapt as well as you do, Ellen," he said, covering my hand with his own. "Will you help me?"

"I'm not sure I understand what you're asking."

"I'm not sure I know what I'm asking," Carson admitted. "I just know that I've been miserable. And the minute I walked through the door and saw you baking cookies, I realized that you're the only person who can help me."

I pulled my hand away, suddenly afraid. Afraid because I didn't know how I could help him when I didn't even know exactly how to help myself. Most of the time I was running on instinct, and I never knew for certain whether or not those instincts were right.

"I'd like things to be like they were," Carson said. "Let's go back and start over."

My heartbeat quickened. It was what I wanted, too. Wasn't it? Yet, I felt as though his turning back to me was a last resort when things didn't work out the way he wanted them to. Or, was I just a port in his storm? "Carson, I don't know if we can go back," I admitted. "A lot of things have happened. People changed. We've changed."

"I haven't really changed," Carson said. "I know I still feel the same way about you that I've always felt."

"Then maybe you need to be sure you know who I am," I said.

"Then let me get to know you," Carson whispered, leaning closer.

Tears filled my eyes as I pulled away. "Carson, you won't get to know me in one evening. Not when you weren't able to do that in nearly fifteen years."

"I thought I knew you."

"I know. But I'm obviously not the person you thought I was. If I were, we'd still be together."

"I'm still trying to figure out what went wrong," Carson said.

"It wasn't one thing," I said. "It hardly ever is just one thing."

"All I know is that I forgot our anniversary. You were rightfully angry, but I wanted to try to make it up to you, and you wouldn't give me the chance."

"You think missing our anniversary was the straw that finally broke the camel's back?" I asked bitterly, turning to face my husband in anger. "Missing our anniversary was nothing compared to why you missed it!"

"I tried to explain. I was busy with work," Carson said defensively, again running his fingers roughly through his hair. "I was working on a project that needed to be finished the following day. I worked late."

"Alone?"

"No, not alone," he replied, his face growing red.

At least he had the good grace to look embarrassed. Now if he'd only confess.

"There were a couple of other people there."

"A couple of people?" I was growing less certain of my righteous indignation.

"Most of the night." He looked away.

"Oh, most of the night," I repeated, my indignation renewed. "So, by what time, would you say, had your little group dwindled down to two?"

"Two?" He nearly choked, his cheeks going from flushed to pale. "How did you know?"

"I called to wish you a happy anniversary that night," I said.

"Jeez, I never heard the phone," he said. "What time? Who answered?"

"About eleven-thirty," I replied. "I remember because I stayed up to watch the news, hoping you'd call me. Instead, you were busy with your friend."

"Okay, I confess that I was with a woman that night," he said. "But not in the way you think. Well, almost—but not quite. I couldn't."

I shook my head. "You can't almost, but not quite, cheat. You tried and you couldn't. That's still cheating in my book."

"She tried. I couldn't."

"Did you want to?"

"I was miserable. I was walking a line between what my life was and what it might become."

He was being evasive and there could only be one reason why. I got up and started to walk away, but he grabbed my hand.

"Let me finish before you jump to more conclusions," he said. "I knew that I couldn't go on the way I was. I was miserable."

"You said that."

He squeezed his eyes closed and sighed. "Please, Ellen, I'm trying to tell you that nothing happened that night because I made a choice. I could move forward or I could go back. In my heart I wanted to go back. I wanted things to be the way they were."

Carson continued to explain that the woman he'd worked closely with for several weeks had stayed behind when the others left. She'd just been divorced and he knew that she was going through a rough time and felt sorry for her. But when she made a play for him, his compassion turned to fear.

"She more or less forced me to make a choice right then and there," he admitted. "I may have gone on indefinitely the way I was. In fact, I know I would've because when you threw me out, that's exactly what I did. I was in limbo between what I thought I wanted and what I knew in my heart was right for me. I thought I'd lost."

As it turned out, Carson never even knew the telephone had rung. After he refused the woman's romantic overtures, she broke down in tears. It wasn't because she felt rejected by him, she told him, rather it was because she just felt so unwanted after her husband had found a younger woman. Carson had assured her that she was a desirable woman, but that there was only one woman for him: me.

He left her alone in his apartment while he went out to warm up her car. It was then that I called.

"She must've answered it," he said.

"Why didn't she tell you I called?"

"She said the phone rang, but that she thought it was a wrong number."

It was my turn to turn red. I remembered that I'd said no more than hello when I called that night. Instead of asking for Carson by name, I gave the woman the number and asked if that was the number I'd dialed. When she replied that it was, I simply hung up the phone.

Carson didn't expect me to believe him. He even gave me the woman's number, handed me the phone, and asked me to call her right then to confirm what had happened that night—or rather, what hadn't happened. But the phone line was dead. The lights were flickering, too.

Maybe it's best to just take some things on trust. After all, hadn't I made the mistake of not trusting him in the first place? Maybe I should've talked to him about it when it happened. Maybe I should've let him explain then.

I wasn't going to let my mind go haywire thinking about maybes. I decided then and there that it was time to concentrate on the moment, just the moment. "You know, if the power goes out, it's going to get awfully cold in here," I said.

"You still have the kerosene heater in the kitchen."

He was so slow sometimes. I tried again. "Yes, but it's awfully uncomfortable sleeping sitting up in the kitchen."

"I could take the heater upstairs, though it's pretty awkward to carry."

"Carson, I thought you'd remember the time the power went out in ninety-six."

Suddenly he smiled and I knew that he finally understood. Just as his lights went on, the lights in the house went out. But we didn't care. We took several extra blankets in for the boys and covered them up before turning back to the room across the hall. We knew we weren't going to need extra blankets for a little while.

That all happened several months ago. Since that time, Carson has made some major changes in his life.

He decided that if I could start a business, so could he. He started his own advertising agency. Thanks to the computer age, he's able to do a lot of his work over the computer and by phone—from home.

Of course, he didn't have to do that for his first customer. He had a lot of good ideas for my company. He still says that someday he's going to take a small business just starting out and turn it into a Fortune 500 company. Who knows? Maybe it will be mine. But even if it's not, I've got more than enough to make me happy.

The End

A HOME FOR THE HOLIDAYS
I used the spirit of the season to help
a homeless boy feel safe at last.

I taught fifth grade in a low-income section of town. The kids weren't poor—they didn't live in tenements or run-down shacks—but their houses were modest, and lots of them lived in one of the three trailer parks nearby. I loved them all.

They were my first class and therefore special to me. Each day brought a new adventure, and as the year went on and I met their parents, I got to know their families quite well. They knew I was engaged to be married in June and that I was only teaching at their school for one year. So, we all treated it special: They made it their business to give me a run for my money and I made it my business to see that they learned.

The kids were tough to teach. About half were below grade level in reading and math, and they were more street smart than I was at the old age of twenty-two. I went home each night exhausted and energized and ready to call my fiancé and tell him about the many things we'd done that day. I felt I was making a difference in their lives and that I was gaining their respect, as well as the respect of my principal and coworkers.

Then Gregory came at the beginning of November and changed everything. There were rumors about him from the moment his mother enrolled him in our school. There was something different about this boy, though not a person in the front office could put a finger on just what was so strange.

But he was smart—really smart. Quiet and shy. He needed a teacher who was friendly, nice, and who had the patience of a saint. He needed someone who had the time to get to know him. After much discussion in the front office, Gregory was given to me.

When he walked into my classroom the room fell silent. He was pale and drawn, and looked like he could use a bath, as well as a few good meals. He had wide brown eyes that looked as if they'd seen too much. And he hardly said a word.

I placed him near some chatty girls and a fairly easygoing boy and hoped for the best. But he never really fit in. He didn't laugh much or crack jokes like the boys in the back of the room did when they thought I couldn't hear.

He didn't tease the girls or get into fights or do much of anything except read.

113

Gregory could read like no other student in my room. After testing him, I discovered that he could read at the high school level. I decided then and there to encourage him as much as possible.

One day at the end of November, during recess, I noticed that he was sitting by himself, watching the other kids. The playground assistants had already attempted to get him to play basketball or foursquare with the other kids, but he just shook his head "no" and sat against the wall. The sight broke my heart.

"Gregory, how about we go to the library?" I asked. "I was just thinking about a couple of books that I think you might enjoy."

He stood up at that, and though he still didn't crack a smile, he followed me to the library. We walked the book stacks, and little by little, we started to talk. I told him how I'd loved mysteries as a girl and how I'd read all the Nancy Drew books before moving on to Agatha Christie novels.

Gregory informed me that he'd never read a Christie book. When we realized that the library didn't carry such books, I told him I'd find him a few from the public library. In the meantime, we chose a few classics and headed on back to class.

That afternoon, I broke my promise. I was on the way to the library, when I thought of the stack of books on my bedside table. I loved to read, too, and I loved to own my books, returning to them over and over again like old friends. I turned left instead of right and went to the mall.

Once there, I picked up three Agatha Christie novels, already imagining the pleasure he'd gain from them. I went to sleep that night so excited; I was hardly able to wait to give the books to Gregory.

Because I didn't want to embarrass him by giving him the books in front of the whole class, I asked him to stay in at recess. Then, when there was no one in the room except for Gregory and me, I gleefully pulled out the novels. His eyes widened when he realized that they were for him.

"These a loan, Miss McGraw?"

"No. They're for you to keep," I said, unable to stop smiling.

His hands shook. "Are you sure?"

"Yep."

He looked doubtful. "What if I don't like them?"

"If you don't, I'll take them back, or I'll donate them to our school library. But I have a feeling that you'll enjoy them," I said, patting his shoulder.

But still he didn't move. "Why? Why me?"

My heart melted. Didn't he get it? He was the reason I'd gotten my teaching certificate! It's every teacher's dream to have a student who desperately wants to succeed. "Because you like to read," I said simply. "I do, too."

114

After a moment he seemed to accept that and went outside, one of the books in his hands.

Days past and I noticed that every time Gregory had a spare moment, his nose was buried in one of those books. Kids asked him about the books, but after finding them difficult to read, they pretty much left him alone.

But one thing that was strange was that Gregory never took the books home at night. Each night his chair would be stacked on top of his desk, and the set of three books would be in the center, his name written in black marker on the corner of each.

I was dying to ask why he didn't take them home, but after deliberating, I decided not to pry. Gregory was a private person, and I figured that if there were a reason why he didn't want to bring the novels home, it was his business.

The school year moved on, and every so often Gregory would be absent for days at a time. He never told me he'd been sick, or that he'd been hurt, so I was naturally very curious about his absences. I took to letting him stay in at recess to make up his work. Gregory was always the type of student to do as much work as possible at school; he'd work feverishly until a task was complete. Sometimes the other kids would tease him about working so hard. They didn't understand why he didn't want to work on the puzzle in the back of the room or just hang out like they did. But Gregory just always ignored them and went about his business.

But one time, after he'd been absent for a whole week, I asked him where he'd been.

"Nowhere," he said, bowing his head.

"What do you mean, nowhere? Was someone in your family hurt or sick?" I'd really begun to be concerned.

"No."

"Then why did you miss so much school? You always work so hard, it just doesn't make any sense that you wouldn't be here."

He looked away. Then, after a long moment, he met my gaze. "Can you keep a secret?"

"I can," I replied, hoping that he wasn't about to tell me a secret that I wasn't going to legally be able to keep. Teachers are required by law to notify social services if they suspect abuse or neglect.

"We had to move. We move a lot."

"Out of your apartment?"

He nodded. "We were living with my aunt and uncle, but they can't afford to keep us no more."

"So, where are you going to stay?"

He shrugged.

What he was saying just didn't make sense. I phrased my question

115

differently. "Where did you stay last night?"

"In our car."

"Your car? All of you?" I asked, trying my best to keep the shock out of my voice.

Slowly, he nodded, a red stain coloring his cheeks. "We parked out at a rest stop and used the bathrooms there."

I was stunned, speechless, and felt completely at a loss. Nothing I'd ever studied in school prepared me for this kind of conversation. What we were talking about was so much more than just a subject in school—we were talking about Gregory's life!

And I felt certain at that very moment that if I didn't try to help in some way, Gregory was going to be the one to suffer for it.

"How long will you be there?" I asked as I fiddled with some papers on my desk, hoping that if I didn't stare at him, he'd be more forthcoming.

He shrugged. "I don't know. A few days."

"Has this happened before?"

"Yes," he said quietly. "My dad has a real hard time keeping a job. He's got a hurt leg and he can't walk real good. Sometimes the people he works for don't like it that he can't run or stay on his leg all day long."

I tried to recall if I'd ever met Gregory's dad, then remembered that it was his mom who'd come to the classroom with him on his first day. His mom, MaryAnn, had been very nice and sweet to her son.

My heart went out to her. How difficult things must be for them if being homeless was a common occurrence in their lives! "Do you need anything?" I asked Gregory, trying to sound pretty casual.

His brown eyes narrowed. "What do you mean?"

I recalled my training from college and the latest workshop hosted by our school nurse. Children needed basic needs taken care of before they could learn. "A shower? There's a shower in the nurse's office."

He shook his head. "No, Miss McGraw. I don't need anything."

Not wanting to embarrass him further, I smiled brightly to him and suggested that he go play a little outside. "We've got a hard afternoon," I reminded him. "Note taking for a social studies test."

He grimaced.

"Yep. Better go run around while you can!" I teased.

As I watched him leave, I knew that I needed to do something to help Gregory and his family without embarrassing them or drawing undue attention to Gregory. I just didn't know what.

I told Steve, my fiancé, about Gregory that night while we were walking in my apartment's subdivision. He shook his head when I told him how I wanted to help.

"I know you do, sweetie, but I just don't see what you can do. I'm afraid if you report them to the authorities, someone might decide that Gregory should be put in foster care, and that won't help anyone."

"Foster care?" I asked, shocked. "I don't see how that could ever be a possibility."

"Some people feel that living in a car at a rest stop isn't the best place for a ten year old, Ashley."

My shoulders slumped as I listened to him, knowing that Steve was right.

He wrapped a reassuring arm around my shoulders and kissed me on my brow. "I know you're worried, but take a break from Gregory for a few minutes, okay? I haven't seen you all day and I'm going to be working late tomorrow night."

His arm felt so comforting and wonderful surrounding me that I turned to him and smiled. "All right," I said. "Thanks for listening. Tell me about your day."

Steve grinned and started to share some stories about his day, which were humorous, indeed. Steve owned his own lawn service and cut grass at several golf and country clubs around town. It was a hot and dirty job, but he always made it sound like there was no better profession than his.

I liked how he never had to worry about anyone at the end of the day. It must be freeing to have such a job where the worries that come with it could be seen to the following day.

A whole week passed. Gregory was absent two out of the five days and gave me a blank stare when I asked where he'd been. I was really concerned about him. Thank goodness we lived in the Phoenix area, where the weather was mild in mid-December. The news was filled with stories of people living in the east who were literally snowed in. How would someone like Gregory survive in those conditions?

Finally, I knew that Gregory's problems were weighing on my mind terribly and that I needed more than a sympathetic ear to hear me. I asked Mrs. Skalka, the principal, if I could speak with her during my planning period. With a look of surprise, she said that she could see me that very day.

At the scheduled time, I sat down in her office and started talking. Mrs. Skalka asked specific, intuitive questions, and before I knew it, I was crying in her office. "I'm just so worried, Patty," I said, calling her by her first name as she'd requested. "I feel like if I don't do something to help them, I'll be letting them down. But if I try to do too much, I'm going to make things worse."

"Do you think Gregory is eating?"

"He's on the school breakfast and lunch programs," I said, "but I don't know how much he gets besides those two meals."

Patty looked at me over her folded hands. "I'm pretty impressed with your willingness to help your students, Ashley. So, I'm going to ask you a question. What is the one thing that you think might help Gregory the most?"

That was a tough one. I knew that there were several immediate needs for Gregory, but there was only one thing that I thought could help his whole family. "His dad needs a job," I said after some thinking. "If they were back on their feet, they could get together some money for an apartment, Gregory would have some stability, and then he could come to school and worry about other things." My eyes closed as I imagined him acting like the other boys in my class. It would almost be a pleasure for him to be talking too much, or to see him goofing off with other kids.

"I agree that that would help." She opened a locked drawer, then pulled out Gregory's personal file. Minutes passed as she skimmed through the information. "It says here that both parents are working."

"Gregory told me that his dad had trouble holding a job because of a hurt leg. I never asked if his mom was working."

Mrs. Skalka looked at me hard, then picked up the phone. My heart raced. Who was she going to call? The police? Social Services? I knew all those people would try their best for Gregory's family, but I also knew that some options government agencies might try could also severely hurt such a sweet, sensitive little boy.

"Hello. Mrs. Albert, please."

She paused, then looked at me. "I called the phone number that she gave the school for emergencies."

I nodded my head, my heart in my throat.

"Mrs. Albert, we're trying to locate Mr. or Mrs. Warner. Any idea where they might be?"

Patty glanced at me with a puzzled expression, and I knew deep inside that Mrs. Albert either didn't know anything or wasn't going to tell the principal of their son's school. My heart sank.

"What are we going to do?" I blurted as soon as she hung up.

"I'm not sure, Ashley. Mrs. Albert seemed to be very surprised that neither Mr. or Mrs. Warner were at the numbers they gave us." She gave me a look then that told all. Mrs. Skalka had been a principal for a long time, and I figured she'd seen cases like this. She was probably trying to find a way to tell me that cases like Gregory's were all too common, and all too hard to wrap up.

"If I were his teacher," she said, shuffling papers on her desk rather nonchalantly, "I would have another heart to heart with my student. Maybe even invite his parents in. If we don't know the truth about their circumstances, we can't offer any help."

What she said was very true, but still my feet dragged all the way back to my classroom. Gregory had confided in me and I'd broken my part about keeping it a secret. Now, if he knew that I'd spoken to the principal about him and still didn't have any constructive suggestions, he might very well turn away from me.

Who would he have then? No amount of books that I could buy for Gregory would make him happy if he thought I didn't really care about him. But then, as I walked into my classroom and stared at the large calendar on one of my bulletin boards, I knew that I didn't have a choice. Sometimes you have to be completely honest with the people who matter to you the most. You have to tell them things that they may not want to hear because that's what real friendship is. I vowed right then and there to have a completely honest and frank discussion with Gregory the following morning.

That evening, I told Steve all about my day over a large pepperoni pizza. He held my hand as I poured out my heart to him, his comforting presence making me want to count the days until our wedding day. Finally, he leaned back and said, "I have a suggestion."

"What?" I asked, not even sure that I wanted to listen. All of the suggestions I'd heard so far were difficult to put into action.

"How about if I join you at your meeting?"

I stared at him in shock. "What?"

He shrugged. "I don't know Gregory's dad at all, but Christmas is coming, and jobs may be hard to find. If he's in need of a temporary job, I could sure use some help for the season."

I was floored by his offer. "But Steve, we don't know him! Plus, Gregory said he has a hurt leg."

"He could ride a riding lawn mower, or even help around the office for a few hours a day." He gazed at me hard, his clear, blue eyes conveying so much love and caring in them that I almost wept. "It's not a great job, but I read that sometimes it's really hard to gain employment if you don't have a phone and an address."

"And it's really hard to get those things if you don't have a job," I finished, grimacing at the catch-22. Steve's offer sounded wonderful, but still I hesitated. "What if the dad is no good? I'll just feel terrible if I hooked you up with someone who you can't trust or depend on."

"Whoa, honey," he said, his eyes twinkling with amusement. "First of all, you've always said that good kids come from good parents. And Gregory sounds like a great kid."

"He is," I admitted.

"Next, you haven't hooked me with anyone. I offered. And believe me, if he's not dependable or a hard worker, he won't be the first guy I've had to let go."

Everything was clicking so fast in my head that I had to breathe deep in order to contain my excitement. "You're right," I said softly, kissing him on the lips. "I love you."

119

Steve looked smug. "You'd better, I'm marrying you in six months."

"I can't wait," I said, meaning every word.

"Good," he replied, then reached out and pulled me away from the table and onto his lap. "Kiss me now," he whispered.

I did, and we did far more than that. When he left my apartment, I went straight to sleep, determined to set things in motion for both Gregory and his dad as soon as possible.

The next morning, I talked with Mrs. Skalka about Steve's suggestion. I spoke to Gregory about it, too. I knew that if I couldn't convince Gregory of my sincerity, we'd never get his dad to come to school to hear Steve out.

At first Gregory looked completely confused. "But Miss McGraw, your boyfriend doesn't even know my dad."

"But you do," I pointed out. Then I leaned forward and gazed at him seriously. "And if your dad is anything like you, then he's sure to be a great guy." I paused then, waiting for my words to sink in. "Tell me if I'm wrong, Gregory. Let me know if you don't want me or Steve to do anything."

He looked at me with wide eyes. "You'd really listen to me?"

"I would. This is your life."

"Why are you doing all of this?"

"Because I want you here in school, Gregory. It's that simple."

His expression fell. "Because I'm your student."

"Yes, you're my student, and I care about you that way, but also because I care about you, Gregory, as a person. As a friend. I want you to be happy. And I have a feeling that you're not going to be happy until your family is."

Gregory sighed. We said nothing for a few minutes, me staring at my favorite student and wondering what he was going to say. Gregory fingered the three books I'd given him. Finally, he met my concerned gaze. "I believe in you, Miss McGraw. I'll ask my mom and dad to come to school tomorrow morning."

Inside, I was practically doing cartwheels! "Thank you, Gregory. I'll tell Steve to come tomorrow morning, too."

The rest of that day seemed to drag. There were so many things that I had to get ready for and think about. But as I glanced at the calendar again, I knew that I was doing the right thing. We only had a few more days until Christmas break. If I did nothing, chances were that Gregory's family would move on over the holidays and I'd never see him again.

I knew doing nothing would be worse than doing the wrong thing. And that's what gave me strength.

I hardly slept that night, but greeted Steve the following morning outside of the school office bright and early. We'd decided to hold the meeting with Gregory's parents in the conference room in the office. That way, we could be near other personnel if things got tricky, or if Gregory's parents asked questions that I didn't know the answers to.

Eight o'clock came and went, but neither Gregory nor his parents arrived. With a scared expression, I stared at Steve. "Maybe Gregory never told them," I said, fearing the worst.

"Give them time, Ashley," he said patiently. "They're not that late."

Minutes ticked by. Mrs. Skalka peered in. "Heard anything?"

"No," I said, feeling almost like I was about to cry. "Not yet."

She glanced at her watch. "I heard there's a lot of traffic on the highway. Could be they're stuck in that."

I nodded, but inside I felt like collapsing on the conference table. Suddenly, I believed everything I'd done had been wrong. Gregory should've been given to a different teacher in November—someone with more experience.

I should never have pried into his personal life! I should have never burdened Steve with my worries and fears. And most of all, I should have never given Gregory such an awesome responsibility! In my naiveté, I hadn't even stopped to think that his dad was probably already doing everything he could to find employment. He wouldn't want his son approaching him about such a sensitive subject. In short, Gregory's life was none of my business.

"Steve, we might as well accept that they aren't—" I began, then stared at the doorway in surprise. There stood Gregory and both of his parents!

Quickly, I stood up. "Mr. and Mrs. Warner, thank you for coming in this morning."

The two people glanced at Steve in alarm, but smiled. "Gregory said it was important," Mr. Warner said. "So we came."

"Please, meet Steve Peyton, my fiancé."

Their smiles broadened as they realized that Steve wasn't a threat to them. "Pleased to meet you," Mrs. Warner said.

Finally we all turned to Gregory. "Gregory, this is Steve."

Steve held out his hand to Gregory and shook it just as he would a grown-up. "It's nice to meet you, Gregory. I've heard a lot about you."

"And we've heard a lot about you, Miss McGraw," Mr. Warner said with a smile. "You have really made an impression on our boy."

"Believe me, it's mutual," I said, motioning for everyone to sit down. Finally, I took a deep breath. "I hope I'm not doing the wrong thing, but I've been really worried about Gregory."

As Mr. and Mrs. Warner leaned forward to hear me, I relayed some of my thoughts, as well as some of the things Gregory had told me.

121

When I finished by telling them about Steve's offer of employment, Mrs. Warner burst into tears.

"This is so much more than I could ever have dreamed," she admitted tearfully. "I had to quit my job at the restaurant to help take care of my husband and Gregory. We honestly didn't know what we were going to do next week when school's out."

Mr. Warner rubbed his leg. "I was in a bad car accident about five years ago. Should've had another surgery, but we couldn't afford it. Things have been pretty hard ever since."

"Do you think you could do some of the things I've described?" Steve asked.

Mr. Warner's face brightened into a mask of happiness. "I know I could. I'm a hard worker. It's just that every once in a while I have a bad morning and might need to come in a little later than usual. Are you sure you won't mind an older guy like me working for you?"

"We could work your hours out," Steve said eagerly. "And to tell you the truth, I'd love to have someone so mature working for me. College kids have a whole other set of problems."

Mrs. Warner clapped her hands with glee. "If I know Andy is going to be okay, then I'll be able to get my job back. Before you know it, we'll be able to move back into our apartment!"

Mrs. Skalka peeked her head into the conference room right then. "That's where I come in. I went around this morning and asked for donations from the staff for a needy family. People gave what they could," she said, clinking a coffee can. "I think it's going to be enough to help with your security deposit and what not."

I squeezed Gregory's shoulder. "You just might have a good Christmas after all."

He looked at me with wonder. "I can't believe how much you did, Miss McGraw."

"Yes, thank you," Mr. Warner said, his eyes glistening. "I've always told Gregory to be proud, to depend on yourself, but this is one instance when I was very wrong. If not for all of you, we'd really be having a time of it." His expression clouded. "We were having a time of it, as a matter of fact."

Mrs. Warner nodded. "That's right. Some way we'll find a way to repay all of you for your kindness."

I shook my head. "Just help Gregory keep coming to school," I said. "That will be thanks enough."

After they left, I kissed and hugged Steve good-bye, then walked off to my classroom, happy knowing that I'd done all that I could for Gregory and his family. Maybe it wasn't going to work out. Maybe everything we offered wouldn't be enough to turn his family's problems around. But I felt certain that years in the future, whenever

Gregory Warner would think of fifth grade, he would think of me, and recall that someone really had cared about him—someone really had cared enough to take a risk and offer help. And knowing that I'd been the one to do that was a gift in itself.

Seven years have passed since my first year of teaching with Gregory. Now I've married Steve and have two preschoolers of my own. And just the other day I opened up the newspaper and skimmed the graduation announcements and spotted Gregory Warner's name. It turned out that he graduated as the valedictorian of the high school in the next town over.

I couldn't help but smile all day long. His success was a wonderful present, indeed.

The End

A Special Christmas Story:
MOURNFUL MEMORIES
Love happens when you're not looking
and least expect it.

"I know it can't be easy for you to coordinate the Christmas toy drive this year," my friend Jewel said.

"No, but charity events are part of my job now, and the toys are for a good cause." I smiled and forced a lightness into my voice that I didn't feel. Giving children toys at Christmas was a wonderful thing to do, but what should be a heartwarming holiday project was like rubbing salt into a bleeding wound. Every day brought tears to my eyes as the pile of teddy bears, dolls, and games in the corner of my work area grew. Each toy was a painful reminder that last year, my daughter Brittany died the day after Christmas.

"Have you called the fire station about dropping off the toys?" she asked. Jewel had led the National Bank's toy drive for years, but she had been promoted into the loan department, and coordinating the bank's charity events was now my responsibility. To help with the transition, Jewel was helping me learn the ropes of each charity event.

"I talked to Chad Stevens this morning—he's their coordinator this year," I said. "I'm going to meet with him on my way home tonight."

"Then you're almost done."

And not too soon as far as I was concerned.

"The guy I worked with last year was really cute." Jewel had a twinkle in her eyes, and I knew what was coming next. "Maybe you and Chad will hit it off." I started to protest, but she continued on. "Don't give me that stuff about not being ready for a relationship yet. You've been divorced for months now."

"I would be interested if the right guy came along," I admitted, "but for now, I want to concentrate on getting through Christmas." My experiences with dating had taught me that finding the right guy wasn't going to be easy. Most guys didn't have any depth and were only interested in partying and getting me into bed.

She chuckled. "Love happens when you're not looking and least expect it," Jewel said as she stood up from my visitor's chair. "Let me know if I can help you with the toy drive."

I appreciated Jewel's offer to help, but nothing she could do would put me in the Christmas mood. I pulled on my coat and got ready to leave for the fire station. On my way, I wanted to stop at the cemetery.

124

I used to go to Brittany's graveside every day. I'd sit beside her grave and remember our happy times together. After a few months, I realized that so many visits weren't helping me to get over her death. If anything, they made me miss her more. Now, I visited about once a month to put a fresh floral arrangement at her headstone. Today, I was bringing a figurine of an angel for Christmas—Brittany's favorite holiday.

.I brushed the snow off the marble headstone and read the inscription as though I was seeing it for the first time. Brittany was only four years old when her life ended. I always imagined my little girl the way she was before she got cancer, with her silky blonde hair that smelled of floral shampoo and her sapphire blue eyes that always twinkled.

From the moment the doctor laid Brittany in my arms, my husband, Sam, and I knew we were blessed. Sam instantly fell in love with his daughter. He created his own song that he sang while he tickled her little pink toes and played with her tiny fingers. He bought her every stuffed animal that caught his eye, and his eyes overflowed with love every time he held her. Sadly, he didn't have the emotional strength to watch her die, or the commitment to our marriage to be with me during those tough times.

When Brittany was diagnosed with cancer, Sam was my rod of support, and he always accompanied me and Brittany to the doctor appointments. "Doctors can cure all kinds of cancers now," Sam had said in an optimistic tone after our first visit with Dr. Morris, a cancer specialist. Dr. Morris had suggested some treatment options, but he hadn't promised a cure. If anything, his diagnosis made my blood run cold with fear.

"Unfortunately, this type of cancer grows rapidly and can be hard to treat, so we'll have to use aggressive treatments," Dr. Morris had said. As he talked, his gray eyes were as hard as stones, and there wasn't a hint of a positive smile on his lips.

At first, Brittany responded well to the chemotherapy treatments. She had some serious bouts of nausea and she lost her soft blonde hair, but the drugs were driving the cancer cells away. I kept thinking that she would get through this rough period of her life and then be able to enjoy her childhood like other children. But then, suddenly, the blood tests stopped showing progress against the cancer.

"We need to try another drug protocol," Dr. Morris had said. Sam and I listened to him explain how a more aggressive treatment might be more effective. His words "might be more effective" tore at my heart as I gazed at Brittany. She lay on the examination table with her eyes closed from the intense fatigue brought on by the chemo treatments. Her skin was colorless, and her pink sweater and knit slacks hung loosely on her body because she'd lost so much weight. Gone was her shiny blonde hair—a pink knit cap now covered her head. She slowly opened her eyes as though her eyelids were weights and her gaze met mine. The sapphire blue eyes that used to dance with life were now dull and expressionless. I swallowed my tears and gave her a soft smile.

"Are you sure that these other drugs are going to work?" Sam was saying to the doctor. He kept pushing Dr. Morris to promise a cure.

I gazed at the doctor. Again, his eyes were serious and his lips made a thin line. "We've had good results with this treatment, but each patient is different and we'll just have to see. The side effects will probably be more severe and Brittany's immune system will become very weak. You'll have to be careful that she isn't exposed to colds or the flu. If she does get a cold, she'll probably need to be hospitalized."

Sam remained hopeful until early November. We were making plans for Thanksgiving when Brittany began having severe side effects from the treatments and had to be admitted to Providence Hospital. The side effects were discouraging enough, but the drugs weren't attacking the cancer cells as we had hoped. Sam stopped coming to the hospital after the first week in November. He was an accountant in business with his father, so he had no problem getting time off to come to the hospital. He just didn't want to come.

One night, I came home after an especially trying day with Brittany vomiting, having high fevers, and dealing with breathing troubles, to find Sam in front of the television, watching a rerun of Law & Order and drinking a whiskey cocktail. I could tell by the deep amber color in the glass that the drink was very strong. I collapsed on the sofa, too tired to even take off my coat. I asked him why he wasn't coming to the hospital anymore.

"There's nothing I can do that you and the nurses aren't doing," he said. His tone was cold and short.

"Brittany would like to see you."

He turned his gaze away from the television and glared at me. "The poor kid's so drugged and tired that she doesn't even know who's there."

"We don't know that for sure," I argued. "Besides, I need you."

"Okay, okay, I'll stop by tomorrow." He turned his attention back to his television program. I felt like I'd made a victory, but a small one.

Sam did come to the hospital the next day, but it was obvious that he didn't want to be there. After a quick greeting to Brittany, who was dopey from pain medication, he paced around the room and looked out of the window. Finally, I suggested that he might want to go to his office. He wasn't making me feel better, and I was afraid his behavior would distress Brittany. He didn't argue and instead made a fast exit out of her room.

It was painful enough to watch my daughter slipping away from me, but I knew I was losing my marriage too. I'd always thought that couples supported each other and grew closer during a family crisis, but I was wrong. If anything, I felt alone, like there was a huge chasm between Sam and me.

On Christmas Day, I went to the hospital while Sam went to his parents' house for dinner. I brought Brittany presents, but she was so tired and ill that I didn't even wake her to open them. I just gently stroked her face and held her hand. Brittany died shortly after midnight.

After Brittany's death, Sam and I were like strangers to each other. He became so withdrawn that conversation was impossible. I suggested that he may want to talk to a grief counselor, but he refused. Instead, he sought comfort in going to bars after work. He'd often come home long after I was in bed, reeking of liquor and stale cigarette smoke.

One night, he came home earlier than usual and I thought that perhaps he'd worked things through. I quickly learned that he'd come home to say that he was moving in with a buddy of his. After a couple months, we both agreed that getting a divorce was probably the best thing.

Snowflakes stung my cheek, drawing me back to the present. I gazed across the cemetery through the falling snow at the nearby homes decorated with colorful Christmas lights. Christmas used to fill my heart with joy, but this year all I could think of was last Christmas at Providence Hospital. Nothing is sadder than a children's ward during Christmas.

I leaned down and touched the headstone as though I was touching Brittany, then I turned away and shuffled through the snowy cemetery to my car. My next stop was the fire station. At least the painful reminders of the holiday would soon be out of my work area.

Fluffy snowflakes were turning the fire station parking lot into a thick white carpet. I parked my car. A fire engine was backing into the station, so I followed it inside. Men dressed in firefighting uniforms leapt out of the truck as it came to a halt. One of the men walked over to me and asked if he could help me.

"I'm Andrea Kellogg from the National Bank." Before I could explain the purpose of my visit, a firefighter within earshot glanced in my direction and strode over. He wore a heavy coat with reflective stripes and carried a helmet in one hand. As he approached, a pungent scent of water, sweat, and smoke surrounded me. There was soot on his face, but I could still see his deep brown eyes.

"Hi, I'm Chad." He started to extend his hand, but then he stopped and smiled. "I'd shake hands, but I think I need to clean up first."

"It looks like you just came in from a fire."

He nodded. "A warehouse down by the docks. No one was hurt, just a lot of smoke and water."

"I can come back," I offered. I didn't want to get in his way and it looked like my timing was bad.

"If you don't mind waiting a few minutes, I'll take a quick shower and then we can talk."

He showed me into a conference room, and I sat down at the table. Chad's back was disappearing out of the doorway when a man dressed in a dark blue paramedic's uniform poked his head in.

"How about some coffee?"

"If you have some made," I said.

He smiled. "The pot's always full."

He came back in a few minutes with a mug of coffee and a plate of brownies. "Dig in before Chad gets back, otherwise you may not get any," he joked. We talked for a few minutes about the snow storm outside. Just as he was telling me how he expected it to be a busy night for him, his two-way radio summoned him for an emergency run.

I was finishing my brownie when Chad walked into the room. In one hand he held a can of Coke, and in the other hand was a file folder. His brown eyes lit up as soon as he saw the plate of brownies. He grabbed a brownie, sat down, and sank his teeth into the chocolate treat.

While he gobbled down two brownies, I tried to still the erratic beating of my heart that this freshly showered man caused. I wasn't sure what had affected me more, the clean fragrance of spicy soap that surrounded him, or his still-damp hair that had small beads of water clinging to it. He'd changed into a pair of jeans and a dark blue T-shirt with the fire station logo, which stretched across his broad chest. I couldn't remember when I'd been more aware of a man's physical presence or his quiet sexuality.

Between bites of brownie, Chad told me about the cook who had made them, and how delicious they tasted after fighting a fire. I asked him about the warehouse fire, and we talked about it for a few minutes before he opened the file folder. "I was talking to the Captain about the toy drive, and we think you should be included when we distribute the toys. That's the fun part."

The last thing I wanted to do was distribute the toys, but I knew that I was representing the bank, so I had to do whatever was required of me. I had hoped to simply drop off the toys at the fire station like

Jewel had done last year, but maybe distributing the toys would be fun. I imagined a Christmas party at the fire station or delivering toys to family homes with needy kids. But the more Chad talked about this year's plan, the more my stomach twisted.

"This year, we're taking toys to the children's ward at Providence Hospital," he said. "It's terrible enough that kids are in the hospital, but to be there at Christmas is even worse."

Just listening to him conjured up visions that I never wanted to think of again. I remembered last year when various groups came to the children's ward and gave out toys or sang. Every time, Brittany was too ill to leave her bed. One time, I walked out to the waiting room to watch, thinking it would lift my spirits. I was wrong—it was too heartbreaking. Santa Claus had sat in a chair by the ward's Christmas tree, with a pile of gifts at his side. Children surrounded him—some in wheelchairs, many with their little arms attached to IV poles, and a few who were carried in their parent's arms. There was no way I could go back to the hospital and give out toys. I never wanted to see the children's ward again, especially at Christmas.

"I'm glad to help," I said, "but you don't need to go out of your way to include me. I know you have busy schedules—"

"It's not a problem. Besides, the Captain and I thought it would be a chance for the children's parents to know that the bank contributed the toys." His words about giving the bank credit for their charitable effort hit home. I had no way out of this.

When I was ready to leave, I was surprised when Chad picked up his coat. "You're going to need help cleaning the snow off of your car," he said. He led me through the area where the fire engines were parked and picked up a snow brush on the way to my car. He was right. The snow had totally covered my car like a fleece blanket. I couldn't even see the color of the paint.

"I love the snow," he said as his arm easily swept the flakes off the top of my car. "Of course, Christmas is my favorite time of year." With his height, he didn't have to stretch to reach the roof like I did. I had gotten my brush out of my car, but my efforts were useless compared to the speed at which he worked. He cleared off my taillights with one swoosh and then he joined me at the driver's door.

"Thanks for the help," I said as I looked up and met his gaze. Standing next to me, his height and strength gave me a safe and comforting feeling that warmed me from head to toe. He wasn't wearing a hat, and the snowflakes piled up on the top of his dark brown hair, giving him a sexy boyish appearance. He opened the car door for me and made sure that my car started before he strode back through the driving snow to the warmth of the station.

As I drove away, the memories of standing next to him in the snow and the power of his freshly showered appearance in the conference room lingered in my mind.

"I'd go to the hospital for you," Jewel said the next day at lunch when I told her about distributing the toys, "but Cindy has her Sunday school Christmas program that afternoon."

There was no way Jewel could miss her daughter's Christmas program, and I wouldn't expect her to. Nor would I expect her to do my job. I added low-fat dressing to my salad as I told her that I could do it.

"Maybe you should ask Paul," she suggested.

It would be appropriate to ask Paul, the bank's manager, if he wanted to participate, rather than assume I should represent the bank. In fact, I should ask him. Paul was a people-person who never turned down an opportunity to make a public appearance, especially if it was in the bank's best interest. If anything, he sought out events where he could be involved.

"Great idea," I said. "It would make him feel appreciated, and it would be good advertising for the bank. I'll talk to him after lunch." I felt more lighthearted just thinking that I had a way to avoid going to the hospital. Plus, it would be great to give Paul an opportunity to feel good too.

"Tell me about the fireman you met," Jewel said. "Any romantic sparks?"

There were sparks, all right. I hadn't been able to get him out of my mind since we'd met. "Chad is cute and sexy," I gushed. We giggled together as I told her how he'd cleared the snow off of my car. As I talked, I remembered how I'd had to fight the urge to reach up and brush the snow off of his hair. Of course, he was very touchable, with or without the snow.

"It sounds like you've met someone to go out with." Jewel smiled as she reached for her soda.

"He's probably married and has a houseful of kids. The good ones are usually married," I said with a sigh.

"Was he wearing a ring?"

I shook my head. "Maybe he doesn't wear one."

"You're going to see him again. You should ask him to coffee," she suggested.

"I'll think about it," I said. I doubted that I would ask him. I may have been interested in Chad, but I doubted a relationship with him was going to happen. He just happened to be a sexy guy assigned to work with me on the annual Christmas project.

I began to have second thoughts when I got back to my office and Chad called. Just the sound of his deep voice made my heart skip a beat. I quickly reminded myself that he was probably calling about the toy drive, but he immediately launched into a different topic.

"Do you have your Christmas tree yet?"

"No," I said, shaking my head even though he couldn't see me. I wasn't planning on getting a tree this year, but I couldn't tell him that. He'd said that Christmas was his favorite holiday, so he'd never understand why I didn't want a tree.

"A group of us from the station are getting trees at the tree farm this Saturday," he said. "I'd be glad to get one for you too."

As much as I didn't want a tree, there was no way I could refuse. Besides, I wanted to see him again. When I hung up, we'd made arrangements for him to come by my house Saturday afternoon with a tree.

After I got off the phone with Chad, I talked to Paul about going to the hospital with the firemen to distribute the toys.

"What an opportunity!" His face broke into a broad smile and his eyes filled with enthusiasm as I told him about the plan. The light in his eyes immediately faded when I told him the date.

He frowned and shook his head. "I can't. My wife's office party is that afternoon. Believe me, delivering toys would be more fun, but Natalie expects me to be there." He went on to explain how he dreaded going to the party every year. "I don't know most of the people, and we always have to stay forever because Natalie's a supervisor. They are a cliquish bunch and are hard to talk to. Besides, they drink too much." As he talked about how much he dreaded the party, all I could think of was that I had to go back to the hospital ward where Brittany had died.

"I hope it isn't too bushy," Chad said as we maneuvered the Christmas tree through my front door and into my living room.

"It looks perfect." It was a perfect tree. It was just the right height, well shaped, and fresh with the fragrance of pine.

I'd been looking forward to seeing Chad since he'd called me about the tree, but my heart still wasn't in the Christmas mood. That morning, I'd gone through my boxes of ornaments. My heart had ached as I'd held the box of small ornaments I'd used to decorate Brittany's tree last year. She'd been too sick to enjoy the tree in the hospital waiting room, so I'd found a tiny artificial tree and miniature ornaments to make a tree for her room. Even now, I could see her smile when we were done decorating her tree.

Chad's voice interrupted my thoughts. "I'll lift the tree into the stand and you can hold it steady while I tighten the screws." With ease, Chad lifted the tree into the stand and then crawled under it to adjust the position.

"It looks straight," I said to him as he made the final adjustments.

He got up from the floor and stood back, looking at the tree from

131

all sides, and then he nodded with satisfaction. He glanced at the plastic boxes filled with decorations. "Do you need help decorating it?"

I hadn't counted on his help, but I welcomed it. Decorating the tree with his help may lift my spirits. Plus, I'd like to spend more time with him. While we were bringing the tree into my house, he'd mentioned he that lived with one of the guys from the fire station, so I knew he wasn't married. "I'd appreciate the help," I said. "If you have time."

"I've got time, and decorating trees is one of the best parts of Christmas." He whipped off his jacket and my breath caught. He was wearing snug-fitting black corduroy slacks and a burgundy turtleneck sweater. He was tall, lean, and sexy. He smelled good too—a soft blend of soap and musky cologne.

Chad had no trouble stringing the lights on the tree—he was almost as tall as it. I was glad that he had stayed to help me. His lively conversation made it easier to decorate the tree, and the more we talked, the more I liked him. We were almost done decorating when I noticed that it was dinnertime. I'd thought that Chad would simply drop off the tree and leave, so I hadn't given any thought to dinner.

"I don't know about you, but I'm getting hungry," I said as I hung an ornament.

"I'm always hungry," he joked.

"What sounds good? Pizza? Chinese?"

"Pizza with double pepperoni," he said, and he flashed me a smile that made my heart skip. Around Chad, my heart seemed to be in a constant state of erratic beats. Between his good looks and great personality, I couldn't hold my heart steady.

When the pizza arrived, the tree was decorated from top to bottom, including a red tree skirt that my mother had given me years ago. Chad answered the door while I went to get my money. I met Chad in the hallway, the pizza in his hands.

"I paid the man," he said as he glanced at the money in my hand.

"But—"

"My treat," he said as he set the pizza on the coffee table.

"Thanks," I said and went into the kitchen for napkins and drinks.

I was walking back into the living room with napkins, plates, and two bottles of beer when I saw Chad standing by the bookshelf. He was looking at pictures of Brittany. In his hand was a picture of me pushing Brittany in one of the swings at the park. The picture had been taken a few weeks before she became ill. Chad turned when I approached, and he carefully set the picture back on the shelf.

"Who's the little girl in all of the pictures?" he asked as he sat down on the sofa.

132

"That's my daughter Brittany," I said as I set the plates on the table. "She died of cancer."

"Oh. I'm sorry." He was quiet while he put a slice of pizza on his plate. Even though I'd only known Chad a short time, I knew that he was a sensitive person. Right now, he probably felt like he'd stepped on a land mine.

"The picture of the two of us at Franklin Park is one of my favorites," I said, putting a lightness into my tone. "That was one of her favorite places."

"How old was she when she died?"

"She was four," I said. I explained how the treatments had always looked promising but then stopped working. "In her case, her body couldn't fight both the cancer and the side effects. The chemo weakened her immune system and she got pneumonia."

"Losing a child has to be the worst thing a parent can ever face," he said. His eyes were heavy with emotion, and I felt as though he was experiencing my pain along with me. "I saw a picture with a man in it. Is that your husband?"

"Yes. We're divorced now," I explained. "For Sam, our marriage died when Brittany passed away. When I look back, I realize that our marriage probably wasn't all that strong even before Brittany was born. She was probably the glue that held us together."

He shook his head. "You've really had a lot of loss."

"How about you? Have you been married?" I was anxious to switch the topic away from me, besides I wanted to know about him.

"Yes, and it ended in divorce," he said. "I married my high school sweetheart right after graduation. We were great dating partners, but we were not good at being married." He paused and took a swallow of beer. "Lynda wanted a husband who worked regular hours at a white collar job. I have scheduled hours, but I can't quit until a fire is out. If there are emergencies and extra men are needed, I have to go to work. She kept pushing me to get a different job, but firefighting is what I do. She's a good person, but we just weren't right for each other."

We talked about marriage, and a hundred other things, as we ate the pizza and drank the beer. Afterward, we found a romantic comedy on television. Unlike many men, Chad liked romantic movies. Even though there were several inches between us on the sofa, I could feel the heat of Chad's body next to mine. The warmth radiated through my body, stirring my senses and making me all too aware that Chad was a sexy man. But there was more to Chad than his sexuality; he had a kind heart, a fun sense of humor, and he shared many of my values. He was the type of man I'd like to have in my life.

All too soon, the movie was over and Chad got ready to leave. "I'm glad we're including you in the toy distribution this year," he said as he slipped his arms into his coat. "After what you've been though with your daughter, you know how much the toys at Christmas mean to the kids."

He looked at me like he'd handed me the opportunity of a lifetime. As he talked about next Saturday, all I could picture was Brittany lying in her small hospital bed, fading from life, and all the other children in their beds facing the horrors of their illnesses. Thinking about seeing all of the children's suffering faces made my heart ache and my stomach turn. I swallowed the bile building in my stomach and forced a smile on my face. "The toys do make a difference," I managed to say.

We stood inches apart, and the heat of his body and the musky scent of his cologne surrounded me like an intoxicating cloud. His gaze met mine and I felt the heat rising in my veins. My heart raced as he moved closer, lowered his head, and gently brushed my lips with his. His kiss was soft and warm, making me ache for more. His arms reached around me and pulled me against his chest, and I wound my arms around his neck. His lips were firmer this time, and the kiss was full and deep. His kiss ignited my body with heat and desire.

We were both breathless when our lips parted. "I had fun tonight," I said as we broke apart.

He smiled and gently ran his fingers over my cheek. "We'll have fun next Saturday, too."

I only wished that were true. I closed the door behind him. All I could think of was the children's ward and its painful memories.

On Monday, Jewel and I went to lunch together. She wanted to hear all the details of my tree-trimming evening with Chad. "It sounds like the two of you really hit it off," she said after we'd ordered two soup and sandwich specials.

"You might be right about finding a relationship when a person isn't looking for one," I said as I remembered her comment last week.

"Did you tell Chad how you feel about going to the hospital?"

I shook my head. "How could I? Chad thinks I'll enjoy giving out toys to the sick kids. He acted like he's doing me a favor to include me."

"I suppose that's a natural assumption," she said. "Still, he sounds like the kind of man who would take your feelings to heart and not expect you do something that is painful for you."

"Even if he understood, I still have to go because it's my job," I said as the waitress set a steaming bowl of tomato soup in front of me.

"It's a shame Paul has plans," Jewel said.

"He sure doesn't seem to be looking forward to his wife's office party."

"No, I'm sure he isn't," she said. "Every year he used to tell me how much he dreaded the annual party. I guess a lot of the people there drink too much and get rowdy. Still, his wife has to go."

"It's kind of like me having to go to the hospital whether I want to or not." I sighed and met her gaze across the table. "It's just that I practically lived there last year. I can still see those kids as they got presents from Santa. They were so sick. And Brittany was so weak—"

We were quiet for a few minutes as we ate our turkey sandwiches and soup—although the memories of last year had dampened my appetite. The turkey sandwich suddenly seemed dry and tasteless, and the tomato soup had lost its spicy zing. Suddenly, Jewel set down her spoon and looked at me. Her eyes were alive, like she'd come up with an idea. "Maybe you need to make some new memories," she said.

"New memories?"

"Right now your mind is filled with sad memories from last year. Maybe if you looked at the hospital differently this year, you'd feel better." She paused and looked thoughtful, and then she continued. "Instead of focusing on the sadness of the sick children and all Brittany went through, think how happy the kids are that Santa came to the hospital."

"It's like looking at the happy images instead of the sad ones," I said.

"Both images are there," she said. "It's a matter of what you choose to see." She reached across the table and covered my hand with hers. "I know it won't be easy to go back to the hospital, but maybe seeing things from a different perspective will help you. Not just for this Christmas, but for years to come."

When I got back to the office after lunch, I sat at my desk thinking about Jewel's advice. She was a good friend, and I knew she wanted to help me. Still, I didn't think her idea would work for me. I knew how powerful the hospital environment could be; she didn't.

Late Friday afternoon, I stood at my desk filling the last cardboard box with toys. I'd told Chad that I'd bring them to the station tomorrow. All the plans were in place. Chad had contacted Providence Hospital, and they were expecting us. He'd reserved one of the vans at the fire station to take me and some of the firefighters to the hospital. Everyone was ready—except me. I was still dreading going back to the children's ward. All I could think about was the children with bald heads, kids pushing IV poles, and little faces that were pasty white.

I was squeezing a small teddy bear into the box when Paul stepped into my cubicle. He was carrying his overcoat. "Would you like some help carrying the boxes to your car?" he asked as he pulled on his coat.

"Sure. If you can carry this box, I'll take that one."

Paul picked up the box and followed me to my car. The trunk was already full of toys, so we put the boxes in the back seat.

"I appreciate your help on this year's drive," Paul said as he closed the car door. "It looks like we collected more toys than last year."

I nodded. "I'm sorry you have to go to the party and can't help at the hospital." As much as I wished he could go in my place, my words were from my heart—I knew he would like to help. I started to open my car door, but his voice stopped me.

"I've decided that I'm going to enjoy the party this year." His voice rang with determination, and he smiled. "Every year, I fuss and fume about going to Natalie's office party—just like I did when I told you about it."

"It doesn't sound like a good time," I said as I remembered some of his comments, along with the other details from Jewel.

"It hasn't been. But this year, I vowed that if I am going to spend three hours at a party, I am going to have a good time. I'm going to enjoy the food, and I'm going to listen and learn more about Natalie's coworkers' lives. Maybe I'll discover that they're more likable than I'd thought." He paused and then continued. "How a person looks at things determines one's feelings. This year, I've decided to be happy." He smiled and walked toward his car.

I got into my car and headed home. Paul was an insightful man. In a way, he was doing what Jewel had recommended that I do—creating new memories. But going to a holiday party was different than going to a hospital ward with the memories of your daughter dying.

Chad made a great Santa Claus. He wore a velvet Santa suit, stuffed with a pillow to fill out his tummy. Several firefighters followed behind us, carrying boxes of toys. I was even wearing a Santa hat, courtesy of Chad.

"Santa's helper has to have a hat," he'd said as he placed the hat on my head. After he'd adjusted the hat, he gave me one of his smiles that made my heart race.

When we stepped into the hospital elevator, my stomach tightened and twisted into a hard knot. We weren't even there yet, and I already felt a hollow ache in my heart. I felt even worse when the elevator doors swept open on the children's floor.

"Santa's here," a nurse in a brightly colored uniform called out from the nurse's station.

"And so is Andrea Kellogg." Toni, the floor supervisor, smiled broadly and came around the counter of the nurse's station. She walked up to me and wrapped her arms around me. I hadn't even thought about the staff I would see today. I was so focused on the children, that I hadn't even considered that I would be seeing many familiar staff. Before I knew it, nurses with happy smiles surrounded me. Their faces sent a flood of memories through my heart. My eyes filled, my lip quivered, and I tried to look away.

Toni's gaze met mine. "It's okay, honey." She gave me a warm hug and then turned toward Chad and the firefighters. "It looks like Santa needs a tree for all those presents." I hung back to collect my emotions while everyone followed Toni to the waiting room where a tree stood in the corner. Several children were already sitting on the floor. Their eyes sparkled and they smiled when they saw Santa. Chad bent down and spoke to each child as he made his way to the tree.

Before long, the scene became reminiscent of last year. The room was full of children attached to IV poles, children with bald heads, and children in their parents' arms. Chad greeted everyone and introduced me as his helper. For the next hour, Chad and I distributed toys while the firefighters talked to the children. I was so busy helping Chad that I didn't have time for my own thoughts, which was a relief.

Toni came up to us after everyone in the waiting room had a toy. "There are some kids who couldn't make it down here," she explained to Chad. I knew all about those children—they were like Brittany, too sick to leave their beds.

"We'll bring Santa to them." Chad grabbed a sack of toys and then motioned for me to follow him. I held my breath as we started down the long hallway and looked into each room as we went by. My heart leapt into my throat as we approached room 1015, where Brittany had stayed those last days. I prayed it would be empty, but it wasn't.

"It looks like we need to go in here," Chad said. He strode into the room, chanting a happy ho-ho.

My feet stuck to the floor. I felt like all of the air had been sucked out of my lungs. A tiny wave from the bed caught my attention. I gulped and slowly approached the bed. A five-year-old boy with a crown of light brown curls was sitting in the center of the bed. He was fully clothed in jeans and a yellow T-shirt. He wasn't hooked up to any IVs or other medical equipment. His mother stood across the room, next to an open suitcase. My heart fell. The boy looked so well—he must have just arrived. My heart ached thinking what painful treatments faced him.

"Mom said I couldn't get a toy because I'm going home today," the boy said to Chad.

"Y-You're going home?" I asked.

His mother nodded at me and smiled. "He's cancer free." Her voice was a whisper, but she probably felt like shouting the news from the rooftop.

"Santa thinks you should have a toy to take with you," Chad said. He reached into his bag, pulled out a game, and handed it to the boy.

"Cool," the boy said as he ripped open the box.

Chad walked out of the room, but I lingered at the door, looking at the happy scene before me. I thought about Paul talking about perspective and how a person looks at things. I'd looked at the boy thinking he was being admitted for treatments when he really was going home. I looked down the hall into the waiting room still filled with children. Many of them were on the floor playing with their toys. Even those with IV poles were smiling and laughing. I'd only been thinking of suffering and death when there was actually a lot more to see. Regardless of the child's medical condition, today's visit from Santa would always be a moment to remember—a time of happiness.

"Are you okay?" Chad was at my elbow.

"I am now." I smiled at him. "I had some emotional issues about coming, because Brittany died here last year right after Christmas."

He groaned and his brown eyes grew serious. "When I saw the nurses greet you, I realized that your daughter had probably been a patient here. I hope it wasn't too painful coming back."

I rested my hand on his arm and met his gaze. "I'm glad I came. Before, I only had unhappy memories of the hospital, but today I've created some happy memories. I'll never forget being here with Brittany, but I'll also never forget how happy the children were when you gave them the toys."

"I'm glad it worked out," he said. "But next time, please tell me if a situation will make you unhappy or uncomfortable. Maybe I can help you."

I nodded and bit my lip so I wouldn't cry—not because I was sad, but because Chad was so kind and understanding. Jewel had been right about telling him my feelings—I should have. I swallowed my happy tears and smiled at him.

He returned my smile through his beard. "I made some new memories the other night at your house." Before I knew what was happening, Chad stepped toward me and kissed my lips. It was a furry kiss because of his beard, but I could still feel the warmth of his lips. "How's that for a memory?"

"Santa's never kissed me before," I teased.

"Just wait until he gets rid of his beard." Chad wrapped his arm around my shoulders and we walked down the hall to another room.

Distributing toys at the hospital taught me a powerful lesson about changing my perspective and looking for happy moments in life. I will always carry the painful memories of my last Christmas with Brittany—nothing can erase them. But looking at the children's ward from a different perspective allowed me to make new memories and enjoy the beauty and wonder of Christmas again.

As for Chad—we're planning a summer wedding. Jewel was also right about love: it happens when you least expect it.

The End

EX MRS. SANTA
TELLS ALL
About who has been very naughty.

Oh, sure, I know what everyone thinks—it had to be my fault. After all, Santa's such a lovable guy, with his "Ho-ho-ho" and twinkling eyes. How could he possibly be responsible for the divorce? Well, let me tell you, everything isn't as it seems with Jolly Old St. Nick. The guy has problems—lots of them.

We first met at the mall, where I was working during the holidays to help pay for my tuition for junior college. The store I worked in was a toy store directly across from Santa's big red and green throne. Each day, I watched as Santa made his entrance just before the mall doors opened for shoppers. He was so impressive. Then again, I've always been a sucker for a man in uniform—even though his uniform was made of red velvet with white, fake fur trim.

After a few days of watching him work his magic with screaming toddlers and frustrated parents, I knew that I had to meet him. Each day at noon, Santa took a break. He'd go to the lunchroom set aside for mall employees and kick back and eat his sack lunch.

I begged my boss to let me take lunch at noon, if only for one day. He grumbled a bit, but then agreed. On the day Santa and I met, I'd made prettily decorated sugar cookies and brought them to work. Once Santa was comfortable at his table, I walked over to him and asked, "Is this seat taken?" gesturing to the seat across from him.

"Please, have a seat," he said. "I haven't seen you in here before."

"This is the first time I've taken lunch at twelve. Usually, I get a break later, and I eat in the storeroom at the back of the toy store." His twinkling blue eyes almost made me forget the cookies I'd made for him. I reached into my insulated lunch bag, took them out, unwrapped the foil they were in, and pushed them across the table to Santa. "I made these for you."

He looked at the cookies that were decorated with red and green sugar. "That's nice of you, but why did you go to so much trouble?"

"Consider it a bribe to get you to bring me everything I want for Christmas. If you like the cookies, there are more where these came from."

Santa winked and played along. "So tell me, little girl, what do you want for Christmas?"

"A Mustang convertible, lots and lots of cash, and a huge diamond ring," I said.

"That's quite an order. Have you been good this year?"

"I've been an angel," I said.

He frowned. "That's too bad. You see, I only bring diamonds to naughty girls. But it might not be too late for you. There are still a couple of weeks until Christmas."

We laughed, and then we ate lunch. Santa finished his by gobbling down the cookies. "These are the best I've ever had," he said. "Would I be too forward if I asked for more?"

"Like I told you, there are plenty where those came from. There's just one tiny problem, though. This is the only day I can take lunch at noon. And if you came into the toy store, it might cause a riot. We'll have to arrange for a place where we can meet and I can give them to you."

"That can be arranged."

"Will I need to bake extra for Mrs. Santa?"

"There is no Mrs. Santa. I live alone with a couple of overgrown elves."

He was a bachelor, and he didn't seem to have a girlfriend. At least he acted as though he wasn't involved with anyone. "Then name the place and I'll be there with a bag full of cookies," I said.

We made a date for the next night after work. It wasn't until later, when I was putting out the new Barbie dolls, that I realized we hadn't exchanged names. I thought of him as Santa, and I hadn't bothered to tell him my name. He hadn't asked, either. I wondered if he really intended to keep the date, or if he was simply trying to blow me off as politely as possible.

My worries were in vain. Santa came to the toy store as soon as he saw his last child for the night. The toy store was five minutes from closing. I spotted him and left the skateboards I'd been arranging.

"Santa, how nice of you to come," I said. "Would you like your cookies now or later?"

"I think I'd enjoy them more after I get out of this costume and into some real clothes. Do you mind waiting for me?"

"Not at all. Where shall I meet you?"

"How about in the employee's locker room?" he said. "I'll get changed and then we can go somewhere that doesn't allow kids. Maybe we can find a place where you can be naughty and earn your diamond ring."

"How naughty are we talking about?"

He winked and gave me a smirking smile. "I'll see you in a few minutes."

After he left, I swiftly finished what I'd been doing, got my things, and clocked out. Just as I entered the locker room, Santa came out of the men's room carrying his red velvet suit. He was even cuter out of uniform than he was in one.

"It'll take me a second to hang this up, and then we can go," he said.

I marveled at how much his costume hid his well-toned body, and I concluded that no one with a face like his should ever cover it up with a long white beard. When he returned, he had his jacket on.

"Mind if we take your car?" he asked. "I let my friend borrow mine."

"Why don't we use the sled and reindeer?" I teased. We laughed together, and then I said, "Of course we can take my car. By the way, I'm Holly Garber."

"It's nice to finally know your name. I've been calling you 'toy store girl' in my head since we met. I'll tell you my name if you won't laugh."

"It's Santa, isn't it?"

He smiled, and I felt dizzy. The man was gorgeous.

"No, it isn't Santa, but it's darn close. I've been teased about it all of my life. I'm Christopher Gringle. Please call me Chris."

Oh wow, I thought, I'm going on a date with Chris Gringle, a mall Santa. My friends would never believe me.

It didn't matter, though, because he was the most drop dead gorgeous guy I'd gone out with in a long, long time. In fact, he was the first guy I'd gone out with in a long time.

We drove to a bar that Chris said was laid back and had good music. Over drinks, I learned that Chris was in graduate school and needed several more credits to graduate. I felt a sense of nagging inferiority because I was only a junior college student working on an associate's degree in accounting.

Time flew by. The bartender finally announced that it was last call, and we decided to leave rather than have another drink. Chris cleared our tab. Once we were back in the car, we discussed where to go, as neither of us wanted the evening to end. I had a bottle of wine in the fridge, and I could think of no one better to share it with than Chris. Besides, I hadn't given him his cookies yet.

"I don't live far from here," I said. "Would you like to go to my place? Your friend could pick you up there."

"It sounds like a plan to me," Chris said. "I'll give Brad a call on his cell phone and you can give him directions."

Chris placed the call, and I told Brad, who was one of his roommates, my address and how to find the apartment. Afterward, I started the engine and we drove to my place. When we reached the building I lived in, I noticed that Chris had a strange look on his face, and he kept gazing about, as though he was trying to avoid someone.

"Do you have a stalker?" I asked.

"Huh?"

"You're acting like someone is following you."

"Oh, sorry. It's nothing. I think I might have known someone who lives here."

He didn't spell it out, but I got the idea that the someone he "might have known" was a woman, and he didn't want to run into her. Chris seemed relieved when we went into my apartment and closed the door.

I got the wine while he made himself comfortable. We settled down on the sofa and talked for hours. Most of the time, we teased or flirted, not going off into anything serious. "How am I doing on the naughty scale?" I asked.

Chris pretended to take out a list that he then read from, listing all of the things I had done that would qualify as naughty. "You're still not there, though. Holly, I don't think you're the sort of girl who does naughty very well."

"Don't underestimate me," I said, advancing on him for a kiss. My arms circled him and our lips met. It wasn't a sweet first kiss but a hot, passionate one. I pulled away from him. "Be sure that goes on my naughty list," I said.

"I have a whole other list for a kiss like that," Chris replied. We kissed again. Still, as much as I liked him, I knew we were going too fast.

"Chris, we need to slow down a little."

He didn't object. Instead, he refilled our wine glasses and kept me laughing with stories about the misery of being a mall Santa. Chris was wonderful in every way. I'd never laughed so much on a date or had as much fun. It was easy to see why the kids liked him.

I was sorry when his friend called and asked if Chris was ready to be picked up. Our date ended with another kiss and the promise to see each other the next night after work. Soon, a pattern developed. Each night, Chris and I ended up at my apartment.

Christmas drew nearer. I hadn't yet earned the diamond ring, though I'd come close a few times. Talking about being naughty and actually doing the deed were two different things. Still, Chris didn't rush me or make me feel uncomfortable.

On Christmas Eve, the mall closed early. Chris told me he had something he had to do with his family. I was a little disappointed that he didn't ask me along—I'd have enjoyed meeting Chris's parents.

As I got into my car to drive home, I saw Chris loading lots of packages into his car's trunk. I smiled and watched him until he slammed the trunk closed. Obviously, like so many other men, Santa waited until the last minute to do his shopping.

It was starting to snow when I reached my apartment. As pretty as the snow was, I hoped it wouldn't cause a problem for me when I drove to my parents' farm on Christmas morning.

Once inside, I put the gifts I'd wrapped earlier in the week into a large box for traveling, and I finished packing my suitcase. Chris's Christmas presents were left under my tiny tree to be opened when we were together again. I'd bought him some CDs and a couple of video games he'd talked about, and I hoped he would like them.

There was some leftover pizza in the refrigerator. I heated it in the microwave, ate it, and then took a hot shower and flopped into bed. The next morning, I awoke early to get ready to go to Mom and Dad's. As I walked into my living room, I stopped cold. My tiny aluminum Christmas tree had been replaced by a fat real one that was straining from the weight of the beautiful, elaborate decorations. On the mantle above the fireplace hung a stocking that was overflowing.

Giggling like a five-year-old, I raced to the mantle and took down the stocking. I pulled out candy and pecans to get to the treasures that lay deeper in the long stocking. First, I found lots of Monopoly money—the cash I'd asked Santa for. Deeper down, there was a toy Mustang convertible that was painted bright red.

I put the small car next to the stack of cash so that I could reach into the toe for another gift. My hand touched a velvet box and a card. I took them both from the stocking. Inside the velvet box was the biggest, most vulgar piece of costume jewelry I'd ever seen. It was a diamond ring like you'd find in a gumball machine.

My ribs ached from laughing. Santa hadn't forgotten anything. I opened the card. Merry Christmas it read. "You have been very naughty, and also very nice. I hope you are happy with your gifts. Look on the tree branch next to the stuffed Santa. There is one more."

With my heart racing, I ran to the tree and looked for Santa. I found him on the fourth limb from the top. Next to him was a slim, rectangular package. I tore the paper from it and found a velvet box, similar to the one the ring had been in. Inside was a white gold charm bracelet, complete with charms. There was a Santa charm, a hundred dollar bill charm, a convertible automobile charm, and, of course, there was a charm of a diamond ring.

By the time I clasped the bracelet around my wrist, I knew that I'd fallen hopelessly in love with Santa. No woman could resist the power of such a romantic man. Happy tears filled my eyes. It was the best Christmas of my entire life.

I tried to call Chris, but he wasn't at his apartment. Leaving town without talking to him first was torture, but my family was expecting me, so I had to get on the road. Thankfully, the road crews had cleared the highway, making driving less hazardous.

All day I was distracted, my thoughts weaving their way back to Chris no matter what subject the family talked about. It was fun seeing my nieces and nephews open their gifts, and I enjoyed visiting with Mom and Dad, talking to my brother and sisters, and thoroughly stuffing myself on Mom's great meal. Still, I couldn't wait to leave.

As soon as I reached home, I called his apartment. "Is Santa in?" I asked.

"He has gone back to the North Pole, but Chris is here," Chris said.

"Would you please tell him that Miss Holly Garber would very much enjoy having him join her for a cup of eggnog?"

"Mr. Gringle says that he happily accepts Miss Garber's invitation and will see her at eight."

It was twenty until seven. I took a fast shower, changed into my sexiest dress, applied makeup with the utmost care, and then prepared the eggnog. Chris arrived exactly on time. I threw myself into his arms.

"I have never had such a wonderful Christmas. You surprised me, and I don't even know how you were able to get in."

"I didn't surprise you," he said. "There's no way I could have. I don't have a key to your apartment. It was Santa. He came down your chimney."

"Chris, I love the bracelet," I said, holding it up for him to see.

He checked it out as though he had never seen it before. "Wow. Santa was good to you. All I got was a piece of coal in my stocking."

"Well, I have a gift for you," I said, and went to get the gaily wrapped box.

Chris opened his gift and a broad smile lightened his face. "These are great," he said. "How did you find this video game?" he asked, holding the game up for me to see.

"I work in a toy store, remember? I have access to all the manufacturer's reps. You said you wanted the game."

"I've wanted it for the past two months, since it came on the market. Holly, you're the best."

"No, I'm not, but I might be second best. How about some eggnog?" I went to get the eggnog, the plate of cookies, and other treats I'd brought from Mom's. When I came back into the living room, Chris was standing at my CD player putting on one of his new CDs.

We settled down onto the sofa and enjoyed the music and refreshments. The Christmas tree blinked, turning lights into different colors. "This is perfect," Chris said.

"I agree," I said. It was perfect. I'd never met anyone more compatible with me than Chris. Being with him was magical. "Chris,

I love the ring Santa gave me, but I don't feel as though I truly earned it. I wasn't nearly naughty enough."

"What are you saying, Holly?"

"Would you do a favor for me and help soothe my conscience? Chris, will you spend the night with me and help me be naughty enough to deserve my new diamond ring?"

He paused for a few seconds, which felt more like hours. I began to think I'd jumped too fast and had rushed our relationship. Maybe Chris wasn't ready for intimacy yet. "Are you sure that you want to sleep with me?" he asked.

"Positive," I said.

Chris took the cup from my hand and set it on the table. He stood, and then pulled me to my feet before sweeping me up into his arms. Like a hero in a romance novel, Chris carried me to bed and carefully undressed me. It was the most sensuous and fully enjoyable sexual encounter I'd ever experienced.

The next morning, we made love again. Then, Chris fixed breakfast for us. We ate it in bed, where we stayed most of that day.

On New Years Eve, we decided to move in together. A year passed, with both of us working odd jobs to pay the bills and cover tuition. I was so caught up in our romance, that I didn't see the early hints of future problems.

In September, Chris proposed to me. I was stunned when he gave me an engagement ring. It was way out of his budget. He told me not to worry because one of the shops at the mall had given him a nice discount.

When, in mid-October, he asked if I would consider moving the wedding up and getting married just before the Christmas season began, I was surprised. We'd talked about having the wedding at my parents' farm in the spring.

"Why do you want to get married so soon?" I asked.

"The manager at the mall has an idea that could be very good for us. He wants to throw us a wedding in the ballroom of the hotel there. All of the stores will give us wedding gifts, and the mall will pay for the wedding and reception out of their advertising budget. It would give them a chance to get the jump on other malls and kick off the season early."

I thought about it. Dad was going to pay for the wedding, but he'd had a hard time lately because of weather causing crops to fail. Also, Mom wasn't in the best of health. It would be selfish of me to take money from them when someone else was offering to pick up the tab for the wedding.

"The main ballroom? It's huge, and we weren't going to invite more than fifty people."

"Actually, the wedding would be in the small ballroom, with the reception in the large one."

"The small ballroom holds six hundred people."

"Holly, we'll have at least that many guests. There are a few catches to the wedding, but nothing we can't deal with."

"You'd better define those catches for me."

It was then that Chris explained that our wedding would be billed as Santa getting married. Santa Claus's wedding would spark a lot of interest. The mall would have a drawing, and customers whose names were drawn would be invited to the wedding and allowed to bring up to three guests.

The reception would be for anyone who shops at the mall on the day of the wedding. They would get refreshments served by elves. They could also have their picture taken with Mr. and Mrs. Claus—for a small fee, of course.

Oh, and I would have to wear a special wedding dress—a white velvet trimmed dress with fake white fur. Chris would wear a suit like his red one, only it would be gold with white, fake fur trim.

I screamed when I heard the suggestion. There was no way I was going to walk down the aisle in a tacky white velvet dress that had dyed fake fur on it for my wedding. What did he expect me to carry for a bouquet—a Christmas tree?

"You've lost your mind, Chris."

"I know how crazy it sounds, but it would really help us out. The mall would pay for everything, so we won't have to go into debt for the wedding or take money that your parents can't spare." He paused. I knew he was gauging my reaction.

"Go on," I said.

"The stores that are participating will each give us a wedding gift. Holly, we wouldn't have to go into debt furnishing our apartment."

"Our apartment is furnished already. It was this way when you moved in, and you've never complained about it."

"Then we'll store the gifts for when we buy a home. Honey, why not go along with it. We could have a wedding at the mall and still have a quiet ceremony at your parents' house."

He gave me the puppy dog eyes and the cherub's smile. Soon, I was persuaded. Chris jumped for the phone and called the manager at the mall. They talked for over an hour, discussing how to get the best bang for their buck.

The next few weeks were the weirdest of my life. A lady who made costumes for dance recitals made my dress. It was more horrible than I had ever imagined. The only thing worse was Chris's costume. Our attendants were all elves, so their costumes weren't any worse than one would expect.

My parents were in shock—not sure if they liked the idea or not. Mom and Dad survived the bizarre preparations, and Dad even agreed to be fitted for a Snow King costume, which would infer to the guests that I came from royalty.

Workers in the publicity staff put together a promotion that was sure to wow the public. There were lots of people shopping early just so that their children could see Santa's wedding.

The day of the wedding came. I looked like a freak, but the mall supervisor was pleased. He even thanked my parents for naming me Holly. It was, in his opinion, the perfect name for Santa's wife. I could only stare at him like an idiot.

My mother came to help me finish dressing. When she opened the door, she let out a whoop and started laughing so hard that her mascara ran. "Holly, you look perfectly dreadful in that getup."

"I have a mirror in here, Mom. I know how I look."

"Why did you go along with this insane stunt? Marriage is supposed to be a sacred communion, not a shopping mall's publicity stunt."

"It was what Chris wanted, and I love him enough to make a few sacrifices."

"Have you thought about how you're going to handle the stares when you tell people you're married to Chris Gringle? The name is so close to Cringle they will assume you're joking."

I had thought about it, but only for a minute. "Chris is a wonderful man, and none of us can help the name we're given."

I suppose she realized how upset she was making me and decided to leave. "They'll be lining up soon to get in. I'm going to find the elf who is supposed to seat me."

Twenty minutes later, Dad took my arm to walk me down the aisle. I told myself to pretend I was back in high school and performing in a play. The wedding planner stood off to the side, waiting to give us our cue. The music started and I almost fainted. They were playing "Here Comes Santa Claus."

I saw Chris step out of a room with his elves and take his place at the snow covered altar. The wedding planner gave Dad the signal to go. I sucked in my breath and began walking. We reached the minister and Chris. My breath burned inside of me because I couldn't force it out.

Exhale, exhale, I told myself. Evidently, survival instincts overcame my embarrassment, and I let out a long breath. Chris winked at me. The minister said something and Dad put my hand into Chris's and then joined Mom. The minister talked on. Had there not been a roar in my ears because I was fighting to keep myself together and not throw up or faint, I might have heard him.

I was savvy enough to know what to do when it came time for Chris and me to exchange vows, and I managed to get the words out. We exchanged rings, which had been donated by Roger's Jewelers on the second floor of the mall. When Chris kissed me after our being pronounced man and wife, children in the ballroom began shouting and clapping. As I turned for our walk back down the aisle, I could see shock and horror on all the adult faces; the kids were deliriously happy.

There was a cake and ice cream reception in the large ballroom. Chris and I cut the cake, and then we went to the throne that had been set up. Lines had already formed for pictures with us. The mall had promoted the pictures as the one and only time that children would be allowed to meet Mrs. Claus and get a picture. According to the mall supervisor, as soon as the wedding ended, Santa would escort me to his sled, where Rudolph and the others would fly me to the North Pole. The next day, Santa would be on his throne in the mall, and the Christmas buying season would officially kick off.

I suppose people never think of Santa having sex with Mrs. Claus, or we might have gotten a honeymoon. Instead, we had to wait until after the holidays for our Hawaiian vacation, compliments of Turner Travel on the first floor.

Since I was scheduled for part-time at the toy store, I couldn't take a trip anyway. Chris and I began our first holiday season as a married couple. Often I would look out the window of the toy store to see him playing Santa Claus. He was so good with the children.

On any given day, there were elves making sure the line flowed as it should. Actually, there were two lines. Any child with a Golden Santa Pass was assured no more than a ten-minute wait. Merchants who participated in the Golden Santa Pass promotion gave them to shoppers that spent a certain amount of money in their store. The toy store where I worked also gave them out.

Having a mall Santa was a major promotional tool, and the mall I worked in utilized Santa to the extreme, my wedding being an example. Another merchandising ploy was the Santa's Special Coupon Book. Children were given coupons to give to their parents, along with the traditional peppermint stick, after talking to Santa.

The coupons were for participating merchants. Merchants that didn't participate in the Golden Santa Pass program weren't allowed to submit coupons. It was said that the pass and the coupons could make or break a merchant's Christmas sales.

Since I wasn't involved in the workings of the mall, I never gave much thought to the promotions. I stacked and sold toys until my shift was up, and then I waited for Chris to change so we could go home together.

Things ran smoothly that Christmas season. Chris and I talked nightly about our upcoming honeymoon. One of the shops had given me a gift certificate to put toward clothes for the trip. During my breaks, I shopped and found some nice things on sale.

On Christmas Eve, the mall closed early. I was surprised when Chris came into the toy store just before closing. He greeted me and smiled, and then he asked where my boss was. The two of them went to the store room together.

I wondered what could be going on. When my boss came out, asked me to go ahead and lock up, and told me that Chris would be home later, my curiosity grew even more.

"Why is Chris staying? I can wait for him. Besides, we rode in together. How will he get home?"

"Holly, I have asked Chris to do a special favor for me. It's against mall rules for their Santa to appear anywhere else, but this is for charity, and I don't see the harm. I'll bring Chris home later. Right now, he's changing so we can make a clean exit. Sweetie, we're borrowing the Santa suit, and there could be problems. Chris doesn't want you involved."

"It sounds crazy to me, but if Chris is set on doing it then I'll go on home and finish wrapping presents. Just remind him that we're due at his folks' later."

I left the mall and drove to our apartment, where I finished wrapping the mountain of gifts for our two families. We'd spend Christmas Eve with his family and Christmas Day with mine. Hours went by and Chris hadn't come home. We were due at his parents. I called his cell phone and when he answered, I reminded him that we were expected.

"Oh, good grief, I've let time slip away, Holly. Go ahead to the party, and I'll join you there. I promise to be on time."

"Chris, you need to change clothes from the Santa suit."

"I'll be fine." He hung up.

I carried the gifts down the three flights of stairs and put them in the trunk of the car. It took four trips. By the time I had everything loaded, my makeup was running and my clothes were a wrinkled mess.

Unless I wanted to look like I'd just run a marathon, I had to repair my makeup and change my dress. Finding something to wear was a problem. I'd been so busy lately that I hadn't made it to the cleaners. Eventually, I settled on black slacks and a sweater that had a rhinestone pin on it.

I was going to be late, and I tried to call, but the line was busy. Not wasting more time, I went to the car and got in. I started the engine and then pulled out into the driveway. At the stop light, I gazed around, admiring the few apartments that sported Christmas decorations on their balcony.

As I was looking at one of the apartments, something caught my eye. A man, wearing a Santa costume, was coming out of a downstairs apartment, a woman clinging to his arm. He kissed her, and then she went back inside. I thought nothing of it until the Santa crossed to the building where Chris and I lived. As he drew closer, I could tell that the Santa I'd seen kissing the woman was my husband.

I reversed the car and parked in our parking spot. By the time Chris had reached our door, I was only steps behind him. "What in the heck are you up to?" I screamed.

"Holly, I thought I told you to go ahead without me."

"I'm sure you wish I had, and I would have if I hadn't had to carry all of the gifts to the car by myself and gotten so sweaty that I needed to change. Still, that's beside the point—I saw you kissing another woman."

"Don't get all bent out of shape. She's an old friend who has a young son. He hasn't been well lately, and she thought a visit from Santa would cheer him up. I brought him a fire truck he wanted, and we shared some milk and cookies."

"That's well and good, but why did you kiss the woman."

"She kissed me, Holly. She wanted to show her appreciation."

"You're a married man. A couple of extra cookies would have served just fine."

"We're late getting to my parents' house. I don't want to drag our problems into their party, so let's knock this off and talk about it when we get home."

Chris and I went to the party together. I could hardly look at him the entire time, and my mind began to take note of all the times he'd go to the library to study or called and said he was working overtime at whichever job he happened to have at the time. Had he been cheating on me right under my nose? If that was the case, then why had he married me in the first place?

I was barely able to eat, and when someone would talk to me, my mind would wander and I wouldn't hear a word they were saying. It hurt to think that Chris was unfaithful, and it made me take a close look at our marriage.

We got through the night, and I made him sleep on the sofa. The next day, we pretended to be a happy couple at my parents' house. When we came home though, I refused to speak to Chris.

"Holly, we have to work this out. After all, our honeymoon begins in two days."

"Take your friend with the kid," I said. "That would cheer them both up."

"I want to take you. You're my wife."

We argued like that until right before we were supposed to leave for the airport. I eventually gave in and agreed to take the trip. We barely made our plane on time. Once we arrived in Hawaii, things changed between Chris and me. I accepted his apology and his explanation, and I forgave him.

The honeymoon was as magical as a honeymoon in Hawaii is supposed to be. When the day came to return home, I was sad. "Holly, we'll come back on a second honeymoon," Chris assured me. "And maybe on our third honeymoon."

"So many honeymoons? Is that proper?"

"Every day will be a honeymoon for us," he said and then kissed me.

Within a week, we were back to the old routine. Both of us attended as many classes as we could afford while taking part-time jobs to pay the bills. After three hectic months, Chris came to me with a proposal.

"Holly, neither of us is getting anywhere. I can't work and go to school and neither can you. Since I'm closer to getting my degree, why don't you drop out of school and work full-time. That way, I can go to school full-time. And when I graduate, I'll be able to get a good job and pay for you to finish school. You won't have to work, and you can concentrate your efforts on getting your degree."

I didn't want to stop taking classes, but his idea made sense. Chris was always persuasive, and I let him persuade me to do something I didn't really want to do. I dropped out of school and went to work full-time at an insurance agency, processing claims.

Chris threw himself into school. He was supposed to have one more year left, and then he decided to change majors. It would be two years before he graduated. One thing that he always managed to do, however, was to work at the mall as Santa. I asked him why, and he said it was a tradition and that he loved seeing the smiles on the children's faces.

"Maybe if you spent the time on school and got your degree, we could see the smile on the face of our own child."

"We're not ready to start a family, Holly. I want us both to have our degrees before that happens."

Sometimes I'd fume in private, but I'd get over it when Chris would do something funny or sweet. It was my dad who pointed out that Chris didn't seem stable enough to stick to anything. Dad called him a professional student, and he thought he was lazy because I was the one supporting us and paying for Chris to go to school.

Defending my husband became a habit, even though the words Dad spoke were the same ones that were in my heart. "Dad, Chris wants to give us a good life. He's going to get his degree, and then he'll be the one working so I can finish school."

"You would have graduated by now if you hadn't dropped out," Dad said. "Holly, I'll help you with your tuition if you'll tell Chris to get a part-time job and pay his own way. Didn't you tell me he has changed majors again?"

"Only because he realized he could get a better job with a different degree."

"He seems a bit old to still be in school," Dad said. "When I was his age, I had a family and a job. When is he going to finish school and go to work?"

Because I couldn't answer Dad's questions, I stopped visiting as often. I threw myself into my job and did my best so that I would earn raises and promotions. If, for some reason, I wasn't going to get a degree, I at least needed a good job.

Christmas rolled around again. This year, there were some changes. Instead of the elves, who had been high school kids for the most part, the helpers were now women who made the Dallas Cheerleaders look like nuns.

And the woman taking the pictures was dressed like the Sugar Plum Fairy—if the Sugar Plum Fairy shopped at Fredericks of Hollywood. I asked Chris why they'd made the change.

"Lots of times it's the dad who comes to the mall with the kids. Dads aren't as sentimental as Moms. We need to spice up the scenery to inspire the dads to wait in line. It's just a merchandising experiment."

"I don't think the moms will like it very much," I said. "And to tell the truth, I don't like it at all."

"Holly, you said that you trusted me. Those women are mostly college girls making extra money over the holidays. I'm too busy with the kids to notice them."

And that was the end of the discussion. The next day, Chris, dressed up as Santa and made his grand entrance when he flew into the mall parking lot in a helicopter, distributing candy canes and wishing a Merry Christmas to the shoppers and their children.

Each year, the company I worked for gave employees a free day off to do Christmas shopping. It was a great gesture on their part, and I appreciated having time to shop without feeling rushed. I went to the mall early and began making the rounds of stores.

"Well, if it isn't Mrs. Santa," Patty Ward said when I stepped into Accessories and More. "You do know that we don't give Santa kickbacks here, or discounts either."

"Patty, what are you talking about? I don't expect a discount. I'm here to pick up some things for my nieces."

"Oh, don't play dumb. I know the game Chris plays with the merchants. And if a merchant doesn't go along with it, then Santa won't be nice to him."

Obviously, she thought my husband was practicing extortion. Her insinuations made me angry. "Any mall promotions are done by the people in charge of the mall. Chris doesn't have anything to do with it."

"Is it possible that you don't know? Holly, the gold merchants are those who pay for the Santa certificates, and anyone who doesn't pay the kickback to Chris and the others running the scheme have a hard time because they can't get discount coupons into the little bag Santa gives the kids. We have to place ads in newspapers, and we get no special treatment from the management."

"Patty, I don't think Chris knows anything about it."

"Then why do the stores give him free merchandise on Christmas Eve? It's pay for promoting them. Chris has a good thing going, thanks to the people who run this mall. Right after the mall was sold and new management came on board, the Santa before Chris was fired because he wouldn't play along."

"I have to talk to Chris," I said, and I walked out the door.

Chris was already busy. Toddlers were lined up waiting to talk to Santa. I had to know the truth, so I went to the toy store to talk to my old boss. After telling him everything Patty had said, I asked him if what she said, was the truth.

He hesitated to say anything, and then he changed his mind, shrugging. "What the heck, you're married to him. I don't think it would hurt for you to know. Chris has a few deals going with merchants to help them move their inventory. In return, we show our appreciation with a few bucks, or merchandise."

I thought of my engagement ring and of other gifts Chris had given me that were way out of reach financially. Thinking that my husband could do anything so underhanded grated on me. Still, I had enough faith in him to believe there was a reasonable explanation. We would talk later, when he took his break.

At lunch time, I went to the employees' lunchroom. Chris was there, and sitting with him was the Sugar Plum Fairy, displaying her heavy cleavage, and a couple of leggy elves. They were talking and laughing. The Fairy occasionally reached over and touched his hand or arm in a possessive way.

I stepped up to the table. "Hi, Santa," I said. "Is there room here for Mrs. Santa?"

Chris's cheeks turned as red as a stoplight. The girls looked uncomfortable and made excuses to go to another table.

"What's with the girls?" I asked.

"Holly, don't make something out of this that isn't there. We were joking around, relaxing since we've spent all morning dealing with screaming kids. What are you doing here at the mall?"

"Shopping for gifts. The company gives us a day off to get our Christmas shopping done. So far, I haven't bought a thing because one of the merchants practically tossed me out of her shop. She says that because she won't pay extortion to you, you cause her to lose business."

"That's insane, Holly. The mall handles all promotions, and sometimes they put together special promotions for the merchants. If a merchant doesn't want to participate, then that's that."

"I see. And do you get anything out of the promotion?"

"Not a thing. I'll admit that at times a merchant will give me a gift to thank me for doing such a good job as Santa, but that's all it is—a gift of appreciation. Hon, I have to get back to work." Chris kissed my cheek and went to the men's room to freshen up. I left the mall without doing any shopping.

Things were stressful between us after that. Sometimes Chris would come in late, after the mall closed, and give me a bogus excuse as to why he hadn't come straight home.

"I'm cramming for the end of the semester exams. The guy who is my study partner works as late as I do, and sometimes it's ten o'clock before we get started." Chris would give me a look as though I was the one who had come in at two in the morning.

"Chris, where are your books? I've never seen you take one with you when you leave each morning, and I haven't seen any in your car."

"I keep them in my locker so I can read on my break."

He would do what he had always done, make it look as though I was a jerk for even bringing the subject up. Again, I apologized and accepted his explanation.

I prayed for the season to end so that Chris and I could get back to normal. He wouldn't be around sexy elves, and he wouldn't have to go to someone's house late at night to study.

Finally, Christmas Eve rolled around again. I'd wrapped the gifts, made a casserole, and was ready to go to Chris's parents. Time passed and Chris didn't come home. I couldn't reach him on his cell phone. I called my old boss to ask if something had happened at the mall to make Chris run late.

"Holly, we closed on time. I saw Chris leave. Maybe Hannah knows where he went. She's my niece and she worked as one of the elves this year."

I'd never heard of Hannah, but I took down her phone number and called her. "Hi, this is Holly Gringle, Chris's wife. Your uncle told me

154

you might know where I can find Chris. We're supposed to go to his parents' house and he isn't home yet."

She hesitated before answering. "I don't want to get involved in a family problem," she said. "Look, you didn't hear this from me, but I think he went to Liza's tree trimming party."

"Who is Liza?"

"The Sugar Plum Fairy. She used to date Chris. I was invited, but I know the crowd and how out of hand things can get with them. My husband wouldn't like for me to be at a party like that."

"Do you know where it's being held?"

When she gave me the address, I could have passed out on the floor. It was the apartment that I'd seen Chris coming out of the Christmas Eve before. So many ideas flashed through my head. I'd go to the apartment and confront Chris, or I'd wait outside until he left and have it out with him. Somehow, I was going to do something. I just didn't know what yet. One thing was for sure, I couldn't just sit in the apartment waiting.

I gathered the trash and took it to the dumpster. When I looked across the street, I saw Chris's car parked in a darkly lit spot, as though he'd intentionally parked where he wouldn't be noticed.

Soon, a group of drunks came staggering out of one of the apartments close to where Chris was parked. I recognized a guy who'd lived across the hall from me when I first moved in. After he moved, we hadn't kept up with each other. I wondered if he'd even remember me. I had to take the chance.

"Larry," I said, "how have you been?"

He stared at me for a few seconds, and recognition came to his eyes. "Holly, you look wonderful. I don't know whose party you're going to, but they're lucky people."

"It's just a family thing. By the way, it looks like you and your friends are full of Christmas cheer."

"Yeah, we were at a party, but it started to get too wild for us. They had a male stripper dressed up like Santa Claus. Liza, the woman who invited us, was way too drunk, and the party was getting so loud we left before someone called the cops. I do not want to spend Christmas in jail."

"I don't blame you. It sounds like a wild party."

"Holly, we have to go. It was great seeing you again. Merry Christmas."

"Merry Christmas to you," I said. Larry and his group got into a car and drove away. I started toward the apartment where the party was being held. As I drew closer, I heard the sound of music and laughter.

Admittedly, I'm a bit timid and hate making a scene, but this time my temper was boiling hot. I heard a car door slam and footsteps coming closer. I stepped into the shrubs, out of the light, so no one would see me.

Two women passed right by me. I recognized them from the mall. They had been elves. When the apartment door opened, I saw Liza and realized she was quite drunk. Then I heard Chris call, "Hey, ladies, it's about time you got here. Come see what Santa brought you."

Without hesitating, I rushed to the door and pushed past the three women. It was easy to spot Chris—he was sitting in a recliner wearing his Santa beard, his pointy cap, a furry red thong, and nothing else—unless you counted the half naked elf sitting on his lap.

Chris was too busy making out with the elf to notice me. I walked toward him, and I pulled the woman off his lap and slapped his face. "You bastard," I screamed, and I ran from the apartment. Chris chased after me, calling for me to stop. I supposed he was cold, running through the December night in nothing but his Santa thong.

"Holly, it's not how it looked," he yelled. "Some of the girls from the mall wanted to have a Christmas party and asked me to play Santa and pass out the gifts."

"You know something, Chris, I might have believed you if you hadn't worn that stupid G-string. And don't expect me to believe that was an innocent Christmas party. Even as dumb as I am, I can recognize a sex party when I see one. And you had the nerve to go to the party in the complex where we live!"

Then it hit me—he'd never stopped seeing the woman I'd caught him kissing a year ago. Chris had probably gotten her the job at the mall. All those nights he didn't come home, he wasn't cramming for his upcoming exams, he was with her.

I remembered how cautious and nervous he'd been the first night I invited him to my apartment. Now, I knew why. He was having a relationship with one of my neighbors and didn't want her to see him with me.

"Tell me about Liza," I demanded while standing in the front of the apartment.

"Can we do it inside? I'm freezing."

I unlocked the door. Chris ran past me to get his bathrobe. He had goose bumps all over and his lips were blue. Chris rubbed his feet. His teeth chattered as he tried to explain himself. I sat still and quiet. And the quieter I was, the more nervous it made him. Eventually, he warmed up enough to talk to me.

"She doesn't mean a thing to me. Honest, Holly, we've been over for ages. We met a couple of years ago and dated, but I broke up because I wasn't able to take on a ready made family."

I raised my left eyebrow, still maintaining silence.

156

"She needed work, so I helped her get a job at the mall as a Santa's helper. Liza and some of the other girls wanted to have a Christmas party. They thought it would be funny to have me come play Santa. As for the thong, that was the girls' idea, and I went along with it to be a good sport."

"Try again. I've put it all together, Chris. I know you were there the nights you came home late and said you were cramming for exams. I'm not as big a fool as you take me for."

He hung his head and slowly shook it. "I'm so sorry, Holly. Please let me make it up to you. Nothing like this will ever happen again."

"Sorry, Chris, but this was the last straw. I've given in to you so many times when I didn't want to. First was that creepy wedding. Then I dropped out of school to support you, even though I knew you were never going to get the degree because you don't want to work. You like staying in school. Maybe it helps you forget that you're a thirty-year-old man who has never completely supported himself."

"Mom told you, didn't she," he said, hanging his head.

"That you really lived with her instead of some roommates until you moved in with me? Yes, she told me soon after we got married. I mentioned that you never saw your old roommates again, and that's when she told me."

"What are you going to do, Holly?"

"I've had it. Rushing into a relationship with you was a mistake. I didn't know you. I was too dazzled to look beyond your charm. Now, I'm going to get my life back the way it should have been."

"You're breaking up with me?"

"Teenaged kids break up. Married adults get divorced."

He began crying. "We can make it work, Holly. I'll change. Just tell me what to do and I'll change."

I knew he wouldn't change. He didn't know how to. Chris was one of those men who had stayed a child much too long, looking to others to take care of him. After the holidays, I filed for divorce. He didn't contest it—I suspected he wasn't able to pay a lawyer.

Within a month, I became the ex Mrs. Santa Claus. Sometimes I think of Chris and miss him a little, but not enough to ever see him again. I went back to school, and because I'd done such a good job at the insurance agency, I was able to work a swing shift so that I didn't have to give up everything I'd accomplished there. They even paid a portion of my tuition.

And when Christmas rolls around, I do my shopping online, avoiding all the malls—and Santa.

The End

A SNOWSTORM ROMANCE
I didn't much care for the thought of
spending Christmas Day with a stranger

It was getting close to Christmas Day and the isolated little town that I called home looked abandoned. Most folks had gone down south to visit relatives over the holidays, but I was left on duty alone. Normally, there were three cops who patrolled the town—my boss, another officer named Mike, and myself—but being the junior person on staff, I got Christmas duty this year.

I wasn't complaining, though, it was an interesting job—one that kept me outdoors in the fresh air a good deal of the time. The worst part about it was the paperwork, and during the holiday I was determined to make a dent in the growing pile of paper on my desk. Keeping myself busy would help me forget that I was alone this Christmas.

My family hadn't been thrilled about me taking a job so far away, but for me it seemed like a great opportunity. I'd graduated from the police academy with honors, but I really had to work hard at it. Police work was challenging for me—it didn't come as easy as it did for some of my friends. That's one of the reasons I chose a rural placement instead of the city. I knew rural people well, having grown up in a small town, and I figured that if I found a job in the same kind of place it would make life easier.

Nettle Crossing was the perfect place. There wasn't too much crime in town, although we did have to patrol quite a large area of wilderness, too.

After three years, though, it was getting easier. To my parents' dismay, I was thinking of settling here permanently. Why not? I liked my boss as much as the people in town. At first, I thought they might not take to a lady cop, but I have to admit I faced a lot more prejudice in the city while I was training than I ever did in this small town in the middle of nowhere.

There was one resident who rubbed me the wrong way, though. I didn't know much about him; no one really did. He'd just appeared in town one summer day when I'd been vacationing with my folks down south. When I came back, everyone was abuzz with the news. Not many strangers came to live here. Sure, there were lots of transient workers with the oil pipeline, but it wasn't every day that someone chose Nettle Crossing as their home. People were wondering what he did for a living, and the single women in town were nearly fainting over the fact that he was so good-looking.

My law enforcement background made me suspicious right away. A man living well in the big Myrtle log house just outside town with no visible means of income was definitely suspicious. I wondered if he was dealing drugs.

"You've got a suspicious mind, Leanne," Bill, my boss, told me. "Why don't you go over to his place and check him out?"

"Yeah," Mike, my fellow officer, piped up. "Get him up against the wall and frisk him. See if he's got anything interesting to hide."

"You two have dirty minds!" I told them affectionately. It was all part of the teasing that was life as a cop. You joked to ease the tension sometimes—and sometimes just because.

"Really, Leanne, when was the last time you had a date?" Mike asked.

"That's none of your business. I'll tell Rhonda that you're being a male chauvinist!"

Rhonda was Mike's wife and was currently very busy taking care of his twin daughters. She would cuff him on the ears if she found out about his saucy tongue.

I did some research and learned that the newcomer's name was Kevin Motts. Everywhere I went in town—to help a cat out of a tree, to chase kids away from the liquor store, or to do the hundreds of other routine things that cops did every day—I heard his name. Kevin was in town today. Kevin said this. Kevin did that. I was sick of hearing about him.

"Now that there's an eligible bachelor in town, why don't you let me cut and style your hair, Leanne?" Eva, the town's hairdresser, urged me.

"I don't need to be pretty, I'm a cop. People have to respect me."

"They do respect you, but it doesn't hurt to put on the dog now and then," she said, walking around me and trying to envision how she was going to do my hair.

"What about that complaint you had, Eva, about Mason St. Pierre always parking right in front of your shop?"

She reluctantly got down to the business I was supposed to be here for. That was life in a small town—you just couldn't separate business from personal.

"Will you come back after work some day, Leanne? I'll do your hair so nicely you won't even recognize yourself," she called out to me as I finally made my escape.

I'll just bet she would. When I was safely inside the unmarked patrol car, I shuddered to think what I would look like after a session with Eva. Frankenstein's bride would look like a beauty queen compared to me.

Besides, what was wrong with my hair? I liked it this way, short and straight—it was easy to care for. Bill wasn't fussy about how I wore my hair at work, even though he made sure his and Mike's hair was always neatly trimmed, so I usually wore it in a short ponytail. If anyone was coming to inspect our little operation, I would wrap it up in a bun off my collar.

That was what I was thinking about when I backed out of Eva's customer parking lot and hit a half-ton truck behind me. I jumped out of the car ready to do battle.

"What the heck were you thinking about, lady? You weren't even looking as you were pulling out!" he said, and then noticed my uniform.

"Oh, just great . . . a cop. This is the best ending to the best day of my life," the man behind the wheel said, his voice dripping with sarcasm.

I knew he was a stranger to town and I guessed that he was one of the oilfield workers. I had to admit to him that it was my fault. We looked at both vehicles and there didn't seem to be any damage. Eva's parking lot had been paved higher than street level so our vehicles weren't of equal height when they hit. The rubber part of my bumper had scraped the side of his truck and there were a few black marks—that was all.

"I'd better get all the particulars just in case," I said. "What's your name?"

I was already thinking about the merciless teasing I would get back at the station. Mike and Bill would love this one.

"Kevin Motts," he said, and I nearly dropped my ballpoint pen.

Then I looked at him, really looked at him, for the first time. I could see why the unmarried women would be interested—he was big, without a spare ounce of flesh that I could see, and I suppose there would be those who would call him good-looking.

"Are you trying to memorize my appearance in case I make a run for it, Officer?" he teased. He knew that I had been taking a good look.

I tried to ignore the comment but I was blushing. Angry with myself for blushing, my face turned even redder.

"My name is Officer Benson, in case you want to make a claim with your insurance," I told him coolly.

"Now that's no fair, you know my first name, why can't I know yours?"

"It's Leanne."

"Leanne." He seemed to swirl my name around in his mouth as if he was tasting it to see how good it felt.

He leaned closer. I'd been bringing in drunks and mean guys twice my size and all of their swearing and threats hadn't bothered me, but this man was setting me off-balance. I took a step back. Every cop knows that moving back is something you don't want to do—it shows that you're nervous.

He leaned back, straightened, and gave me a mocking salute.

"See you around, Leanne," he said. Then he got back in his truck and roared away.

I made a mental note to avoid this character from now on. I was mad. Even though the accident had been my fault, he didn't have to enjoy it so much. If he so much as drove through town one mile per hour over the speed limit, I was going to nail his hide.

It took about three weeks for the laughter and teasing to die down at the station. Mike and Bill came up with all sorts of jokes. They talked endlessly about Leanne popping in to get her hair done and running smack dab into the man she was getting all dolled up for.

Now, working alone on the holidays by myself, I kind of missed those big lugs. It was a couple of days before Christmas and I was alone at the station. A wind was blowing outside, and it looked like we were in for snow.

Then I got a call from Lyndonville, the town to the south of us. Someone had stolen an old lady's car. A trucker had called in from a truck stop between our towns, reporting a man acting suspiciously. The man was driving an old Cadillac in mint condition, just like the one Mrs. Harris owned. The trucker said he was headed our way.

What really struck me was the man's description of the driver. He was depicted as a big man with dark brown hair wearing a very distinctive looking ski jacket—one with blue with red trim and unusual patches with some kind of insignia on the arms.

That sounded just like the jacket Kevin Motts was wearing on the day we bumped into each other. My cop instincts took over. I'd always wondered how Kevin supported himself in that big log house that the Myrtle family had built. The Myrtles had been one of the biggest merchants in town before Frank Myrtle sold his business and moved the family down to Florida. Too many years of snow and ice had finally gotten to them.

Their home must cost half a million dollars. What did Kevin Motts do for a living that he could afford to buy a place like that? You sure couldn't buy it on a cop's salary. I thought about my own little apartment. I was trying to save to get a place of my own, but it wasn't easy—even being single with no kids. Houses up here were expensive.

I shook my head to clear my thoughts. Maybe I should just pay Mr. Motts a visit. If he was home, then he couldn't be the one who had stolen the car. Since the trucker had just spotted the guy less than half

161

an hour ago, he wouldn't have had time to get here.

I drove out to the Myrtle property. I parked the car, got out, and was nearly toppled over by a big gust of icy wind. We were in for a blizzard. I began to yearn for my nice warm office and a big cup of coffee.

Kevin Motts wasn't home. That didn't prove anything by itself, but it meant that he was still a suspect. I decided to wait a few minutes to see if he turned up.

Sure enough, in the time it would take for a person to drive a stolen car from the truck stop into town, hide it somewhere, and switch vehicles, Kevin showed up. I'd figured it out, timing each leg of the trip. Kevin Motts was my number one suspect.

He got out of his truck and stared over at me. I got out and pulled myself up to my full height. We didn't get many criminals like this in town—mostly drunks and domestic disturbances—but this could be a man who made a lot of money from stolen cars. A man like this wasn't about to let some small-town cop ruin his operation. My hand moved to check my service revolver.

Kevin stood still, seeing my slight movement.

"What's this about, Leanne?" he asked softly, like he was afraid to make me angry. Don't upset the crazy cop.

"There's been a car stolen just south of here. I need to bring you in to ask a few questions."

"A car was stolen? What has that got to do with me? You don't think—you can't think—that I did it?" he asked, his voice amazed.

Suddenly, he started to laugh. The sound was caught by the wind and thrown at me.

"If you'll just get in the car, Mr. Motts, I'm sure we can settle this thing in a few minutes."

I wanted to get him down to the station. I wanted to tape his answers—there was no way anyone was going to say I didn't do this by the book.

"I can't go right now," he said, and a strange look came over his face.

Maybe he needs to call an accomplice to tell him to pick up the Caddie before someone spots it.

"Why not?" I asked, a thread of fear in my voice. He was twice my size and if he chose to resist, I didn't want to have to bring my gun out.

"I can't really explain. Come inside and see for yourself."

I let him lead the way, keeping him in my sight at every moment. He walked through the house to the back. I'd been in it once or twice before when the Myrtles were still in town—they gave great Christmas parties and invited the whole town.

Kevin stopped at the back porch. He opened a door to a small room that was probably once used to store vegetables.

"They don't seem to like the light, so I only keep a dim bulb in here. Can you see them?"

I looked, straining my eyes. I couldn't see anything. I looked up at Kevin, fully expecting him to try to jump me.

But then I heard it. Little whimpering sounds.

"What the—" I began, and then knelt down to a box of writhing fur.

Puppies. I reached out, picked one up, and brought it to my nose to smell the newborn animal scent.

"They were abandoned on my doorstep the other day. Someone in town figures I need a dog out here, maybe."

"Abandoned!"

My heart lurched to think that someone in my town would do such a thing.

"Well, you don't have any kind of animal shelter here."

"I know, but to just abandon these little guys? Whoever did this should have called the station. We've found homes for lost animals before. It's better than having them roaming the streets."

Kevin laughed.

"I didn't know that dog catcher was part of your duties."

I put the puppy back and straightened up. Was he laughing at this small town and at me? Well, he would soon find out that we did other things than rescue animals. We caught car thieves, too.

"You still have to come in to the station, Mr. Motts."

"Oh, I forgot, I'm Public Enemy Number One. Well, you can see that I have a family to take care of now," he told me, feeding the puppies from a bottle even as we spoke.

"I promise it'll only take about an hour. I'll send someone to look after them if you're not—"

"If I'm not released, you mean," he said. Sighing, he put the last of the puppies down.

A part of me stirred at the sight of the big man handling the little guys so gently. Could he really have just dumped off a stolen car and then calmly gone home to feed puppies?

"I'll see that someone feeds them," I said.

"Is that actually a crack I see in that armor of yours, Officer Benson?" he said, his smile not quite reaching his striking blue eyes.

"No cracks. Now, get in the car."

He was silent all the way into town, which was fine by me. The storm was getting worse. I had the wipers going full blast but they only seemed to be making a mess of the windshield. At this rate, I'd never get him back home tonight—if, of course, he proved to be innocent.

163

He came along quietly enough. As I walked behind him into the station, I couldn't help but give a little shudder. This guy was big, and if he chose to turn on me, I'd better be ready.

As I questioned him about his whereabouts, I couldn't help but notice the snow pelting against the windows. Just as I was wrapping it up, I got another call from Lyndonville.

"Leanne? We got the guy who stole the Caddie. Turns out he was heading south—not your way."

"Oh," I said, and looked over through the glass at Kevin sitting there waiting impatiently for me to return.

Kevin was innocent. At least, it didn't look like he was a car thief.

"You're free to go, Mr. Motts. Lucky for you, they caught the real thief."

"That's what I've been trying to tell you. I don't steal cars for a living."

"Then what do you do for a living?" I asked. I told myself that it was just police business—knowing all about our citizens.

"I'm a writer. I write books about nature, mostly. I came here to follow a pack of wolves and study their habits."

I stared at him. You can make a living by writing about wolves?

He shrugged as if it was no big deal.

"Can you take me home now, please?"

I felt my face burning. So he was an author and I thought he was a car thief. Well, he could still be lying. If not a car thief, he might be into drugs or something else. Part of me just didn't want to trust Kevin Motts.

The wind was howling now. I remembered the puppies and remembered my promise to get him home.

"All right, let's go," I said, hoping he wouldn't see how embarrassed I was.

"No apology, Officer Benson?" he asked.

"I don't have to apologize for anything," I said defensively. "I was just doing my job."

"What made you think it was me, anyway?"

I told him about the ski jacket.

"Oh, so you did actually have something to go on—you weren't just dragging me in for questioning for the hell of it."

At the image of me trying to drag him anywhere, I had to smile a little.

"I don't think this is funny. You've had it in for me since that first time we met. Do I have to remind you that you bumped into me? I've done nothing wrong."

"No you haven't, Mr. Motts. Of course, the department apologizes for any inconvenience this may have caused."

"The department apologizes, huh? Well, that's about as close to an apology as I'll get from you. All right, take me home."

The ride back was silent. With the storm just about at full tilt, I had to concentrate on finding the road. I just wanted to get him home. Then I'd walk back to the station if I had to.

There wouldn't be much crime tonight—every sensible criminal would be sitting snug in his little house—only a fool would go out on a night like this. As we drove, I got a call from a Lyndonville cop sitting in his car at the truck stop—the highway was being closed.

Still, it was almost Christmas, and if you didn't have to go anywhere it was a nice way to spend it—at home with your loved ones, snuggled up tight with a mug of hot chocolate. I began to wonder what my family was doing.

We got safely to his house with Kevin's help—he told me where the edges of his driveway were. Without his help, I would have slipped off the road and into a ditch. He got out of the car with a curt good-bye.

Now, I just had to turn the car around and head back to town.

The wheels began spinning helplessly. The more I pressed the gas, the deeper I would be digging into the snow. I sighed and buttoned up my collar. I'd have to get some gravel from the trunk—we kept some there for just this purpose.

Mike was the last one to have the duty of cleaning up the two patrol cars, but from the looks of things he had done too good of a job. The trunk was empty.

I groaned, and the sound was whisked away by the wind. My fingers were getting numb in my gloves. I looked at the house and then at the road. If I thought I had half a chance of walking back to town, I would have done it.

Suddenly, the back door of the house swung open. Kevin stood there, his arms around his body to keep himself warm.

"You're not going anywhere tonight in all this snow. Come on in."

Those words sent a little chill through me, which had nothing to do with the freezing weather. I didn't want to give in so easily, though. Most of all, I didn't want to owe this man anything.

"If you could maybe just give me a push?" I asked.

"Nope. I'm not going to freeze my extremities off for some dumb cop. Now get inside."

I bristled against his tone. My face was freezing now—it felt like I'd been to the dentist for some major work. If I sat in the car to keep warm, there was a good chance I'd get carbon monoxide poisoning—the snow had already covered the tail pipe. If he was not going to help me, I wasn't going to get the car out of this mess.

"All right, all right," I said irritably.

My decision to bring him in for questioning was coming back to haunt me—big time! I followed him in and heard the door close behind me with a heavy thud.

When we got to the living room, Kevin turned to look at me. He didn't seem at all happy about having an unexpected houseguest.

"If you'll feed the puppies, I'll make us something to eat," he said.

I was glad to have something to do. He watched as I took off my winter coat—standard cop issue—and he took it from me.

"I'd feel a whole lot safer if you took off that gun," he grumbled.

"I'm still on duty," I told him. I still didn't trust him.

"There's no arguing with you, Officer. Just don't shoot one of my puppies with that thing."

"Don't worry. The puppies are safe from me," I said, and he threw me a look that told me he knew what I was implying.

"I won't make any fast moves. Do you watch too many cop shows or what? You talk like a stereotype."

"I do not!"

"Have you ever really listened to yourself, Officer Leanne?"

I had a retort on my tongue but I stopped. It would be no sense in getting in an argument with him; it would be a long enough night as it was. I turned to go see to the puppies. I could hear Kevin chuckle and I fumed inside.

So, let him mock me. I knew I was a good cop. To tell the truth, I acted differently with him than with any other suspect, citizen, or fellow cop I'd ever known. There was just something about Kevin Motts that really got to me.

The puppies were so sweet, and it was such a nice break away from that horrible man. It was hard to believe that he could be so gentle with them and such a pig to me. In fact, everyone in town seemed to like him, but he definitely brought out the worst in me.

If only Bob, the tow truck man, hadn't gone on Christmas holidays down south. I'd talked to him before he left and he'd figured that not many people would need a tow over Christmas since so many people were away. If I could only call him up now I'd be out of this mess.

But no, I had to try to act like a gracious houseguest with Kevin Motts. That didn't sit well with me at all.

Kevin had to call me back when supper was ready. It wasn't anything fancy—beef stew and biscuits—but after a long day it tasted like the best gourmet meal I'd ever had.

"Good appetite," Kevin said, as I emptied my plate. He quickly started dishing out more from the pot of stew on the stove.

"Oh, no, I couldn't," I said.

"You could," he told me, and put another full helping on my plate. He was right; I was very hungry. I hadn't eaten since breakfast.

"Is it true that cops live on coffee and donuts?"

"Now who's talking about stereotypes?" I shot at him.

"Okay," he said, laughing. "You win."

The sound of his laughter was unexpected. I looked over at him. His whole manner changed when he laughed; he looked like a different person.

"So, any idea who might have left those puppies?" I asked.

"Always looking for a crime, huh?" he asked.

"No, just curious."

"I don't know. Someone who figured me for a soft touch."

"I can't imagine anyone thinking that," I said, then clamped a hand over my mouth. I couldn't believe I'd said that to him.

"For your information, Ms. Smarty Cop, there are a few people in town who like me."

His tone was teasing, but I didn't smile back. He sighed.

"You really did have it in for me since the moment I got to town."

"I wouldn't say that," I said defensively. "It's just that you moved into the most expensive house in town and didn't seem to have any way of making a decent living."

I still wasn't convinced that he was writing about wolves. As though he read my mind, he got up and picked up a couple of magazines from the counter. He tossed them over at me.

I looked at the cover lines of the magazine. Sure enough, there was something about wolves. I flipped through the pages and found the article. It had Kevin's name on it.

I closed it and looked at the cover. It was a well-known nature magazine—the one that a lot of people read up here. No wonder he was popular in town.

I tried not to look too impressed, but Kevin wasn't even interested in my reaction—he was more interested in his stew.

"Would you like more?" he asked, and I quickly shook my head.

"Good. On to dessert then."

"Dessert? Oh, no. I couldn't."

But he was already bringing over a big apple pie.

"Were you expecting an army?" I asked.

"You never know who might get stranded with you in a storm. It's better to be prepared," he told me with a twinkle in his eye.

"Well, maybe just a sliver of a piece," I said, leaning over and taking a sniff of cinnamon and nutmeg.

"You are really quite domestic," I told him.

He laughed.

"Now, if I'd said that to a woman, I'd be up on charges of male chauvinism or something."

"As far as I know, that's not on the books," I replied.

Something was happening here—I was actually relaxing and enjoying Kevin's company. I should be more on guard, but I was just too tired for that.

"Good thing for me," he said, as he looked at me.

I looked away. The wind was still howling outside, reminding me that I was stuck here with this man. It wouldn't do to get too friendly.

"I'm sorry to put you out like this, Kevin. If you have a spare blanket, I can sleep on the couch."

"There are lots of rooms here. You can stay in a guest bedroom."

After we cleared away the supper plates, he showed me to a room. It looked like it may have belonged to one of the Myrtles' daughters. The whole place seemed to be a froth of mint green—from the curtains, to the bedspread, to the rug on the floor.

"There is a bathroom through here—your own," Kevin said, opening one door and revealing a mint green tub, sink, and toilet.

"This is great. Thanks," I said.

"Come on back downstairs when you're settled in. I'll make us some tea. There won't be any TV reception in this storm, but we can talk."

Talk . . . with Kevin Motts?

Suddenly, I felt shy. I waited until he'd left, took off my gun, and set it on the feminine dresser. It looked so out of place there. I was off duty now. I was still on call and had my pager, but there was little I could do if somebody called in for help.

Not that there would many calls for help. The car thief call had been the only one all day long.

I went back downstairs and joined Kevin in the living room. I couldn't get over how magnificent this house was.

"You don't have a Christmas tree," I said.

"No. When you live alone, you get out of the habit," he said, sipping tea from a big mug.

"I have a tree," I said, "and I live alone."

In fact, I was a Christmas junkie. I loved the songs, the smells, and the red and green decorations. Each year, December was barely here before I got out my decorations and transformed my small apartment into what looked like Santa's workshop.

When Mike or Bill happened to come by, they were amazed. They couldn't quite see me as the kind of person who loved all the hoopla—not when they'd seen my no-nonsense attitude on the job.

"Too bad you didn't bring it with you. We could be snowed in here for a couple of days."

No! That couldn't be. I looked outside, willing the snow to stop so that I could at least try to get home. I didn't much care for the thought of spending Christmas Day with a stranger. It would be much better

168

to spend it alone. I would make a long phone call home to talk to my folks and to my nieces and nephews. It wasn't the same as being there, but at least it was something.

"You didn't go home for Christmas," I said suddenly.

"I am home," he said, and there was a strange tone to his voice.

"No folks? No one to see down south?" I asked. I could have kicked myself for probing into his personal life. I blamed it on the cop in me.

"Not unless you call an ex-wife family. I don't happen to," he said tiredly.

Kevin got up and made himself busy by making a fire in the big fireplace, which stood in the center of the room. It had been one of the things I liked best about this house. This place was meant for a big family, I wondered how he could live here all alone.

Then again, for tonight, he wasn't alone. That made me think.

"Kevin, I have kind of a favor to ask of you."

"Ask away," he said, poking at the fire and watching as little flames licked around a log.

"Please don't tell anyone that I had to spend the night here. You know how cops are. I'd never live it down," I said, biting my lip.

He straightened and turned to look at me.

"As a matter of fact, I know exactly how cops are. My dad was a cop."

"He was?" I asked. Somehow I didn't think of his parents as being ordinary, everyday people.

"Yeah. He never approved of me, though," he said.

An ex-wife and a family who didn't approve of him—I was beginning to understand why he was alone for Christmas.

"So you won't say anything to anyone about this?" I prodded.

"Sounds like a perfect opportunity for blackmail."

"Kevin! You wouldn't dare!"

"Wouldn't I? Well, maybe I could keep my mouth shut about this—for a price."

"What?" I asked.

"How about dinner at your place after we dig ourselves out of this blizzard?"

I was shocked. Why would he want to have dinner with me?

"I—uh—I don't think so."

"Okay. We can go to Katie's Diner. I noticed it's Bill's favorite place to eat—and everyone else's in town."

"All right! All right! Dinner at my house," I grumbled. "I hope you like corn flakes."

He laughed then, a low sound in his throat that reminded me of those wolves he studied. He abandoned the fire and walked slowly toward me.

"Since we're stuck here, alone together, why don't we get better acquainted?" he asked.

"Uh, I'm kind of tired now. I think I'll just call it a night."

"Suit yourself," he said, but the look he gave me made me certain that he didn't think I was tired at all.

The next morning, I woke up after a wonderful sleep. I looked around expecting to be in my own bed and saw mint green everywhere. Then I remembered the day before. I groaned.

Today, I was determined to get a snowplow out to this road. I was leaving here, one way or another.

It was Christmas Eve. I felt a touch of homesickness. I'd be better off in my own apartment with my Christmas tree and all the old, familiar decorations.

After a quick shower, I got back into my uniform and went downstairs. I could smell bacon and coffee. I followed the smells to the kitchen where Kevin was whipping up breakfast for an army.

"Are you expecting someone else?" I asked, sitting at the kitchen bar and watching him.

"Just us," he said, and somehow that sounded too intimate.

"I've got to try to see if I can make it into town today," I told him.

Kevin looked over his shoulder. The window was at his back, and he was looking at the snow. It was still coming down and showed no signs of letting up.

"Why the hurry?" he asked.

"I'm on duty. I've got to get back."

He slid some eggs onto a plate, added bacon, and handed the plate over. Then, he did the same with his own, and he sat down across from me.

"I was kind of hoping—"

"Yes?" I asked, my mind on the snow and my patrol car.

". . . that we could get out the snowshoes, walk into the woods a little ways, and find a nice tree . . . since you're an expert on all this Christmas stuff."

I froze with the fork halfway to my mouth. Was he crazy? This wasn't just a picnic here. I was the town's only cop at the moment and I was stranded—I had to get back.

However, when I tried calling the guy who drove the town's snowplow, I found out from his recorded message that he was on vacation. He'd left an alternate number for a man who was supposed to be covering for him, but there was no answer at that number. No tow truck and no snow plow—terrific.

"Damn," I said softly.

"Should I get out the snowshoes?" Kevin asked.

I still couldn't believe that I was stuck here. I went out to see my car. I could barely get Kevin's front door open, the snow had piled up so high. The car was covered! Even if I managed to shovel it out of the drift, then what? The road was impassable.

"What are you worried about, Leanne?" Kevin asked, coming up behind me. "You didn't get any calls for help on your pager last night, did you?"

"No," I said.

"Then, relax. You weren't on duty anyway, just on call, right?"

"Yes," I said reluctantly. I didn't like to be so helpless, but there didn't seem to be anything I could do at the moment. Kevin was right—not a soul had tried to call me.

"Then I'll get the snowshoes," he said.

He sounded like an eager little kid and I had to laugh.

"After we bring in a tree, we'll have hot chocolate and bring the puppies out to the living room for entertainment."

He left for a few minutes and came back with two pairs of snowshoes.

"I haven't been on those for years," I said, and then I got an idea. "You don't suppose I could make it into town on these?"

"Possibly, if you didn't sink into a big drift or fall off the road, wherever it is. Also, you should never snowshoe alone if you're not used to it."

"And of course you wouldn't want to snowshoe into town with me?"

"Of course not," Kevin said.

I shrugged my shoulders and we went outside to strap on the shoes. Kevin was right, I didn't think I could last all the way to town. The snow was fluffy and even with the snowshoes we sank down pretty deep.

"The best trees are over here, just behind my place."

We headed toward the trees and I began to relax. There really wasn't anything I could do about getting back to the station right now, so I might as well enjoy the day a little. Besides, I was in Kevin's house and it was Christmas. There was no need to make it miserable for him.

To my shock, I had a great time. Kevin was right about not snowshoeing alone. I got close to the base of a big pine tree and fell into a hole made around the tree's base. He had to pull me out.

"You weigh hardly anything," he commented, as he pulled me up to my feet.

"I can hold my own," I said. Was he saying I was too small to be a cop?

"That's not what I was implying," he said, impatience in his voice. "Why do you always take everything I say the wrong way?"

"What way was I supposed to take it?"

"As a compliment, maybe? I never saw anyone look so good in a cop's uniform. I think I'd like to get to know you a little better, Officer," he said, still standing close.

In the cold of the day, with the snow melting on our faces, I felt a rush of heat inside. I turned away. This couldn't be happening—only yesterday I was questioning this man about a car theft.

He would have kissed me then if I'd let him, but I made a really awkward about-face on the snowshoes and headed back towards the house.

"Hey, wait a minute, we haven't got the tree."

"What difference would it make?" I grumbled. "You wouldn't have decorations for it anyway."

"You're wrong, Officer. The Myrtles left a box marked 'Christmas Decorations.'"

"Oh."

So we went a little farther and found a bushy tree. Kevin brought out a small hatchet and cut it down. I always felt a little guilty cutting down a tree for decoration.

Then, we went back to the house. By this time, it had gotten colder and I was starting to yearn for that hot chocolate. Walking behind Kevin and the tree, I was thinking that this must have been what it was like for the pioneers, bringing the tree home for Christmas.

As soon as we got back, we found we had another thing in common with the pioneers—the electricity had gone out.

"I'll start a fire in the fireplace. We can heat the hot chocolate over the fire," Kevin said.

I brought the puppies out so they could be warm, too. Once they were walking around on their pudgy little feet and the fire was roaring, Kevin came over and sat down beside me on the floor.

It was just too domestic. Too much like a loving couple sharing Christmas Eve together.

Then, Kevin jumped up and said he would be right back. I watched as he went upstairs. In a few minutes, he came back with a big box.

Sure enough, it was marked "Christmas Decorations."

"Who knows . . . maybe it's full of old clothes," he said.

It wasn't. It was stuffed full of every kind of Christmas ornament you could imagine. I couldn't believe it. I was in heaven, bringing out one after another. I even found a rubber ball that the puppies immediately fought over.

At one point I stopped, noticing that Kevin was watching me closely. All the time I had been fascinated with the ornaments he had been looking at me. I blushed.

"You must think I'm acting like a kid," I said self-consciously.

"No, not at all. This is a side of you I haven't seen before," he said.

"Well, I love Christmas," I said.

"You don't have to defend yourself. Enthusiasm is an honest emotion, Leanne. Why hide it?"

I hid my embarrassment by turning my back on him to decorate the tree. My emotions seemed so raw around this man.

We spent the day doing practical things. Kevin had a little wood stove, which we fired up to add more heat and to prepare meals. It had been a long time since I'd done any cooking on a stove like this, but between the two of us, we came up with a decent supper. We ate in front of the fireplace. By the time we finished, the puppies were asleep around us, warm and snoring.

"Are you going to keep one?" I asked.

"Probably. Would you like one, too?"

"I don't know if my landlord would approve," I said laughing.

As the evening passed, I was reminded of Christmas Eve with my family. I had to admit I was a bit homesick. When Kevin asked me what was wrong I told him, and that led to each of us telling stories about other Christmas Eves we'd lived through. Kevin had a grandmother who had practically raised him, and some of his happiest memories were of her.

We talked long into the night. The fire burned low and the puppies slept on. It was too cold to go to bed in the bedrooms upstairs. Sometime during that long night we both fell asleep, and as we slept we snuggled into each other for warmth.

I didn't hear the snowplow. I didn't even hear the knock on the door at seven on Christmas morning, but Kevin heard it and leaped up from a deep sleep.

It was the alternate snowplow man. Not only had he had plowed the road all the way to Kevin's place, he'd also found my patrol car and shoveled it out, too.

I groaned as I looked out the window at Kevin talking to the man. In minutes, it would be all over town that I'd spent at least one night here, snowed in at Kevin Motts's house. There would be no living this down.

Kevin came back in and I heard the plow make its way back to town.

"Here's your Christmas present," he told me. "You're free to go."

"Right," I said. "I just have to gather my things and put my coat on."

"You don't have to go, Leanne," Kevin said, giving me a long look.

"I have to. I have to check in," I said, avoiding his eyes.

"All right you have to, but that doesn't mean you can't come back."

173

I thought of my empty apartment. I looked over at the embers of the fire and saw one of the puppies wake up. Inevitably, he would wake all the others, too. I had to smile.

"See . . . you're not entirely immune to us," Kevin whispered, coming close and kissing my forehead. I didn't draw away.

I didn't want to.

Instead, I leaned toward his warmth and strength.

"You know, I just can't resist a woman with a gun. Do you want to arrest me again, Leanne?"

My breath caught in my throat. I'd heard similar lines from men before, but from Kevin it stirred something in me that I hadn't felt in a long, long time. I held my head up to read the expression in his eyes—there was enough passion there to scorch all my inhibitions.

"Your reputation is shot in this town anyway, darling. Why not come back and spend Christmas with me?"

I did.

By the time my cop cohorts got back into town the rumors about Kevin and me had spread like wildfire. By that time, I had to admit that most of them were true.

It all came to a head the day Mike and Bill drove out to Kevin's place and "arrested" him, bringing him to a jail cell and demanding that he make an honest man of himself by marrying me. By that time, though, Kevin didn't need any persuading—from the other side of the bars, he got down on one knee and produced a ring.

I agreed, of course. After all, this was one lady cop who was head over heels in love with a supposed car thief.

The End

SANTA'S RELUCTANT HELPER
I should think of our temporary jobs as
an early Christmas present

I needed a moment to take in Derrick's surprising announcement—that he finally had a job. I put down my fork and stared at my husband. "What do you mean, you need me to work on your team?" I asked. "Why should I have to work with you at the mall?"

"Come on, Meghan," he answered. "Everybody knows that Santa's married. You'll be Mrs. Claus."

No words came to me. Had my husband completely lost his mind?

After four years of being married to Derrick, I had learned to interpret his facial expressions perfectly. I searched his face for clues that he was kidding around with me, making a silly Thanksgiving Day joke. He looked as serious as could be. That was worrisome. Why didn't the man crack a smile to let me know he was only teasing me about working in a Santa suit? Not that landing a job, any sort of job, was anything to poke fun at. Certainly not after almost five grueling months of unemployment.

If this was a legitimate job offer, I guess I'd be proud of him. In fact, under normal circumstances, I'm sure I would have thrown my arms around Derrick, kissed him, and congratulated him about the job. I would have ignored our turkey dinner and danced around the kitchen with him. But these weren't normal circumstances.

For starters, when had my husband even applied for the job of impersonating Santa Claus? And why? That remained a mystery. As for me, I'd never given a thought about playing the part of Mrs. Claus—not at the Meridith Mall, not anywhere. I wasn't the grandmotherly type. To make matters worse, I just couldn't picture a twenty-four-year-old slender-built man such as Derrick masquerading as Santa Claus. I doubted he could even utter a convincing ho-ho-ho.

I bit my tongue to hold back my negative comments. I was tiptoeing on eggshells because unemployment had become a sore topic in our household. Paid work was paid work, true, but Derrick was a computer nut and had an associate's degree in computer science. That was his chosen field. His dream job would probably be writing adventure games for computers, certainly not parading around in a fake white beard and handing out candy and toys to screaming kids. What in the world was going on? What was happening to our otherwise festive Thanksgiving celebration?

Derrick, you see, had worked in computer sales and figured that

175

would be his career for life. He was great in retail, earned above-average commissions, and loved his job. He figured he'd be named assistant manager in a few years, possibly the store manager later on, if things progressed well.

But big business squelched that career dream in a hurry. At the peak of our July heat wave, his store got sold to a big electronics chain, and they announced immediate plans to cut back on computer stock and to specialize in televisions. So, computer-genius Derrick was out—out of luck and out of work.

He took it hard. It was a complete shock for him not to have a job to go to every morning. It hurt his ego as much as his wallet, but we both figured he'd find something fast. There were plenty of openings around town, which was clear from seeing signs posted and from news reports about corporations in our region begging for applicants. We put on our rose-colored glasses and proceeded to try and find Derrick a job.

Derrick asked me for help in searching the newspaper want ads. We found quite a few possible jobs every week, but some were quite a distance away, and we didn't want to have to buy a second car, nor could we afford to move to a different location. Many of the jobs that sounded interesting turned out to be very part-time or they lacked benefits, such as health insurance.

It was uphill all the way. Still, we kept at it. We sent out Derrick's resume by mail and fax, and he called about many of the ads. I tried to cheer him up, but it was discouraging for us both—week after week, month after month, with hardly a request for an interview.

Ever since graduating from high school in 1999, I'd been cashiering full-time at the Brookwood Community Cinema, selling admission tickets. Except for being regularly scheduled on Saturdays, I liked my job. I didn't have to dress in office attire and could wear jeans every day if I felt like it. I got free movie passes, too. My boss was a pleasant sort of guy, very fair. I counted my lucky stars to have such a comfortable job.

Luckily, my job allowed Derrick and me to continue paying our rent. We used our savings for everything else, assuming that his unemployment was nothing but a temporary setback for us. I didn't say anything to Derrick, but I started to resent being the sole earner in our family. Then, just as Thanksgiving turkeys started appearing in area grocery stores, Derrick began getting calls for interviews left and right. Suddenly, he was Mr. Popularity. We felt luck was on our side, that our fortune was about to change for the better. Each time he headed out, usually in his lucky blue-striped shirt, he kissed me good-bye and promised he'd come back with a job by Thanksgiving Day.

He interviewed at a hardware store, a cell phone company, a public library, and a dry cleaners. Nobody hired him. Next he interviewed at the telephone company, a trucking firm, a corporate headquarters, and a toy store. Nothing happened.

Derrick was getting more desperate by the day. "Meghan, what's wrong with me?" he asked. "Is my hair too long? Am I wearing the wrong shirt? Do I need a tie?"

I assured him he was presenting a clean and professional appearance, just what employers wanted. His resume was letter-perfect. He had job experience, a college degree, and favorable references. I couldn't pinpoint what might be preventing him from being selected for any one of the jobs.

It would happen soon, I assured him. I knew our future depended on it. As a last resort, Derrick spoke to an army recruiter about the possibility of enlisting. On a whim, he also applied at the temporary employment agency located in the same building.

Days before Thanksgiving, my place of employment went up in flames. While the residents of our town were sound asleep and totally unaware of it, the Brookwood Community Cinema burned to the ground. Faulty wiring or a short of some sort was suspected. The building was empty, so nobody was hurt. But a dozen of us were out of a job, just in the blink of an eye.

Not having my job all of a sudden put me into panic mode. I'd been the one covering our rent for months. I was the one holding us together. I prayed Derrick would get hired soon—something, anything. He was on a whirlwind of interviews, sometimes going to two or three in a single day. Surely something would click and he'd get selected soon.

Mom was shocked at hearing that neither of us had a job. She invited us over to have Thanksgiving dinner with her and my stepfather, but I didn't need her pity or her tears. Derrick and I had to dig our way out of this crisis ourselves. Besides, I'd already bought our frozen turkey and most of the trimmings.

I assured Derrick that we'd have our traditional Thanksgiving celebration together, no matter what. I'd bake us a pumpkin pie like always. I'd stuff the bird the way I learned from Mom. Somehow we'd cheer up enough to celebrate Derrick's favorite holiday of the year.

The table was set with our best plates. Just as we took our first bites of turkey breast, the telephone rang. It turned out to be a job offer for Derrick from the temporary agency. He was given the once-in-a-lifetime opportunity to play Santa at the mall. He accepted the offer enthusiastically, without a moment's hesitation.

As I helped myself to dressing and sweet potatoes, I quizzed Derrick about this new job of his. "How does a skinny guy like you fit into a Santa costume, even with a big pillow? Have the boots been worn by other Santas? How does the beard stay on? And what sort of a crazy organization calls people to set up jobs on important holidays?"

Derrick held up his hands. "Hold on, Meghan," he said. "I don't know much yet, except the pay is great and they need me to bring you to be Mrs. Claus. They'll send me more information about the job duties. We start next week, that's why they were in such a hurry to get things settled. The job is for a whole month. We'll be working from noon to seven at night. The agency hired for a dozen different malls, and I was lucky enough to get my first choice, practically in our back yard—Meridith Mall."

As tickled as I was that Derrick finally had a job, I wasn't convinced I could do my part of pretending to be an old lady. After all, I'd only been out of a job for a few days. I didn't feel that desperate yet. "Don't they usually hire older people for this sort of work?" I asked Derrick. Try as I might, I just couldn't picture him with white hair and a long beard.

After we ate and took a much-needed break before serving the pumpkin pie, Derrick suggested that we keep an open mind and try to have fun dressing up in the costumes and playing our assigned roles. He assured me it would be no harder than appearing on stage in high school musicals.

I wasn't buying it. "Have fun? What do you mean? Derrick, I don't know if I can," I answered. "I've never found work particularly entertaining. I mean, how exciting is handing out movie tickets and giving change?"

"Then don't think of this as work, Meghan. View it as play-acting," he said, a note of desperation creeping into his voice.

To me, that sounded even worse. "I can't act, Derrick, you know that," I said, my voice getting louder. "I'll probably get stage fright." I threw down my napkin and left the table.

I stared out of our bedroom window at the snowdrifts in the parking lot. Even for northern Illinois, this was a ton of the white stuff. It did nothing to improve my rotten mood.

Derrick tapped on the bedroom door. "Meghan, please," he called out. "Let's not have a fight. Not today, not on Thanksgiving."

I knew he had a point, but I wanted to pout a little. It was my right. My crazy Santa-impersonating husband had offered my services without even bothering to consult me. I'd be embarrassed to appear at the local mall in a long dress and a gray or white wig that made me look a hundred years old. Even with make-up, I doubted I could play the part of a sweet old lady. Plus, Christmas shopping was about to begin, and all my friends would be at the Meridith Mall. They'd know right away Derrick and I were fakes. They'd make fun of us.

I heard the telephone ring. Oh, great, another employer. Maybe Derrick would be offered a part in a Broadway musical!

"Meghan, it's your mom. Come out and talk," Derrick yelled from the kitchen.

I'd been backed into a corner and had no choice but to go. I couldn't refuse to talk to my own mother and stepfather on Thanksgiving Day, could I? I swallowed my pride, unlocked the bedroom door, and walked into the kitchen, avoiding Derrick's eyes.

"I hope you cracked open a bottle of wine, you two," were the first words out of Mom's mouth.

She knew. Derrick had told her his news.

"Not yet, Mom" I said, trying my darndest to sound cheerful. "Actually, Derrick got the call just as we sat down to eat."

Mom offered her congratulations and Dad's congratulations. "Meghan, you two will be so cute dressed up as Santa and Mrs. Claus. We'll come see you to take pictures. Should we alert your aunts and uncles so they can visit you at the mall?"

I bristled. The last thing I wanted was to have a bunch of relatives pointing cameras at me. I didn't share her bubbling enthusiasm about what was looming before us, but, for Derrick' sake, I didn't offer my opinion.

After we finished the usual holiday chitchat, I reluctantly returned to my chair. Derrick was smiling and cutting the pie for us. "Meghan, it's okay," he said. "Don't worry. Not only is the Santa gig offering great pay, but they cover all our meals on breaks at the food court."

I glared at Derrick. Did he really think I was going to waltz over to the food court dressed like a complete idiot and order a taco with him?

After the pumpkin pie, I felt slightly better. Maybe I was being too hard on poor Derrick. His ego had suffered greatly when he was out of work, and he needed praise and encouragement from me, not a crybaby attitude. He was all worked up with enthusiasm about having a job again.

I looked up and realized he'd been talking. "Plus, the agency has plenty of work for me after this," he said. "So I expect to keep on working after our month is up—probably in a warehouse. They need some people to input stock via computers, and I'm their man. I have good vibes about this, hon."

I half-smiled at him and collected our plates to head to the sink. Our dinner had been a blur. I was living a Thanksgiving nightmare.

Derrick danced around me, grabbed the sponge, and filled the sink with hot water. He announced I should go sit down and watch television, that he was going to clean up. He kissed me on the cheek.

I hardly thought to thank him. In a daze, I wandered into the living room and plopped on our sofa. I switched on the TV, not caring what the program was. My mind was being bombarded with mixed emotions, all jumbled together. While I was relieved Derrick would be bringing home a hefty paycheck soon, I was less than enthused at his chosen career, impersonating St. Nick. That I had been dragged into his bizarre Christmas performance amazed me, confused me, and angered me.

What did Derrick and I, both only children, know about entertaining kids anyway? The mere thought of impatient, crying children usually sent me running to hide. That's why I'd never tried much babysitting, despite many requests from neighbors during my early teen years. Would Mrs. Claus be responsible for drying tears, wiping noses, maybe even talking baby talk? While dozens of eager, squirming youngsters waited in line to talk to Santa, I was pretty sure Mrs. Claus was considered to be the official babysitter.

The scenario made me feel woozy and dizzy. My stomach felt like it had been tied in knots. Nerves. Usually I was the happiest woman in the world on Thanksgiving. Today, I hadn't even wanted seconds. Most of our turkey and dressing would be waiting for us tomorrow.

The whirring of the fax machine interrupted my daydreaming. The computer table was too far away for me to see what was arriving by fax for us. Derrick had been expecting his folks to fax us a holiday greeting from their vacation in sunny Florida.

I called to Derrick that his parents' Thanksgiving wishes had come in, but then a second page started. That was odd. Maybe the hotel desk clerk where they were had pressed send twice by mistake.

Derrick whirled past me, took the paper out of the fax machine, and announced, "It's not from my parents at all. It's our new job descriptions." He did a little dance around me to accent his message.

I felt a sense of dread. I was starting to feel queasy about this. Holding my stomach, I rushed past him to the bathroom.

Soon I returned to Derrick to watch a comedy special on TV. I glanced at the job descriptions he'd put on the coffee table, but I just didn't have the heart to study the words.

Maybe tomorrow. Maybe never.

We switched off the TV early. Derrick asked if I wanted to open a bottle of wine, but I declined. What I needed was sleep, about twenty hours of it. My movie theater had burned down, my husband thought he was Santa Claus, and I was supposed to parade around in public as a granny. What next?

The next morning was sunny. Maybe if some of the snow melted, my mood would improve. I still felt unwell, strange, and a little blue—just generally out of it. I couldn't explain it. Being offered a job was supposed to feel like a compliment. Maybe I had the flu.

After breakfast, Derrick and I sat down and reviewed our

respective job descriptions. Maybe I'd made an elephant out of a molehill. Everything sounded cut-and-dry. Maybe it wouldn't be such horrible work after all. At least Derrick would get to sit down most of the time. Me, I'd have to stand for hours. I was used to that from my ticket sales booth, where I alternated standing and sitting.

I could do it. The money was more than convincing, and the temp firm would cover some extra expenses, such as our gas to the mall and back every day and our on-the-job meals. It wasn't such a bad offer at all. Maybe I should think of our temporary jobs as an early Christmas present.

Maybe all the kids at the mall wouldn't be sniffling and complaining while waiting. Maybe they'd be controlled by their parents, and everything would be smooth sailing. Polite kids, smiling parents with cameras at the ready, Derrick ho-ho-ho-ing and handing out picture books, me handing out candy canes . . . I could dream, couldn't I?

Before I knew it, the big day came, and Derrick and I reported for our day of job training. We signed some papers and showed identification, and then everyone got issued costumes, wigs, and what-have-you. Then we split into two groups to change—Santas to the left, wives to the right.

I stood in the room with about a dozen other nervous Mrs. Clauses. We helped each other get ready and we tripped over our long red dresses. It felt crazy putting on the curly wig. It itched. I looked in the mirror, and it wasn't me who stared back. How in the world had my nutty husband convinced me to do this?

Everybody had brought black shoes, as the info sheet had specified, but some of us wore loafers, others wore leather pumps, and a few of us wore tennis shoes. Half the women in the room were my age or younger, and none of us was a convincing grandmother type, despite our wire glasses and the rouge on our cheeks. We were a motley bunch.

Timidly, we filed into the large auditorium to be paired up with our disheveled, bearded Santas. Some of the belly-stuffing pillows left a trail of down feathers. Derrick looked downright silly with his extra-large boots, ill-fitting suit, and patent leather belt. He held his cap in his hand; it wouldn't stretch over his unruly wig.

While we wives practiced waving to the imaginary crowds and smiling at the invisible children, the owner of the temp agency tutored the plumped-up Santas on how to achieve the all-important jolly laugh. Most of the noises that came out of the Santas resembled more of a cry for help than a convincing guffaw. All uttered a ho, some got as far as ho-ho. Nobody had perfected a ho-ho-ho, and that was sorry progress considering it was almost December.

In just a matter of days, malls throughout northern Illinois would set up Christmas trees, decorated top to bottom. Near the tree would be a chair designated for Santa himself. Derrick and I were glad we would be working at Meridith Mall, so close to home. I was still nursing a mild case of the flu, but I figured I'd be in tip-top shape by the time our debut rolled around. Also, I wasn't completely over my case of the jitters about appearing in front of all my friends and neighbors.

At night, all I could dream about was being a very unfortunate Mrs. Claus, where everything went wrong. An irate child pulled off my wig, and then Derrick couldn't find his boots and had to appear barefoot. In another dream, Derrick ran out of gifts, the kids rebelled, and the mothers hit him with their purses.

As we had a leisurely breakfast of blueberry pancakes before reporting to our gig for the first time, I told Derrick about some of my strange dreams.

He laughed and said, "Meghan, remember, this is just an ordinary job. Plenty of people wear uniforms to work. Not even our worst enemy is going to criticize us for accepting paid work. Don't worry so much. Just keep smiling as much as you can and entertain the kids a little while they wait. I'm sure you'll do fine."

I took a long look at my husband. He was twitching a little and tapping his foot. Santa had a case of nerves, too! Somehow that made me feel slightly better.

Hours later, we were dressed and ready to become public spectacles. We weren't perfect, not by any means. Derrick's beard stayed off-center, and his cap looked ridiculous perched on top of his wig. Somehow I'd bent my glasses, so they kept sliding down my nose. We giggled at ourselves in the bedroom mirror and off we went.

The mall arrival of Santa and Mrs. Claus had been widely publicized, and we discovered that all the neighborhood kids as well as all the kindergarten classes were already in line. We stood next to the twinkling Christmas tree amid applause and merry laughter.

So far, so good.

Derrick sat down in his designated chair as if he belonged there, and he placed his bag of toys near his feet. "Ho-ho-ho!" he boomed. The perfect Santa. Go figure. I stifled a giggle as the crowd cheered him wildly. My Derrick was a star.

As if on cue, Christmas carols started playing from a loudspeaker overhead, adding more merriment to the holiday feeling. I found myself whistling along. I couldn't help it.

My eyes scanned the hundreds of children waiting to see Derrick. They were full of smiles, with hope glistening in their eyes. This was an important moment in their young lives. Moms and dads stood by, holding jackets, scarves, hats, and mittens.

How wrong I'd been about the kids. I figured they'd only be thinking about themselves and would beg Santa Claus for endless games, dolls, puppies, computers, and ponies. Not this bunch; these kids didn't have a selfish bone in their bodies. The first little boy climbed up on Santa's lap and whispered that his daddy was in the army and he wanted him to stay safe.

The next child asked Derrick for a hospital bed for his ailing grandma. On and on it went. The kids wanted mommies to stop crying and daddies to stop yelling. The only tears I had to wipe all day were my own.

Derrick was doing great, a real pro. He was handing out the picture books after listening briefly to each child. He accepted lists from those who brought them. Sometimes he handed out candy canes, and other times I did it. We played it by ear. Several local newspapers had sent photographers, but Derrick was so busy he hardly noticed the extra attention.

After a few hours, we both took a break and got something to eat. Our instructions were to pick up more books when Derrick started to run out, but he didn't want to enter the designated store dressed as Old St. Nick. He knew every kid in the place would stop him to chat and he'd never get back to his workplace.

I understood his predicament, and I offered to go instead. Who'd bother a feisty old lady in a velveteen gown? I knocked on the store manager's door and a familiar voice called for me to come in.

I stood directly before my neighbor, Anna Andrews, secretary to the store manager. Without a moment's hesitation, I announced, "Good afternoon. My name is Mrs. Claus, and I'm here for more picture books for my husband to hand out to the children."

Anna blinked. "Meghan, is that you?" she asked.

I nodded a yes.

"Well, you look great," my neighbor said. "I hear you two have record crowds out there. All the mall managers are very impressed. This is our biggest day ever. Way to go, guys! I have another box of books right here."

I handed over the toy sack and Anna filled it three-quarters full. Suddenly, I was feeling on top of the world, almost like a celebrity.

"How's the candy cane supply?" Anna asked.

I told her we had about twenty left.

"Here," she answered. "Let me stick a package in your sack. Better to be safe than sorry."

I thanked her and rushed back to my Derrick, eager to tell him that everyone was satisfied with our job performance.

He grinned widely at the compliment.

I'm not exactly sure when my change of heart came about. At first, I was 100 percent opposed to Derrick's crazy job scheme. When I first heard about being shoved into the spotlight, it frightened me. I'm not much of a public speaker, and I likened the work to being on stage. Maybe I'd open my mouth and no words would come out. I was afraid I'd forget all my lines and the audience would throw tomatoes at me. Then it hit me—there were no lines to rehearse, no script to learn. Everything Santa and Mrs. Claus had to do centered on making the kids feel comfortable and accepted. We had to listen to them and maybe encourage some laughter. That was all.

When seven o'clock rolled around, it was time for us to leave, and there were still a few hopeful children waiting in line. We knew we had to keep on working, so that's what we did. I ignored my growling stomach. We didn't want any disappointed youngsters. Only when the last little girl had her picture book and candy cane did Derrick and I yawn and head for home.

The next day was much of the same for Santa and me, except the crowds were even larger. A popular radio station covered the event live, reporting on the incredible number of happy children at Meridith Mall.

Again, the kids were well-behaved—little Christmas angels. A few store managers were so impressed that they donated dozens of other gifts for Derrick to hand out—card games and music CDs, spinning tops and soccer balls. How the presents got wrapped so fast was beyond me. Maybe little elves were secretly at work in the basement.

Each day, more and more kids showed up. Store managers responded by donating plastic dump trucks and play microscopes. Soon they were up to camping gear and pull-wagons.

"Look at all the generosity circulating around Meridith Mall. This is exactly what the spirit of Christmas is supposed to be about," reported a local TV anchorwoman. She interviewed smiling parents and happy kids waiting in line to see Santa. The segment got aired all over the state of Illinois.

The owner of the temp agency called us to rave about our enthusiasm and said we'd get paid for all our undeclared overtime. Derrick was ecstatic. It meant we could pay off the car in full.

Two days later, Derrick and I received a note of thanks from the governor's office, along with a fancy engraved Christmas card. The love continued to flow. One day, children from a nearby homeless shelter came to sing Christmas carols at the mall. Store mangers rushed out and presented them with gift certificates and bicycles.

The days at the mall passed by quickly. We worked up a storm and enjoyed every single minute of it. Derrick and I realized our time was about over, and soon we'd have to fondly pack up our wigs, caps, and clothes to give back to the temporary agency. The mere thought left a lump in my throat. It was hard to fathom, but I'd miss the sweet little kids.

On our final day of work, I told Derrick I had some important business to tend to on our break. He smiled, since Christmas was hours away, assuming I was going shopping for a unique Christmas gift for him.

In a way, my husband was right. If my gut feeling was correct, this would be a unique, very surprising gift.

While he ate a corned beef sandwich alone, I dashed off to the pharmacy. Going on a hunch, I bought a pregnancy test. Minutes later, I squealed at seeing the results. Santa and Mrs. Claus were going to have a baby.

The End

www.ingramcontent.com/pod-product-compliance
Lightning Source LLC
Chambersburg PA
CBHW051512170626
46811CB00002B/774